Galactic Defenders

Endurance
Book One of the Defenders Trilogy

Michael Mishoe

Copyright © 2018 Michael Mishoe

All rights reserved.

ISBN-13: 9781983352355

Prologue

Date: July 6, 2132.

    The question of whether other life lives out in outer space has been answered. Alien life does exist. But they are not our allies; they are our conquerors. They came to Earth without warning or announcement. By the time our satellites picked up their starships, they were already in orbit. The President of America along with several other representatives around the world, attempted to contact them, but their calls ware unanswered, other than an announcement that they were a robotic species called the Ribiyar. After all their ships arrived in orbit, many of them descended into our atmosphere, and began attacking all the major civilizations of the world, targeting everything from Russia and Japan to the Netherlands and America. When the attack began, the united armies of the world attacked the invaders vying for control of their territory. Though they fought relentlessly, their fighter planes and battleships could not hold back the gigantic Ribiyar warships, the relentless attack cruisers, and a seemingly endless supply of oval-shaped fighters.

The Secretary of Defense urged the President to use the nuclear warheads the United States possessed, but the President refused, believing the warheads would do more harm than good. Other countries did not believe that and used their own warheads against the battleships and cruisers that brought the Ribiyar warriors to the surface. The countries using the warheads quickly discovered a weakness in Ribiyar starships as the warheads impacted with the ships. Somehow, the nuclear energy started a chain reaction in the alien ship's power core, causing the cores to explode, and bring the ships down in a thundering explosion of fire.

But the victories were short lived. For every Ribiyar ship destroyed, dozens of fighter jets, military ships, and cities were destroyed in return. In one day, much of the world's main defenses were largely weakened. Now, in the days after the initial assault, the Ribiyar had sent their soldiers to the planet, hunting down the population and imprisoning them in fortress-like holding camps they were creating.

But not all hope was lost. There were still people free, calling themselves the Defenders, and fighting for the freedom of Earth. Somehow, with already limited resources, they must find a way to expel the robotic Ribiyar from Earth.

And, in the chaos of the invasion, a warrior is born. A warrior that just might have a chance to save humankind from enslavement, and destruction.

Chapter 1

Date: July 8, 2132.
Location: Secret base on Hawaii.

The mood was grim when Admiral James Hofkins, a tall, heavyset man with brown hair and a bushy mustache, entered the room. Hofkins noted grimly the weighed-down appearance of the officers manning the base. The newly started war for survival was not going well. Earth's spy satellites that the Ribiyar had not yet destroyed have shown the beginnings of what they believe will be prison camps for the several thousands of people that have been captured. These buildings, large structures that resemble fortresses, are being constructed by a legion of Ribiyar soldiers, aided by swarms of flying, spherical machines that place and secure the structures into place, and are working at such a pace that in mere days they have progressed to a point that would have taken years to build under human devices and resources. The satellites also show that the military installations around the world, regardless of which nation they belonged to, are being located and destroyed by the Ribiyar's fighter squads. Only the best hidden and secure facilities are safe, for now.

"Report," Admiral Hofkins ordered as he walked to the center of the room, where display monitors showing the Ribiyar troop movements hung from the walls, indicated by maps of the world covered in red indicators. The room was rectangular, with one of the long ends holding a window that gave a hidden view of the island outside the base. The other three walls held doors that led to other parts of the base, but this room held all the computers that processed the information that the satellites collected, making this room one of the critical tools that admirals and other commanders used to plan their next steps against their foes.

One of the officers, hearing the admiral's entrance, walked away from the consoles, and approached Admiral Hofkins.

"The *U.S.S. Thunderfox* has docked at the port 7 miles from this base, Admiral Hofkins," Lieutenant Oakland, or Olo, as he liked to be known as, a some-what thin officer with black hair and a tan from the island sun, who oversaw the base's intelligence and logistics, reported. Olo's nickname originated from his odd, given name, Otlin Levry

Oakland, the first name a combination of his father's parents, and his middle name a combination of his mother's parents. To lessen the burden of his outlandish name, he preferred to be referred to as Olo, and while it wasn't perfect, it was better than going with his given name.

"However, the nuclear sub *Atlanta* has still not reported in since the invasion began, or shown up on any Defender vessel's radar or sonar, sir. It is possible that the sub was destroyed, but it is also possible that the sub has simply sustained damage to her propulsion and/or her communications system. The *Atlanta* could be simply stranded somewhere, and unable to contact us."

Admiral Hofkins considered this information, and then ordered, "Lieutenant, you are to call off the search for the *Atlanta*, and log the ship as destroyed in the military records."

"Sir," Olo protested, "I believe that we should postpone giving up on the *Atlanta* for just a few more days. I know Captain Jack Vade personally, and he wouldn't have let his ship be destroyed so easily in the initial assault by the Ribiyar."

"Lieutenant, we can't waste our time looking for ships that are not there to be found. Discontinue the search, and note the *Atlanta* as destroyed at once. Is there any information on the outpost in Delaware? Last I heard, the Ribiyar search parties were getting close to their position."

"Our data from the spy satellites show a crater where outpost DE-13 was located. It does appear that they found them, sir, and I didn't see many wreckages from the Ribiyar fighters. It appears they had a near-casualty free strike against our forces, again."

The admiral sighed as he skimmed through the images of outpost DE-13 on a small tablet Olo had handed him. The tablet showed a clearing in a forest, completely charred and burned from energy cannon fire and bombardment from Ribiyar fighters. Though there were a few Ribiyar wreckages among the battle field, it brought little comfort considering how many brave soldiers, along with the civilians taking refuge at the base, were annihilated in the carnage. "We can't afford to keep letting the Ribiyar bleed our forces dry with this death-by-a-thousand-cuts stunt. We need to send a ship to the Atlantic Ocean, and, hopefully, put a dent in the Ribiyar forces stationed there. Contact the captain of the battleship *Ocean-Walker* and have him report to my office at once. And, Lieutenant, be sure you don't forget to call off the search for the *Atlanta* and make the changes to her file the first chance you have." The admiral then left the room and traveled to another part of the base.

"Yes, sir," Olo said as he saluted the admiral's departure. After instructing one of the other officers to contact the captain of the *Ocean-Walker* and report to the admiral, Olo returned to his post to fulfil the task that Admiral Hofkins had given him.

Jack, where are you? Olo silently asked himself as he logged onto the military database. He desperately hoped that Jack was still out there, bringing the fight to the Ribiyar, not just because of his proven experience in military endeavors, but also that he didn't want anything to have befallen his old friend.

After informing the few patrol ships in the sea to consider the *Atlanta* destroyed, Olo selected the *Atlanta's* file and began making the necessary updates to it, noting the time and position last known to be, somewhere in the Atlantic Ocean, and that all hands where presumed lost with the vessel. After he completed his task, he walked to the radar screens and continued to track the Ribiyar movements across the globe using the satellites in orbit. Though he didn't want to admit it, the admiral was correct. Everyone had to be focused on the task at hand to win this fight for survival. If they weren't, no one would be left to protect this planet from the robotic invaders.

Location: Aboard the Ribiyar Warship *Ji'Co*, in orbit of Earth.

High above Earth, a large Ribiyar Warship hovered over the planet. The warship's form consisted of two massive domes that comprised the top and the bottom of the ship, and in the middle of the domes was a trench in the hull, where thirty-six large spherical cannons where placed around the circumference of the ship. The ship was encompassed by a massive dual ring, that acted as the ship's main propulsion drive, powerful enough to traverse the vast reaches of space faster than other engines. The rings were held in place through a complex gravimetric field created by the ship's power core and supplemented with magnetic paneling placed along the hull. Adding to the ship's offensive capabilities, there were also a vast amount of energy cannons placed along the engine rings hull, ensuring anyone who went against the beast wouldn't find any gaps in its arsenal.

The corridors within the ship were triangular, with the ceiling arching sharply down to the floor like an up-side down V. The corridors were coated silver, glamorously reflecting the pure white light that shone from the illumination panels within the V arcs.

Echoing softly were the footsteps of a Ribiyar warrior as he made his way through the corridor. His skin was completely metal, lightweight, and nearly as strong as diamonds, and was coated with the same silvery color of the corridor. The alien possessed two arms, and at the end of the arms were circularly shaped hands, with four fingers evenly distributed along the circle. The alien walked on two legs, with bulky boot-like objects for feet. Among the obvious uses such as walking, the feet were also simultaneously used to store power packs for weapons and other objects. Other small storage crevices were hidden over the body to maximize adaptability to a large range of situations. The alien had the body mass of a sumo wrestler, big and bulky, and possessed the strength comparable to 10 humans.

The alien's head was dome shaped and sat directly next to his shoulders without a neck, though the front and back of the base could be raised and lowered to adjust his view. On his domed head were two rectangular holes, glowing a bright blue, which contained the optical sensors that allowed it to see. Its mouth was a rectangular speaker located beneath the eyes, and it possessed no ears on its head, its audio receptors hidden within the structure.

The alien was Tactical Analyst Cha'Hawk, a warrior with a standard height of 8ft 9in, with only his name, rank, and the symbol of his clan (a grey half circle standing alongside a blue 7-pointed star) branded onto his chest armor differing him from other Ribiyar. He walked to the Battle Coordination Hall (or "The Scheming Chamber", as some of the officers had recently began to secretly call it) as he thought about the information he was going to report during the meeting. Soldiers operating Holding Facility Tri'La, the imprisonment camp nearest full completion and operation, had detected the possible crash site of a Ribiyar troop transport ship in the mass of liquid the natives of this planet have labeled: the Atlantic Ocean. If the data is correct, the ship is most likely the *Ra'Ta*, which had last reported to be converging on a submerged vessel that carried the weapon that destroyed many of the starships during the start of the invasion. Because the *Ra'Ta*'s signal was lost, it was possible the alien vessel fired an energy-disrupting weapon on the *Ra'Ta* as they were being attacked. Or, possibly the more likely scenario, the organic lifeforms, or 'organics', as many throughout the ranks referred to them, managed to fire their devastating weapons, known as nuclear warheads, on the *Ra'Ta* before the vessel could overtake the aliens, though a great amount of debris and radiation should be present if it was the case.

Cha'Hawk approached the entrance to the chamber and raised his arm to the scanner. A cylindrical, snake-like object called a Data Module ejected from the middle of his right arm. Cha'Hawk positioned his arm in front of the scanner and the module went into the scanner, linking him to the *Ji'Co*'s computer network while the computer verified that he possessed the clearance to enter the chamber. While he waited, he used his connection to search the database to see if there was any data about the *Ra'Ta* he was not already aware of. Cha'Hawk knew he was in a high position in the military, but he knew from experience that he was not always informed of new information, and he refused to be surprised and humiliated before his superiors during the battle briefing because of his limited knowledge.

Finally, the computer completed its scan, and the computer transmitted the information to his internal Heads-Up-Display, reading: **TACTICAL ANALYSIST CHA'HAWK; JKL LEVEL 7 CLEARANCE: ACCESS AUTHORIZED.**

Cha'Hawk removed his arm from the scanner and the data module retracted back into his arm. The door split open and he walked into the room. Several captains, squad commanders, military coordinators, and a few battle supervisors had already entered the large, three level, ovular room. The metal surface was colored the same gleaming silver as the corridors, and the illumination panels built into the walls made the room shine brightly, making the room feel 'enchanting,' though Cha'Hawk felt that it didn't possess the aura of seriousness that should match the importance of the matters discussed in this room. On each level near the center of the room, there was a large gap in the floor, the size of the gap increased as the level decreased, so that the leaders stationed around the center of each floor could view each other on the floors, making it easier to have large meetings.

Cha'Hawk walked to his podium on the second floor, a stand with a flat surface facing him with a Data Module port, so he could connect with the joint server that would be used for the meeting.

Though Cha'Hawk and the other officials could have simply connected to the mainframe from their stations and conducted this meeting there, a disconnected data network that was placed in this room would be used, insuring that no prying eyes hacked into the gathering and spied on them. Though Cha'Hawk found this unnecessary, as the organics, or any other warriors with false intent, were doubtful to breach into the meeting in its short duration, protocol needed to be followed. And while they could simply connect to the network and transfer their thoughts and conversation through it, thus exponentially increasing the rate they could convey their information at high-processed speeds, their leader had deemed that these meetings would be held orally, reserving the data network for data transfer and Hall holographic controls only, as he preferred to draw moments out for maximum suspense. Which was one of the many reasons Cha'Hawk despised him; for delaying progress because of the needless element of drama and production, though few others would admit their distaste of their exalted leader.

After waiting only a few minutes, the last officers entered the chamber, and the door on the 3rd level opened, echoing around the chamber, immediately silencing anyone talking to each other. High Order Ki'Ra, leader of the invasion of Earth and coordinator of the Try'Lar expansion fleet, entered the room and approached his podium that was located on the third level. Because of his position in the Hall, Ki'Ra would be looking down at the officers he commanded, giving a clear and intimidating image of leadership. Though all Ribiyar were built identically, Ki'Ra equipped himself with thicker and more resilient armor, and a taller appearance as well, to further strengthen his image of authority.

"How goes the invasion of Earth?" Ki'Ra asked, his synthetic, slightly gravelly voice echoing through the room as he approached his podium. When Ki'Ra reached his podium, he inserted his data module into a port that was placed on the podium and activated the holographic displays in the Battle Coordination Hall. Many displays activated along the walls in the Hall, but in the center of the second level, a large holographic image was created, showing a live image of Earth from orbit.

"It goes well, High Order," one of the generals responded. "The strength of the organic's resistance decreases as the invasion progresses. Our analysts have studied the progress of our efforts thus far in the invasion, and they have estimated that the planet will be completely conquered within 10 *Qat* (Ribiyar equivalent of days)." The general went on to explain the brilliance of the plans he put into action, and the other officers also shared what they had contributed to the campaign as they gave their reports as well, and Cha'Hawk thought it would never end when he finally got a chance to speak.

"High Order," he began, presenting orbital close-ups of the Atlantic Ocean surface, "troops operating the Holding Facility Tri'La have detected the possible crash site of the *Ra'Ta*, a troop transport that we lost contact with during the initial attack. I believe that we should investigate this immediately and obtain the ship before the organics do."

Ki'Ra computed this data and then replied, "I do not think that will be required. If the ship is still intact, one of the soldiers on board would have activated the ships homing beacon."

"It is possible that there were no survivors, High Order," Cha'Hawk countered. "We have seen for ourselves that the organic lifeforms possess Electro Magnetic Pulse weapons, devices capable of disrupting us, and all of our equipment. It is possible that the warriors were destroyed by the pulse, but leaving the ship disabled at the bottom of their Atlantic Ocean."

Ki'Ra again computed this data and responded, "I do not believe that we should trouble ourselves with this matter. Even if the ship is intact, it is unreachable to these 'organics', because of its location beneath the liquid surface. I will not tolerate unnecessarily diverting our resources to prove your claims while there are battles to be won elsewhere on this planet."

"But Ki'Ra-"

"*That* is *High Order* Ki'Ra to you, Tactical Analyst Cha'Hawk. Do not forget your place. Are there any objectives that need to be discussed?" Ki'Ra asked as he glanced at the officers below. "Good. The invasion shall continue as planned. Disperse, and return to your posts." Ki'Ra disconnect from his podium and quickly exited the Hall. Cha'Hawk waited by his podium as most of the officers left, and then stopped one of the last squad commanders, a warrior with green-red armor, as he was leaving the Hall.

"Squad Commander Tau'Ka, I have need of your squadron. You are to search out the *Ra'Ta* and confirm its destruction."

"Are your audio receptors in need of adjustment? High Order Ki'Ra-"

"*I* am your superior officer Squad Commander. Do not concern yourself with High Order Ki'Ra."

"Very well, Tactical Analysist, but I cannot immediately comply with your orders. I already have orders from another commander to hunt down and destroy one of the organic's puny sea machines. I will start the search after their little toy is destroyed." Tau'Ka then turned and left the room, leaving Cha'Hawk alone in the Hall.

Cha'Hawk pondered these developments; especially why he just went behind Ki'Ra's back and defied his orders, but the highest of his concerns was that Ki'Ra was willingly allowing their enemy a chance to obtain some of their technology. The organics may be weak, but they should not be underestimated either. If Ki'Ra was going to let the organics gain the Ribiyar's own resources to fight back with, Cha'Hawk was going to take matters into his own hands.

"Soon, Ki'Ra," Cha'Hawk muttered as he went back to his post, "Soon we shall see who is the better warrior."

Chapter 2

Date: July 8, 2132.
Location: Aboard the *U.S.S. Atlanta*, at the bottom of the Atlantic Ocean.

"Captain, may I come in?" Lieutenant Commander Trisha Hayley, a slender, African American woman with shoulder-length brown hair, stood at the doorway of the captains' quarters. Like all personal quarters on a ship this size, the room was small and filled with only essential furniture, normally only big enough to hold two or three people. The captain's quarters however, was reserved for the captain's residence only, and the room also had a small table and a desk for his computer interface, where he could access ship logs and information on the computer. He could also use the computer to talk to other officers by either accessing the ship's communication system or talking to a person using another computer on the ship. In addition to the table and desk, the room also held a bed and a small bathroom, as well as a closet. Hearing Lieutenant Commander Hayley speak, Captain Jack Vade, a fit, young-looking man with dirty-blond hair, got up from his bed and stood to greet her.

"Yes, come in, Lieutenant Commander. What do you need?"

"I just left the Research and Development room, and I have been informed that the Genetic Modulator is almost ready for testing. Once it is completely operational, how do you want us to proceed?"

"For now, simply let me know when the GM is ready. In the meantime, continue to run more computer simulations while we wait. Have you heard from Chief Lexton yet? Do you know if they were successful in restoring our communications systems?"

"I am afraid that Chief Lexton was unable to restore the communications systems to full functionality, Captain. It appears that the communications, along with many other systems on the *Atlanta*, has been partially disabled or rendered inoperable by the Electromagnetic Pulse from the Korean ship, but we can still communicate within 5 kilometers with our communications operating at the rate they are now. Not that there is anyone to talk to down here. I also am here to report that the

Atlanta has detected something on sonar, about 4 kilometers away. We've tried communicating with them, but there had been no response And, since we are still trapped, we cannot move closer to see what it is. Should we continue trying to contact it, Captain?"

"When we get free, and we get a chance, we will investigate it further. But until then, don't worry about it."

"Understood, sir. Is there anything you need me to do, Captain?

"No, Lieutenant Commander. You can return to your duties."

"Yes, sir. Enjoy the rest of your day, Captain." Lieutenant Commander Hayley saluted Captain Vade, then turned on her heels and left the quarters, keeping the door open as she exited the room.

Once Vade was sure she left, he left his room and went down the corridor of the hallway. The hallways in the *Atlanta*, like any other sub, were very compact, only giving enough room for two people to barely walk alongside each other. Throughout the corridors, doorways were periodically placed so a part of the ship could be sectioned off to avoid the sub from sinking from a hull breach. The hallways were lit by lights built into the ceiling, shining white light onto the gray metal plating that comprised the walls and the floor. Though the mood of the furnishings would be considered 'dreary', 'dull', or 'uncomfortable' for civilian standards (even though they were technically right), military vessels are designed primarily for functionality and durability during battle, not for the comfort of its crew.

While walking to the operations center, also known as the secondary bridge for use if the main bridge was damaged or flooded, he hoped he was making the right decision about using the Genetic Modulator. With all standard and orthodox means exhausted trying to free the sub from the debris of the Korean ship that was destroyed above them, they had to attempt any unorthodox method they could think of to free the submarine. The hull of the Korean ship kept the sub pinned to the ocean floor, and because they were so deep in the ocean, they couldn't send people to remove the wreckage off the *Atlanta* because of the water pressure. To add to the list of options they couldn't use, they couldn't fire any explosives at the Korean ship because the debris would most likely land on the Atlanta and damage her even more, possibly putting the safety of the crew in even greater jeopardy. While it is unlikely that the GM would somehow be able to free them from captivity, it was the only option besides hoping an allied vessel stumbles upon them at the bottom of the ocean.

What none of the crew knew, however, was that Captain Vade himself would be using the device. Even though he felt it was the right choice, he imagined that many of his officers would object, and his first officer and Ambassador Shaan would most likely have the loudest objections to his plan.

Shaan was the Indian ambassador from the tribes in Naee Aasha, Indian for 'New Hope', a nation born three years ago in eastern Africa that was devoted to preserving Indian tradition. Though the opinions of his crew were something that he valued, and he would likely spend much time considering their arguments, it was unlikely that they would change his mind about his decision. He was the captain of the ship after all, and what he said goes.

He walked to the end of the hallway and turned right to face a doorway with an elevator door held behind it. After pressing the button to call the elevator, and entering it once it arrived, Vade selected the level that would bring him to where the operations center was located. After waiting roughly 20 seconds for the elevator to complete its journey, the door chimed as the door slid into the wall, and Captain Vade exited the elevator as he continued his trek to the operations center. After walking down the hallway and turning right at an intersection, he reached the main entrance of ops. By the entrance to ops, a scanner was built into the wall on the right side of the door frame, where Vade placed his hand on the palm scanner moving his eye to the retina scanner. After he completed those scans, he then typed in his personal password on the keyboard bolted on the wall beneath the scanner: Vade, Captain, A789, B217, D793.

After waiting a moment while the computer processed the information, the screen above the scanner reported: "SCAN AND PASSWORD

ACCEPTED. ACCESS GRANTED: CAPTAIN JACK VADE."

The wall in front of him then slid up into the ceiling, allowing him to enter. The door was built this way for two purposes. If an intruder was attempting to gain access to the room, he would first have to find the part of the wall it was at, and then get through it, a process usually long enough for security teams to intercept them, in theory, anyway, as the *Atlanta* had been fortunate enough to not yet be boarded by aggressive forces. The wall was also built that way for the door to close quickly: gravity would usually pull the door down along with the door machinery at the same time, closing it in less than two seconds.

The operations center was shaped like a half circle, with a door on each end of the flat end of the circle: one leading to a briefing room and the other door leading to a small supply room that held some food, water, and other supplies. In the circle part of the room, several computer consoles and displays were spread throughout it, some showing updates on the *Atlanta*'s current status, others showing visuals of the ocean outside from cameras equipped on the outer hull, but of course, all those monitors were dark because of the sub location at the bottom of the ocean.

As Captain Vade entered the operations center, one of the officers noticed him, jumped to his feet, and announced "Captain on deck!", causing the rest of the crewmen in the room to jump to attention as well.

"As you were," Vade said as he made his way to his first officer, Commander Adam Rickman, or "Rick" as many of the officers called him, who was overseeing an officer operating the radar equipment in the corner of the room. Rick was a white man with muscles that made him look like a body builder, and his crew cut style tan hair made him seem like a drill sergeant fresh from boot camp in addition to that.

Rick saw Vade coming and walked over to him. "Did you need me, sir?"

"I do, Commander. I want you to assemble a meeting of the senior staff in the briefing room at 1900 hours." (Half an hour from now)

"Aye, Captain. I'll get to it." Commander Rickman walked away from the captain, reached a computer console, and sent a message to their communicators, small wrist devices that resembled watches, that functioned as 'cell phones' for officers that allowed them to interface with the *Atlanta*'s communication system, connect with the sub's computer for status updates, activate a tracking device if they were captured, and many other features.

While Rick sent the message, Captain Vade went to the briefing room to prepare for the briefing, and most likely a heated debate, that awaited him.

30 minutes later…

"You can't be serious!!"

The voice came from Lieutenant Commander Hayley, who had been assigned to lead the development of the GM, who was sitting near the end of the other side of the table where all the officers were sitting. "Sir, no disrespect, but we don't know what the genetic modulator will do to you. While the results from our computer simulations may be promising to say the least, the information isn't clear on what the effects of the device will be to the person using it, or if using it will result in later problems to your biological systems."

"I appreciate your concern, Lieutenant Commander. That is the same for all of you," Vade said as he glanced at the other officers. "I take all of your concern for my wellbeing very seriously, and I would never want to dismiss any of your suggestions without thoroughly examining them. But, I believe I am the logical choice. I will not send other officers to this machine without knowledge of what it will do to them."

"Why do we have to use the device at all?" This came from Rick, who sat closest to where Captain Vade was seated. "I still doubt that we have explored every possible option. There just has to be some other way to get the *Atlanta* free."

"And we may find that option Rick, but we don't have the time to wait while we look for it. Our food reserves where already low before this started, and we only have a week's worth of food left, and that is with us rationing it." Vade took a deep breath and pushed forward with his argument. "You all now I have commanded the *Atlanta* for over a year now, and I have commanded two ships before this. I have gained what I set out to achieve. If my end has come, I need it to end by doing everything I can to guarantee my crew's safety, even if that means sacrificing my life to do it. Lieutenant Commander Hayley exactly how does the device work, and what are the advantages predicted from using the Genetic Modulator?"

Trisha paused a few moments while she gathered her thoughts, and she then responded, "Well, theoretically, the GM device is supposed to emit an energy beam at the subject, using the nuclear core of the ship to power it, until the person's body changes into a state of pure energy. When the subject reaches that stage, we then use the Genetic Modulator to alter their genetic code, allowing us to alter their physiology and genetics. After we have made the alterations, we then reconfigure the beam to 'reassemble' the person's body from its energy form to its physical form. That is the predicted best-case scenario. But, Captain," she warned, "we haven't tested it on live subjects yet, never mind humans. All that I have told you is heavily based on computer simulations. I again strongly recommend against this course of action."

"I know, Commander. And be assured, I have made plans if things do not go well. Commander Rickman, if something happens to me during the experiment, resulting in me being unfit to command the ship, you will be the captain of the *Atlanta*. You will also oversee reassigning officers as you see fit."

"Understood, Captain" Rick replied, his voice slightly hoarse with emotion.

"I know you all are concerned about me, and I am not blind to the risks involved. I am aware that I might not come out of that room alive. But I feel it is what I need to do. Does anyone have anything to add before we dismiss?" As he looked at the officers, Shaan, the Indian ambassador, who was deeply tanned, muscular, was bald expect for his pony-tail, and wore red animal fur pants and vest, stood and addressed the officers in the room.

"Many suns ago, my chief saw Indian traditions fading like the paint on an old car. He knew he had to act, and he requested a territory where Indian tradition could thrive away from outsiders. Many thought him mad. Many tried to stop him. And he faced many trials to achieve Indian sanctuary. But through his efforts, we Indians now have true home. Captain Vade, if you have same conviction chief had, pursue it with all strength, and never waver in that task."

Shaan nodded to the captain, and then sat back down. The room was quiet for a moment, reflecting on what they heard. Captain Vade cleared his throat and said, "Thank you, Ambassador." He paused and said, "If no one has anything else to discuss, that concludes our meeting. Lieutenant Commander Hayley, when will the device be ready?"

Lieutenant Commander Hayley shook her head to clear her thoughts, and replied, "The device will be operational tomorrow, by 0700 hours, Captain." (7:00 am)

"Understood. Expect me to be there around that time. You are all dismissed." As the officers left, Vade sat back down at the table. *Why was he doing this?* He asked himself. His father had always said he was a risk taker: leaping before he looked. Was it that, or was it more?

"Captain?"

Vade looked up to see Rick standing beside him. "Are you sure that this is the right choice, sir?" Though the commander was trying to hide his emotions, Vade could faintly see hope in his face that he hoped that Vade would reconsider his decision to use the Genetic Modulator.

"Yes Rick, I am," Vade replied, smiling softly as he said it.

"Then, I respect and will support your decision, Captain. You've gotten us this far, you can get us out of this mess. Sir, if you don't mind, may I be present to witness the procedure?"

"Of course, Rick. I would want you to be there. But Commander, make sure you're prepared if something happens to me. I'll need you to be at the top of your game if that happens."

"Understood, sir. I will see you there." First Officer Rickman then left the room, leaving Vade alone with his thoughts, and concerns about the looming operation.

Chapter 3

Date: July 9, 2132.
Location: Aboard the *U.S.S. Atlanta*, at the bottom of the Atlantic Ocean.

"What if we used the emergency surface protocol? It might be enough to get us free and closer to the surface." Rick was standing next to the captain, who was sitting on a chair next to the operating table as he prepared to get strapped to it. The operating table was designed to keep Vade up in a near up-right position during the 'operation', if you could call it that. They were both in the Research and Development room, waiting as the GM was being prepared for activation. The Research and Development room was shaped like a rectangle, with numerous tables and shelves displaying a wide assortment of devices and machinery scattered throughout the room, though it was still cramped as it was built in a submarine. The Genetic Modulator was in the center of the room, with the operating table in its range. The GM was built with black, shiny metal, and shaped like a cone, with a barrel at the end of the narrow side of the cone. Several cords were attached at the end of the larger side of the device, linking it to the computers in the Research and Development room, and other cords were connected to the conduit that would transfer power from the nuclear reactor into the Genetic Modulator. Several engineers were scattered around the room, or performing modifications to the GM, making final adjustments for the operation.

"We have already discussed this, Rick. Several of the air tubes were punctured when the *Atlanta* landed on the ocean floor, and the remaining tubes wouldn't be able to free the sub. Besides, using the tubes would most likely breach the hull from the stress. It would just make the situation worse."

"Sorry, Captain. I am just going through our options to make sure we didn't miss anything" Vade stood from his chair and leaned next to the operating table. The Captain had decided to wear his uniform during the experiment, instead of the civilian clothes he had in storage. Just because he was the 'guinea pig' of this project didn't mean he couldn't wear the clothes he worked so hard to acquire. Rick was also dressed in his uniform, though it was wrinkled, and it looked like it was the one he wore the previous day.

Lieutenant Commander Hayley entered the room and took a deep breath. "All of our diagnostics on the GM report that all of its systems are operational and standing by. Are you ready, Captain?"

"Yes, Lieutenant Commander, I am."

"Very well. I want you to know that if things look bad while we are making the modifications, we can revert you back to normal and terminate the project. But once we have made the modifications and start to reassemble you, we can't turn back. Your body will be too fragile after the alterations to reverse the process. I just wanted you to be aware of that before we begin."

"Thank you, Hayley. I am ready to begin when you and the rest of the crew are."

"Understood, Captain. I will go into the control room and apply the settings for the alterations. After I am done, we should be ready to begin the countdown to GM activation." Hayley left Rick and Vade, walked to the door on the side wall that contained the control room, a small room that had monitors and a window that allowed operators to know what was going on in the R&D room while being safety protected within the room.

Hayley entered her code and entered the control room. The room was shaped like a rectangle, and, while it was small, the equipment in the room was positioned in a space-saving way that allowed up to

12 people to occupy the room, and with the operation, the room would be very close to its full capacity.

Commander Hayley approached a 65' inch display screen on the center of the wall and used its touch screen feature to enter her commands. She pulled up the captains' bio readings and reconfigured the screen's setting to divide into several sections, allowing her to monitor his readings while using the interface for other purposes. She then pulled up the alterations that were to be made to Captain Vade, among which were bone enhancements which would increase strength, and would also increase blood production and white cell strength, strengthening the immune system. More enhancements would be strengthening muscles to increase stamina, endurance, and increasing skin strength, making it more difficult to puncture. Though the skin strength would make it difficult to apply surgery if the need arose, she figured that her and the crew would simply have to deal with that problem in the future when and if it happened and do what they could to help him.

Just as Hayley was about to send the data to the Genetic Modulator, she heard her communicator beep, indicating someone was attempting to contact her. She lifted her right arm and interacted with the watch-sized device. Touching the call notification on the screen, the device routed her to whoever was contacting her.

"Lieutenant Commander Hayley reporting. Do you need something?"

"This is Lieutenant Bedford in Operations. We are possibly detecting a ship on sonar. There are no responses to attempt of communication, and it is emitting unusual signals toward the *Atlanta*. Some the computer systems are offline, and others are not working properly. Since Captain Vade and Commander Rickman are currently occupied, I assumed that you would be the proper person to notify."

"Understood. I am on my way." As Hayley headed for the door, it occurred to her that she hadn't confirmed the procedure settings to the Genetic Modulator. She thought about confirming the settings now, but she decided she could do it when she returned, since they couldn't start the operation without her experience with the Genetic Modulator. As she left the room, the computer automatically activated the password portal and blacked out the rest of the information, a safety precaution installed so no one would accidentally leave the system unsecure, creating the possibility someone could access classified information. After she left the control room, Trisha exited the R&D room, and after briefly explaining the situation to Captain Vade, headed to the operation center to see what was happening.

Unknown to Hayley, as soon as she left the control room, the password portal on the display screen suddenly deactivated, and files and information began to be rearranged, selected, and altered, as the officers in the R&D room continued about their duties, unaware of what was happening.

(Computer alerts on screen)

WARNING. UNAUTHORIZED ACCESS DETECTED. ATTEMPTING TO SECURE SYSTEMS AGAINST INTRUSION.

REPORTING FIREWALL BREACH TO SECURITY IN 5 SECONDS.

Scans of the Captain Vade's retina and palm appear on the screen.

(Unknown User Inputs)

Authorization code: Vade, Captain, A789, B217, D793.

ACCESS GRANTED: CAPTAIN JACK VADE. DISCONTINUING SECURITY ALERT.

Show Genetic Modulator Settings and Allow Alteration.

FILES SELECTED: BEGIN WHEN READY.

Alter Genetic Modulations to These Specifications.

New physical parameters show up on the display.

WORKING...ALTERATIONS COMPLETE.

Select New Alterations and Apply Them to the Genetic Modular Operation Program.

WORKING...APPLICATION COMPLETE: SETTINGS CONFIGURED TO SPECIFIED PARAMETERS.

Alter Settings to Appear as Previous Settings but Keep Current Settings the Same.

WORKING...TASK COMPLETED: VISUAL SETTING PARAMETERS ALTERED.

Confirm Changes.

The previous parameters for the Vade's operation appear on screen.

CHANGES CONFIRMED.

Discontinue Computer Link and Delete All Logs That Show Alterations Were Made by Anyone Other Than Lieutenant Commander Hayley.

TASK ACCEPTED: DATA PURGE IN PROGRESS.

TERMINATING COMPUTER LINK.

"Report," Lieutenant Commander Hayley said as she walked into the operation center. Lieutenant Larry Bedford led the Commander to the display in the middle of the room, showing her the unknown object on the radar screen.

"Lieutenant Commander, we have unknown contact on sonar in grid..." The officer stopped and started to input several commands into the computer when the contact on sonar suddenly blinked off the display on the radar screen.

"Is something wrong, Lieutenant?"

"I don't know Commander. I believe that we were detecting something on sonar, but we aren't detecting it any longer, and the computers are returning to normal." He turned toward the Commander. "I apologize for bothering you, sir. It appears the sonar is malfunctioning. I will run a diagnostic on the system"

"It is all right, Lieutenant. Under these conditions, something is bound to malfunction eventually." Hayley left the control center and headed back to the Research and Development room. It was time to get the show on the road.

"Are you ready, Captain?" Hayley spoke through an intercom system in the Control Room. All the engineers that had been working in the R&D room had either returned to their stations on the ship or gone into the Control Room to monitor the procedure, with Commander Rickman and Ambassador Shaan also present to monitor the procedure. In addition, the medical staff and the engineering crews were standing by at their posts elsewhere on the *Atlanta* in case something went wrong with the procedure. Lieutenant Commander Hayley didn't want to take any unnecessary risks that she had to, and preparing for the worst-case scenario was the least she could do to minimize the potential danger the procedure presented.

"For the hundredth-time, Lieutenant Commander, I'm ready. Are you sure you aren't stalling?"

"Only partially, sir," she replied with a small grin on her face. "I am just making sure you are really ready to do this. We are t-minus three minutes to the procedure." She turned toward the officers in the room. "Begin activation sequence."

"Yes, Lieutenant Commander," they responded as they began inputting their orders through their computer interfaces.

She turned back toward Vade. "Captain, we are going to make you unconscious during the procedure, and we are going to administer some numbing medication. We don't know if it will be painful, but it will be easier to endure any possible pain if you are unconscious. I am administering medications now." She pressed a button on the display screen and the drugs began to be filtered into the air vents in the R&D room. While using an IV could be more effective, it was easier to administer the medications through the air, rather than hooking him up from an IV, so they wouldn't have to unhook the cords after they sedated him. An air vent that was positioned above Captain Vade started to pour down a white mist onto him, containing the numbing and sleep medications.

As the mist was being released, Hayley spoke through the intercom, "Captain, I know you may have the urge to hold your breath, but you need to inhale as much of it as you can." She saw Captain Vade nod and he started to take deeper breaths, breathing as much of the misty air as he could. Nearly thirty seconds later, Captain Vade's eyes started to close.

"Rick," Vade softly spoke through the intercom.

Rick approached the microphone. "Yes, Captain. I am here."

"Do me…. Proud, Commander." Vade's speaking began to slow down, his drowsiness increasing by the second. "I know you... can save… the crew. I... believe... in you." The captain then went into unconscious, his head resting back on the table. Hayley stopped administering the medications through the air vent, and the white mist slowly began to evaporate off Captain Vade's body, and the area around him.

"Safe travels, Captain Vade," Shaan spoke as he watched Vade from the Control Room's window. "May you find what you seek for."

"T-minus one minute to the procedure." Hayley said as she approached the computer console on the back wall. With the procedure nearing its beginning, the operators and technicians began announcing a multitude of updates.

"T-minus 30 seconds. Genetic Modulator is online."

"Begin rerouting power from nuclear core to the GM."

"Power transfer in progress."

Hayley activated the ships communication systems. "All hands. Prepare to switch to auxiliary power. Main power will be unavailable in 20 seconds. Primary computer systems will also be rerouted. The secondary computer core will be online momentarily." She cut the communication and activated the computer transfer. Moments later, she had the primarily computer core completely dedicated to the Control Room's systems. She immediately began to input her instructions.

Activate Genetic Modulator program in 15 seconds.

"T-minus 13 seconds," Ensign Laura Matthews, one of the technicians, announced.

ACKNOWLEDGED. LOADING PROGRAM NOW...

"T-minus 10...9...8…7...6…5…4…3...2...1."

PROGRAM ONLINE. INITIATING PROCEDURE.

"T-minus 0."

Chapter 4

Date: July 9, 2132.
Location: Secret Base on Hawaii.

"May I come in, sir?" John Whitefield, an officer with an average height and well-groomed blond hair, captain of the *U.S.S Ocean-Walker*, stood at the door of Admiral Hofkins' office.

"Come in, captain. Please, take a seat. We have much to talk about." Captain Whitefield entered the room and sat down in the chair in front of his desk. The office appeared to be small in its size, and it was even smaller with all the files and file cabinets scattered around the room. Ironically, the admiral's desk was in perfect order. Even the pens on his desk were lined in a straight row.

"I have a mission for you, Captain Whitefield. I need you to patrol the islands deep in the Atlantic

Ocean. If there are Ribiyar in the area, your orders are to take them out."

"Understood, admiral. I will get on it right away." He started to stand but then asked, "Is there anything else, admiral?"

"There is, captain." Whitefield sat back down. "I have decided to assign Lieutenant Oakland to you for this mission. He has been posted in the base on this island, and has been tracking Ribiyar movements across the globe. He may be able to keep you informed of their possible troop locations, so you know the best place to patrol and take out the Ribiyar posted in that location. He also has a good measure of combat experience, so he should be able to make a fine addition to your crew."

"Is that the only reason, sir? No disrespect, but I have officers onboard that have been tracking the Ribiyar as well, and they are quite capable of keeping is on top of their movements. In addition, my ship is filled with officers who have a great deal of experience running a ship of this class. Why are you assigning him to my crew?"

Admiral Hofkins sighed and said, "The lieutenant has been struggling with accepting the loss of a former comrade he had served with in the past. He has been reluctant to face the reality that he may have died during the first assault, and being out there where they last reported might give him a chance to move on."

"So, reassigning this lieutenant is more about rebuilding his morale and confidence, instead of what he can contribute to my crew?"

"No, captain. I meant what I said. He has been closely studying the movements of the Ribiyar, and has been closely monitoring the Atlantic Ocean, where Olo's comrade disappeared, and where you will be taking the *Ocean-Walker*. And from what I've seen of him he is a very experienced officer, and will likely be a valuable asset to your crew. This is just my way to kill two birds with one stone."

"Very well, admiral. Is that all, sir?"

"There is one more thing, Captain. I want you to take my cat with you."

Puzzlement was clear on Captain Whitefield's face. "Your cat, admiral? May I ask why you would want me to take your pet with us?"

"It is a prototype anti-personnel device. I want to field test it to see how it works. If it acts like it is supposed to, it will be very helpful if your ship is boarded."

"If you say so, sir. What is the device called?"

"It is an E.V.A.N. unit. It stands for..."

"An E.V.A.N. unit!!!" Captain Whitefield proclaimed, jumping to his feet. "Sir, why would you even have that device? The entire military knows of the E.V.A.N. incident of 2078!" Because of faulty programming in the unit, the E.V.A.N. disappeared while officers at a military base where showing several commanders possible military devices for future combat. The E.V.A.N. unit then attacked the compound a few hours later after activating the 20 other prototypes they had in storage, which led to a full-on invasion of terminator-like cats attempting to take control of the base. They were eventually all neutralized, but not before they virtually destroyed the compound and killing over 5 dozen officers and wounding 150 more. As the news spread, it was understandably proclaimed that dogs were officially 'man's best friend'.

"Captain, I understand your hesitation of using these devices. But the programming of the E.V.A.N. has been altered so it will only attack the Ribiyar. That is why we need to test it. If it works, it will be extremely helpful in ground combat. Don't worry, Captain; I also have added a function that can deactivate the E.V.A.N. with a remote, insuring that you can deactivate it if it goes out of control."

"I don't like this, sir, but I will follow your orders. I do, however, want to note in the logs that I recommend against this action."

"As you wish. When can you depart?"

"We are scheduled to leave in a few hours. We are still loading supplies aboard the *Ocean-Walker*. May I see Lieutenant Oakland before we depart?"

"Of course, captain. Talk to Officer Flier, and she can arrange for him to meet you before boarding the ship."

"Thank you, admiral." Captain Whitefield stood and saluted the admiral. Admiral Hofkins returned the salute, and Captain Whitefield left the admiral's office.

Location: Onboard the Ribiyar Warship *Ji'Co*, in orbit of Earth.

Squad Commander Tau'Ka walked into the hanger where his squad was docked on *Ji'Co*. The hanger was a huge, oval-shaped room that had a ceiling high enough to hold four additional levels in the space above the hanger floor. The area above the floor was filled with a large number of catwalks that were used for storage space, small repair bays for the fighters, and additional landing pads for the ships to be stored on. Along one side of the oval of the room were eight entrances placed on the ground level of the hanger, along with several other entrances above that deposited a person on the upper catwalks. On the other side of the oval was a large hanger door, which would split in half and move out and on top of the outer hull of the ship when the hanger was opened.

"Squad Commander." Tau'Ka saw one of the fighter pilots of the squad approach him. When the pilot reached him, he saluted Tau'Ka by raising his right arm in the center of his chest and closing his fist, slightly bowing as he did so.

"We are ready to fight, Squad Commander. What are your orders?" The other pilots saw Tau'Ka and scurried over, all of them saluting and repeating the phrase when they arrived.

"Warriors, our orders are to destroy one of the organic's sea vessels. When we encounter it, we are to disable it, and then board the ship and determine if there is any useful data that will aid our superiors in the invasion. After we have extracted anything of use, we will purge the organics aboard, and then the vessel itself. Our target is titled, the *U.S.S. Ocean-Walker*."

"It won't be walking when we get through with it," one of the officers remarked.

"Save your comments for the battle. Better for our enemies to hear it themselves," Tau'Ka responded. "Board your vessels, and depart at once!"

Immediately, all the officers hurried to their fighters. Ribiyar fighters were oval shaped, with its six engines along the middle of it. The fighter also had four, rectangular cannons that were placed between the engines along the middle of the ship as well. Though flying in the atmosphere was more difficult than space flight, particularly because the ships didn't possess wings, the Ribiyar quickly adapted to the conditions and continued to use the fighters during the invasion.

Tau'Ka boarded his fighter with his crew and activated the engines. The interior of the craft was, as was the exterior, shaped like an oval, with control panels positioned all around the cockpit, even on the ceiling and the walls, as Ribiyar could magnetize themselves to the surface of the craft, allowing them to fully utilize the space, and the zero gravity of space further facilitated their defiance of standards for organic ship construction. In the front of the interior was holographic display that showed footage from visual sensors on the outside of the fighter, giving a realistic view of the hanger bay in front of vessel.

While his crew oversaw the startup sequence, Tau'Ka inputted the codes that would open the hangar doors. Because Ribiyar didn't require air to breathe, their ships didn't have to depressurize in order to take off, though some of the larger and more equipped ships in the fleet could produce an air-filled atmosphere air if an organic prisoner was brought aboard.

As he and his squadron departed from the ship, Tau'Ka considered Tactical Analysist Cha'Hawk's orders. It didn't make sense for Cha'Hawk to risk his post simply to satisfy his curiosity about a 'mystery', but who was Tau'Ka to refuse Cha'Hawk's orders? Even if he went behind Cha'Hawk's back and informed High Order Ki'Ra of his plans, Cha'Hawk would most likely find a way to bring Tau'Ka down with him, and he had worked too hard to become squad commander to lose his post that way. He decided that it would be best if he submitted to Cha'Hawk's wishes and comply with his orders.

For now.

Chapter 5

Date July 9, 2132.
Location: Aboard the *U.S.S. Atlanta*, at the bottom of the Atlantic Ocean.

The GM produced a whining sound as it powered up, and with a flash a flash of blinding light, it was activated. The Genetic Modulator fired a white beam of energy infused with nuclear power at the captain. His body jerked from the energy, but otherwise he remained still.

"Life signs are stable," One of the technicians announced.

"Bring the device to full power," Lieutenant Commander Hayley ordered

"Right away, Lieutenant Commander. Bringing GM to full power now. Genetic alterations will begin in 20 seconds."

Though she knew what to expect the device to do, Lieutenant Commander Hayley was caught off guard when she saw Vade's body start to glow. She cleared her eyes to make sure her vision wasn't fooling her, but she realized that Captain Vade was…changing. His body was slowly being altered and turning into energy, just like they had hoped would happen.

The energy slowly covered the captain's body, starting at the center of his chest, where the GM was focusing its energy, until his entire body was just a bright white light. To say that her captain turning into a human light bulb was discomforting was an understatement. It felt, wrong somehow, messing with his genetic code. But it wasn't like she could do anything to stop it now.

"Lieutenant Commander, Captain Vade has successfully entered genetic suspension. (The term they choose for when he was completely in an energy state) We are ready to start altering him.

Hayley took a deep breath and said, "Begin the genetic alterations."

On the display screen Hayley saw that the captain's genetics were beginning to be altered, just as the device was supposed to. Though everything was going as planned, Hayley wished she didn't have to rely on computers for the operation. She understood that the alterations were so specific a computer had to do it to avoid human error, but she still held her belief that it was too risky depending solely on them. That thought gave her an idea. She should check the program to make sure there were no errors. She also mentally kicked herself for not checking it sooner.

"Alterations are 49% complete and rising steadily." She heard Ensign Matthews announce, but she was paying more attention to her display. The alterations that were being made to Captain Vade were different than she had programmed, further rising her concern levels from worried to near-panic. She quickly checked the computer to see what had been changed in the parameters to account for these differences.

Computer, has anyone made changes to the procedure other than myself?

NEGATIVE. NO CHANGES TO PROCEDURE PARAMETERS OTHER THAN LIEUTENANT COMMANDER HAYLEY.

Scan the database for any missing time logs, or corruption in the files.

WORKING... SCAN COMPLETE. TIME GAP DETECTED BETWEEN 1254 HOURS TO 1257 HOURS ON JULY 15. NO CORRUPTION DETECTED.

That was the same time I was called to the command center about that unknown object on sensors and when the computer malfunctions were happening, Hayley thought. *Only a three-minute gap, but with this program, only slight alterations need to be made to result in the death of Captain Vade.*

Feeling panic begin to grow inside her, Hayley quickly typed: Computer, scan the procedure program. Are the alterations on the file the same that are being made?

"83% complete." Ensign Matthews announced. "We are in the home stretch." Hayley couldn't call off the operation without something more substantial than a suspicion, they couldn't pause the procedure without risking damage done to Captain Vade if he was held in suspension for too long, but she had to work quickly. Once the procedure was complete and they started reassembling the captain, there was no turning back. The captain wouldn't survive being pulled back apart after we started putting him back together.

ATTEMPTING TO SCAN FILES...

ERROR: UNKNOWN FIREWALL IN PLACE.

UNABLE TO SCAN SPECIFIED FILES: UNABLE TO DETERMINE ALTERATION SIMILARITIES.

She assumed that whoever changed the program was attempting to keep them from changing it back. Hayley had to hurry. If she could stop the procedure and alter the parameters…

"Alterations are 100% complete. Molecular reassembly has begun."

"NO!!" Hayley yelled. She saw some of the operators glance over in surprise of her outburst, but quickly diverted their attention to their duties.

"What is it, Lieutenant Commander?" Commander Rickman asked as he rushed over to her.

"The program has been altered, Commander Rickman, and there is nothing I can do to revert the operation to its intended parameters."

"WHAT!!!" Rick proclaimed. Now half of the room was looking at them, but Rick paid them no mind as he continued. "Then, what is the captain turning into? Never mind, that's not important. We have to stop the procedure!"

"Commander, it's too late. Once the molecular reassembly has begun, we can't turn back. Captain Vade won't survive."

"He won't survive if the operation is completed!" He realized he was yelling, but he didn't care. "Isn't there a small chance that the captain will survive if we pull him back?"

"Rick, there is *no* chance. It isn't just Captain Vade. The genetic modulator can't maintain the field for that long. We just have to hope that he can survive as whatever he is becoming"

"Molecular reassembly at 56%" Ensign Matthews softly reported, her voice thick with fear of what they had done to their captain.

"Can't you use the equipment in the Research and Development room to scan what he is turning into?" Rick asked

"We can try. Look at what the readings show. I'll try to access the real procedure settings."

"Does it matter if we can find out?" Ensign Matthews asked. "We are going to find out in a few minutes anyway."

"If we find out now, we can prepare for what we may need to help stabilizing Captain Vade when he re-materializes." Hayley answered.

Computer, circumvent current file display settings and show procedure settings.

TASK ACCEPTED. WORKING...

"Trisha, the readings are inconclusive. In fact, they don't show any readings at all. Could he already be dead?" Rick asked

"No. While a person is being altered, the GM keeps the person in a state similar to suspended animation. It shouldn't be possible to be dead before the procedure is complete. Theoretically, anyway." Hayley said, not completely sure of her facts.

"Molecular reassembly at 87%."

ERROR: UNKNOWN FIREWALL IN PLACE. UNABLE TO ACCESS SPECIFIED FILES.

Hayley fought the urge to scream. Or punch her fist through the computer screen. Or both.

"Molecular reassembly at 100%."

Everyone in the room turned to look through the window. There was a blinding flash as the GM converted Captain Vade's body back to normal, whatever that was now. Everyone held their breath as they waited.

And when the light faded, Lieutenant Commander Hayley opened her eyes, and saw that her worst fears had become a reality.

Chapter 6

Date: July 9, 2132.
Location: Secret base on Hawaii.

"Lieutenant Oakland reporting for duty, captain." Olo said, saluting to Captain Whitefield, who stood near the dock where the *Ocean-Walker* was anchored. The ship was almost finished taking on its supplies and was prepared to leave in less than an hour. The *Ocean-Walker*'s hull was long and shiny from the metal plating that composed its surface. Though most of the top deck of the *Ocean-Walker* was empty, there were various weapons mounted on it, aimed up at the sky, ready to blast away any Ribiyar who approached. Farther down the deck, after a large open area, lay a tower that stood a few feet high. The tower consisted of various equipment for the ship, such as housing the communication system, and at the foot of the tower was the bridge, which could be accessed from the deck by walking up one of the two stairways that led from the deck's surface and up to the level where it was located. At the end of the ship, hoisted high above the deck and hung over the water, were three airplane-size rocket engines, which would give the *Ocean-Walker* the speed needed to arrive at their destination much faster.

"Permission to come aboard, sir."

"Permission granted, Lieutenant Oakland. Welcome aboard. It is good to have you with us Lieutenant Oakland. After you board the ship and store your belongings in your room, I have an assignment ready for you. Were you aware that Admiral Hofkins has a cat?" Captain Whitefield started to walk to the ship, and Olo tried to keep up with him, while he carried his luggage with him.

"No, sir. Should I have known?"

"No, lieutenant, just curious. The admiral has ordered us to take the cat with us, and I want you to be its supervisor, along with your other duties I assign to you while you're onboard the ship." They reached the ship and started to walk across the boarding ramp.

"Understood, Captain. I think I'll do fine. I have handled animals before."

Captain Whitefield chuckled to himself and said, "This animal is a little…different than what you have been used to. I have had the cat sent to your quarters." They reached the door that lead inside the ship. "I will have an officer escort you there." The Captain opened the door. "Good luck cat sitting Oakland. I hope you survive the experience."

Olo chuckled. "Good one, Captain. That *is* a joke, right, sir?"

"I never joke when it comes to military affairs, lieutenant. Report to the bridge tomorrow at 0700 hours. See you then." The captain entered the doorway, leaving a nervous Olo standing by the door.

"Captain, we are ready to depart." Commander Joseph Jones, an African American with jet-black hair, who served as the *Ocean-Walker*'s first officer, reported. Captain Whitefield observed the crew from his position at the doorframe of the bridge. The bridge had various control consoles scattered around the room, with crewman operating them, preparing to set a course for wherever they were headed. In the front of the room, there was a large window, that showed the sea before them, and there was also a large computer interface that ran the length of the window.

"Commander, once we are a mile from the island, engage H-mode and set a course for the Atlantic Ocean, full speed ahead. Alert me when we arrive." Captain Whitefield left the doorway and headed below deck.

"Aye, Captain. Helm, bring us out of the dock."

"Aye, sir. Reverse speed at 25%."

While the helmsman did his job, Commander Jones activated the communication system and set the system to broadcast to the crew of the ship. "Attention crew, prepare for ship to go to full speed and initiate H-mode in five minutes. All crewman on the main deck, batten down the hatches and report below deck as soon as possible."

"What's that H-mode he talked about?" Olo stood by the entrance to his quarters, preparing to see what kind of animal he was assigned to. The corridors in the *Ocean-Walker* were fairly standard for a military ship: metal plating comprising the wall, ceiling, and floor, no windows, lights bolted to the ceiling emitting white light in the corridors, and doorways periodically placed to section off a portion of the ship in case of a hull breach.

An ensign stood beside the door holding some of his luggage. "Don't you know what kind of ship this is, lieutenant?" She asked.

"I didn't have time to do any research on the vessel. I was assigned this position on short notice: I barely had time to pack my bags before I had to get out here."

"Lieutenant, this is an H-class battleship. Didn't you notice the big engines on the back?"

Olo thought back, thinking he should have noticed them, but then remembered he had been too busy talking to the captain to take a good look at the ship.

"I have heard of H-class ships before, but I have never been on one. Could you tell me what is so special about it?" The ensign took a deep breath, clearly frustrated at Olo, but then explained, "The H-class battleship is capable of hovering about 12 feet above the water surface. Many ships can lift themselves up somewhat these days, to reduce the amount of vessel in the water to increase its speed. But what is special about this ship, is that it has three airplane engines attached to the ship: allowing a maximum speed of 250 miles an hour, the first ship ever to achieve that high a velocity. That is why it's standard protocol for the crew to be either secure in the rooms above, or below deck before we go that fast. I have to report to my station, Lieutenant. Enjoy the ride."

The officer quickly walked away, and Olo didn't think it was her duties that were compelling her to walk at that speed. *What kind of monster was he assigned to?* Olo thought. Holding his breath, he opened his door to find…nothing. *Was this whole thing a joke?* It was after Olo entered the room and closed the door that he heard a meow come somewhere in the room. He looked around to see if he could find the cat.

"Here, kitty, kitty, kitty." He called, aware of how stupid he sounded. While he was looking, he saw a letter and a manual of some kind on the bed. He walked over to the bed and read the letter.

Dear Lieutenant Oakland.

I wanted you to be aware of what this animal is. It is an E.V.A.N. unit. If you are not familiar with the device, you can read the technical manual, though you should read it even if you know about the device. Your objective for this device is to bond with it, let it learn to be able to trust you. Its programming is adjusted for that bond; so, in combat, it will have the instinct to 'protect its master'. It is vital for this trust to be present so the device will work properly, in theory anyway. This device is highly experimental, and is *dangerous: so be aware of the possible risk in bonding with this machine. If you don't think you can handle it, let me know and I will assign someone else to train it. Come talk to me if you have any other concerns.*

Captain Whitefield.

An E.V.A.N. unit. That explains why everyone wanted to stay away from him. And why would Olo not be aware of E.V.A.N.? Though he hadn't yet been born when the incident occurred, its infamous tragedy was known to virtually everyone, and even included in many R&D department lectures, as 'Don't do This so Your Project Doesn't Become This' kind of lessons. Developed by freelance researcher Evan Adler, the term E.V.A.N. stood for

Enemy Vector Analyzer and Neutralizer. Though the incident with the device went by many names, Olo was more familiar with the "kitty catastrophe" than anything other title for the disaster with the E.V.A.N. prototype disaster. Olo briefly considered taking up the captain on his offer to let someone else take care of the cat, but then decided against it. What would everyone think of him if he backed out just because the task looked challenging? He would need to suck it up and go along with it.

He set the letter down on the bed and looked around for the cat. After almost a minute of looking for it, he finally saw the cat walk from behind the dresser beside the bed. Olo was momentarily stunned from the sight of the cat. The cat was slightly larger than other cats usually were, and curiously, the cat also wore a Batman mask on his face, modified to fit him perfectly. If the mask wasn't odd enough, the cat also wore a black cape that covered most his body, but the cape had a crease in it so the cat's tail could be seen. The cat's fur was also black, probably to accent the black mask and cape, or the other way around.

What was wrong with this cat? Olo asked himself, still trying to get over how crazy the cat looked.

"Meow," the cat spoke softly as he walked up to him, purring as he walked between his legs. Olo thought it odd that a cat, dressed like Batman, supposedly carrying enough weaponry to make even a Terminator jealous, was purring beside him and acting like a real cat.

Let's hope I turn out to be a fan of cats, Olo thought as he considered how to start 'bonding' with... Batcat.

Chapter 7

Date: July 9, 2132.
Location: Aboard the *U.S.S. Atlanta*, at the bottom of the Atlantic Ocean.

UNIT IS ONLINE.

RUNNING DIAGNOSTIC CYCLE:

MEMORY: FUNCTIONAL AND OPERATING AT 100% CAPACITY.

WEAPONS SYSTEMS: OPERATIONAL.

MOTOR FUNCTIONS: OPERATIONAL.

OPTIC, AUDIO, AND SENSORY RECEPTORS: OPERATIONAL.

SCANNING... UNIT FUNCTIONALITY IS AT 100%.

WARNING...POWER CORE IS UNSTABLE.

POWER IS AT 7% AND DROPPING.
SHUT DOWN EMINENT.
ATTEMPTING TO ACTIVATE UNIT CONSCIOUSNESS TO INITIATE REPAIRS ON POWER CORE.
ENGAGING...

Rick couldn't believe what he was seeing. Captain Vade was still on the operating table, but he had been completely transformed. All off his skin appeared to have been replaced with ink-black colored metal, so much that Captain Vade looked completely like a robot of some kind. The uniform he had worn to the operation, but most of it had been torn apart from where his body had increased in size, which was apparently most of his body. The bulk of his upper body had doubled in size, giving him a broad form, and his arms had nearly tripled in width, and while his lower half of his body had gained mass as well, it wasn't as drastic an increase.

Rick was the first person out of the Control Room as everyone ran behind him. Only Lieutenant Commander Hayley stayed in the room, rapidly typing commands into the computer console. Rick was the first to arrive to the captain, though he didn't have a clue what to do now that he was beside him, wanting desperately to bring Vade back to what he had been.

"Is there anything we can do for him?" Rick asked.

Ensign Matthews walked up behind him, concern firmly planted on her face as she concentrated. "I don't know sir, but we will do what we can for him." She gave directions to the other operators in the room, assigning them to begin various tests on Captain Vade, the Genetic Modulator, and the computer program, hoping to find what went wrong with the procedure. Ensign Matthews grabbed a scanner, a tri-angularly shaped sensor with a handle on the face of the tri-angle, and near the handle was a cord that connected the scanner to a tablet where the information was displayed, and where the settings for the scanner could be adjusted. After the ensign activated the scanner, she slowly moved it up and down the captain's body, slowly collecting data about his infrastructure. The device was a modified version of an x-ray machine, scanning in small, low level pulses to minimize the radiation the subject would get from the device.

"Sir, if these scans are right, then the captain's entire body has been turned into machinery. His heart, lungs, blood vessels, even his brain and nervous system: everything has been replaced with technology!"

"Increase your scan pulses to continual; that will give you better scan quality. We need to get as detailed information about him as we can."

"Sir, if the captain is alive, he may suffer radiation-"

"I am aware of the risks," Rick interrupted, "But we need to use whatever means we possess to get as much information about Captain Vade as we can. And if what you said is correct, if he has turned into a machine of some kind, he shouldn't receive any side effects from the radiation." Ensign Matthews nodded, adjusted the X-Ray scanner to emit more intense scans, and continued to collect more information about Vade.

"Commander Rickman," Lieutenant Commander Hayley called from the control center, "I have something I need you to see, sir!" Rick hurried into room, which had again filled up as the crewman operated the equipment.

"Look at these readings," Lieutenant Commander Hayley said as she pointed at a datafile that showed Captain Vade's biological information. Normally, this file would show the subjects blood pressure, heart rate, and other readings to help doctors keep track of their patient's status. But on Vade's file, he was showing no blood pressure, no heart rate, and completely void of any brain wave activity.

"I thought you couldn't access Vade's information because of the firewall blocking the data," Rick said as he viewed the information.

"This information isn't from those files. This is coming from the scans that the crew is taking of Captain Vade, and what the equipment in the room is collecting about him." Rick examined the readings and then looked at Hayley.

"Lieutenant Commander, if these readings are right, then, biologically speaking, nothing is left of the captain. Is that right?"

"That's what it looks like to me. It doesn't appear that there is any of Captain Vade's genetic code left, meaning we can't reverse what the Genetic Modulator did to him. I was hoping that you might find something that would prove my suspicions wrong." Hayley sighed and looked on the verge of tears. "If only I could have checked the program earlier. I might have able to save the captain from this."

Rick put his hand on Hayley's shoulder and turned her toward him. "Lieutenant Commander, don't go down that road. We need you to help us if there is any chance to save the captain, or help him adjust to his new form. Will you be able to pull yourself together?"

Hayley cleared her eyes and said, "I'll do what I can, sir. Thank you."

Ensign Matthews ran to the control room and said, "Sirs, I found something that you need to see!" Mathews led Rick and Hayley back to the operating table, and the Ensign pulled up the information the she found from her scans.

"I have completed my scan of the Captain, and I have detected some sort of power core inside him."

"And?" Rick asked, not understanding the significance of this find.

"Sir, his power source is unstable, and he's quickly running out of power. I hooked him up to a power generator, but it wasn't even close to being able to recharge him. It's only barely slowed down the rate of power depletion"

"What will happen if he runs out of power?"

"I don't know, sir. It is possible that we could re-activate him once we find a power source that recharge his systems, but it is also possible that we won't be able to reactivate him once he runs out of power."

Lieutenant Commander Hayley thought hard to find a solution as she looked around the Research and Development room to see if anything could help them. When her eye's focused on the Genetic Modulator, an idea finally blossomed in her mind. She turned back toward Rick and Laura and asked,

"What if we used the GM's connection to the nuclear core? Could it be possible that could contain enough of a charge to stabile the captain's power source?"

Ensign Mathews was silent for a moment as she considered this option, and replied, "It is possible it could work, Lieutenant Commander Hayley. But, we will need to work quickly to recharge his before Captain Vade's power core is depleted."

"Then let's get to work. Everyone, help us hook the captain to the *Atlanta*'s power core! I need some of you to monitor the power transfer from the control room." Everyone snapped into action, dispersing throughout the Research and Development room and the Control Room to do their part to prepare for the power transfer.

"Re-activate the Genetic Modulator," Hayley ordered. "Adjust its settings to only channel power into the captain. Do what you can to minimize the power output; we need to make sure we don't feed him to much at once and overload his circuitry."

"Understood, Lieutenant Commander Hayley." One of the officers responded through the intercom in the Control Room. "We are readying the GM now and will soon be standing by to initiate the power transfer on your orders."

Rick stepped back as everyone did their job, just as he did when the procedure had started. "An unexpected turn of events." Rick jumped as he turned to see Ambassador Shaan standing beside him.

"Sorry, Ambassador. I didn't see you there."

"Do you think Captain Vade has the strength to endure this trial?" Shaan asked.

"I don't know, Ambassador. I just don't know."

"Lieutenant Commander, the Genetic Modulator is ready," Ensign Matthews called over the intercom. "We can begin on your order."

"Everyone, get back in the Control Room, quickly!" Hayley said. Everyone needed to be in the Control Room so there wouldn't be a risk of someone being infected with nuclear radiation, or something else happening to them. When everyone was in the control room, she said, "Let's hope this works. Activate the Genetic Modulator and attempt to recharge the captain's power core."

"Understood, Lieutenant Commander." Ensign Matthews replied.

Come on, captain, Rick silently spoke to himself. *Have the strength to make it through this.*

POWER AT 0.1%.
    SHUTTING DOWN IN 3... 2...
    ...
    ...
    ...
POWER CORE STATUS: STABILIZING.
POWER INCREASE DETECTED.
    POWER AT 9%...21%...47%...63%...
    POWER CORE HAS REACHED MAXIMUM CAPACITY.
    ATTENTION: BOOT-UP SEQUENCE COMPLETE.
    UNIT CONSCIOUSNESS IS NOW ONLINE.

UNIT WILL BE RESPONSIVE IN 3 SECONDS.
    2...
    1...
    0...

As the blinding light faded while the Genetic Modulator powered down, Rick focused intently on the Control Room displays, trying to examine the results from the power transfer to determine if it successfully stabilized Captain Vade. Though it looked like the transfer had successfully stabilized and filled the captain's power source, he still couldn't tell if the captain was conscious. He turned to Lieutenant Commander Hayley to ask her what she had determined from the information on the screens, when he heard, "Where... am I?"

He looked around to see where it came from, and then he realized: it was from the captain, his voice coming through the intercom, though it was deeper than it had been before, and it sounded computerized and artificial. Rick hurried out of the control room and went to where Vade was laying on the table. As he got closer, he saw his captain slowly open his eyes, which still looked normal, but also had a more mechanical appearance like a camera lens, moving his head to look at Rick as he approached.

"Sir?" Rick asked, not wanting to let his hopes rise just to be disappointed again, though he felt them rising despite himself.

The captain lifted his hand, the restraint long ago torn open from his size increase and looked at it for a moment. Setting it back down, he finally said, "Rick, what happened to me?"

Sadness for his captain weighing heavily on him, Rick responded, "I don't know captain. I just don't know."

Chapter 8

Date: July 9, 2132.
Location: Unknown

In a dark meeting room, far from the chaos, two generals were quietly conferring with each other.

"Are these rumors true? Has other life been found?"

"It would appear so, but we may have found out about them too late. Our scouts report the planet they inhabit is under siege by the Ribiyar. They also report that High Order Ki'Ra is leading the invasion."

"It is curious to see him venture so far from the safety of his world."

"He must believe he is in no relative danger to himself to take this action."

"Indeed. Do we have the ships required to liberate this world?"

"We do. I must ask though, you would risk the lives of our warriors to help these people? We don't know if they would retaliate against us."

"It is possible we might not arrive in time to save them. But whether or not we arrive in time to save them, we will be able to destroy many Ribiyar."

"So, no matter how we play this, we win?"

"Basically, but we still would need to win the battle first. I need you to personally approach the War Council and make a case to fight the Ribiyar forces on this planet."

"Understood. I will notify you when they are ready." The officer then left the room.

"Have strength in your fight against the Ribiyar, brave alien warriors," the officer still in the room said. "Have the strength to survive."

Location: Aboard the *U.S.S. Ocean-Walker*, at the border of the Atlantic Ocean.

"Helm, all stop." Commander Jones ordered.

"All stop, aye sir." Lieutenant Jacob Johnson, the *Ocean-Walker*'s helm officer, replied as he pulled down on the throttle on the ship, and it eventually slowed to a stop. When they were stopped, the *Ocean-Walker*'s jet engines powered down to conserve fuel.

Jones turned on the ships communications system and called the captain on his communicator. "Captain Whitefield, we have reached the Atlantic Ocean. What are your orders?"

"Hold our position until I arrive. I am on my-"

A loud explosion rocked the ship. Jones and a few other officers got knocked to their feet. The combat alert automatically sounded, announcing to anyone who was too deaf to hear the explosion that the ship was under attack.

"Report!" Commander Jones yelled, though he was fairly certain of the answer.

"Ribiyar fighters detected!" Lieutenant Ryley Forrest, the radar operator, reported.

"Why didn't we detect them earlier?"

"Unknown, sir! They must have radar jamming technology!" Lieutenant Forrest responded.

"Of course they do. Like they need any more technological advances over us." He turned to Lieutenant Commander Haruto Zu, a Japanese officer with a shaved head and his name tattooed on his left cheek in Japanese symbols, who had recently been assigned as the *Ocean-Walker*'s Chief Tactical officer, and said, "Return fire immediately. Power-up the *Ocean-Walker*'s Laser Array, and prepare to fire at the fighters."

"With pleasure, sir." He said as he sent orders to the weapon operators below deck. The *Ocean-Walker*'s cannons immediately opened fire at the

Ribiyar fighters flying around the ship, but because of the maneuverability of the fighters', only a small number of the ships were shot down.

Jones continued to issue orders. "Comm, send out an alert to the Defenders that we are under attack by Ribiyar fighters." Another explosion rocked the ship, but he was able to steady himself. The *Ocean-Walker*'s cannons continuing firing at the Ribiyar fighters, but many of the fighters still managed to avoid the cannon fire.

"Helm, take the ship's engines at full throttle. We can't afford to be a sitting target." Jones ordered as he attempted to set a course to travel through the fighters circling around the *Ocean-Walker*.

Lieutenant Johnson attempted to use the engines, but the *Ocean-Walker* didn't gain any speed. "The engines are not responding, sir. One of the engines have been destroyed, and its destruction has disabled the other two engines. I can't get them to activate.

Jones sighed, and ordered, "Then get the *Ocean-Walker* in the water, and get us moving as fast as you can."

"Aye, Commander," Lieutenant Johnson responded as he began to input instructions to the computer. The ship immediately started to descend onto the ocean surface.

"Sir, boarding parties on deck!!!" Zu announced. Commander Jones looked out the bridge window to see two fighters landing on the ship.

"Lieutenant Commander, blow them away."

A cannon on the front of the deck turned toward a fighter and fired its payload. The fighter blew off the deck in a burning wreck. The cannon rotated towards the other fighter to destroy it, but the other Ribiyar craft reacted first and used its weapons system to completely obliterate it. More fighters began to land on the *Ocean-Walker*, destroying the ship's other weapon platforms as they approached, and the ship was slowly being covered by the alien robots boarding the deck.

"Security teams, report to deck one at once. Boarding party protocols are in effect," Zu ordered as he punched in more commands. When a ship is boarded, the officers are instructed to engage Boarding Party Protocol, which locks down the lifts, and engages the computer encryption sequence; tripling the firewall protecting the data in the computer core.

Commander Jones considered what his next action should be, when he suddenly realized that Captain Whitefield hadn't gotten to the bridge, or called in for a status report. Something must have happened to him.

"Haruto, have a security team-"

The bridge suddenly tore itself apart as it was being fired upon by Ribiyar fighters. Jones was knocked on his back and parts of the bridge started to fall on top of him. The last thing he saw was Ribiyar fighters flying overhead as they came back around to fire upon the *Ocean-Walker* again.

Olo was playing with Batcat (the name he decided to call the cat: if the name fits, use it.) when he was thrown against his bed as an explosion rocked the ship. He heard Batcat "MEOW!!!" as he was thrown on top of Olo and landed on his lap. Red emergency lights lit up as a loud alarm start to blare out of the speakers. As Olo lifted Batcat off him, he decided he needed to report to someone, and request instructions, since Captain Whitefield had yet to give him a post on the ship to report to if the *Ocean-Walker* was attacked. Olo activated his wrist communicator to activate it and tried to call the bridge, but he was denied as the officers were in contact with other officer that maintained a higher priority. With no other ideas, Olo decided the best thing for him to do was to personally find someone who could direct him to where he should go to help.

He got off the bed and put his hand on the handle when he thought of something. If the ship was under attack, he should activate Batcat's combat abilities. During the day's trip to wherever they were headed, he had studied some of the manual Captain Whitefield had given him, and he knew Batcat would probably be a good body guard for him. He fished a small device out of his pocket, a small cylindrical trigger, flipped the cover off the top, and pressed down the red button it contained.

He watched Batcat and waited for a minute. Nothing happened. Then, Batcat closed his eyes, and when he opened them, they were brightly glowing a deep red, signaling that he was primed for combat.

Okay... that isn't creepy at all, Olo thought as he and Batcat left the room. He wished he had a better weapon with him, he only carried a standard-issue pistol at the moment, but it wasn't exactly ship protocol to have a machine gun or a bazooka as part of your luggage. Olo figured he was probably lucky to have been able to keep his pistol, being new to the *Ocean-Walker*'s crew.

The ship rocked beneath him another time, reeling from whoever was attacking them, likely the Ribiyar, and then the noises of combat above him stopped. Wondering if they had already defeated the Ribiyar, he tried contacting the bridge again, but he received no response. Realizing something was wrong he quickly but quietly continued his way up the decks using the stairs with the lifts locked down. After only a minute of traveling, he approached an intersection in the hallway, and turned to the right, only to jump back behind the corner when he glimpsed a Ribiyar soldier enter one of the rooms in that hallway, probably hunting crewman down.

How did they get down here so fast? Olo asked himself. He took a deep breath to gather would courage he could muster under the circumstances. Somehow, armed with only a standard pistol and a

Terminator cat dressed like Batman, they had to bring this guy down.

"Let's do this, Batcat." He whispered. He looked down and saw that Batcat wasn't by his feet or anywhere in the hallway. He must have run away when he wasn't paying attention. *Terrific,* Olo thought. *Some bodyguard you turned out to be.* He turned the corner and was instantly punched in the chest by a metal fist, his combat-specialized uniform absorbing a portion of the blow so it didn't kill him. Olo flew down the hallway behind him, and collided into one of the doorways, 7 feet away from the intersection in the hallway. Dazed and heavily bruised from both the impact and the attack, he looked up to see the Ribiyar soldier approaching him. He grabbed his pistol and quickly emptied out his ammo at the alien, but the bullets just harmlessly ricocheted off it onto the metal plates of the corridor.

"Time to be purged, organic."

Olo was about to say something, but then he noticed something that brightened his mood. Batcat was standing were Olo had just been, though he didn't know how the Ribiyar hadn't seen the cat in the corridor, since the alien stood in the middle of the intersection only a few feet away from it. Batcat brought up his front arms, but on his arms, were… mini machine guns? He liked were this was heading.

The Ribiyar aimed his weapon at Olo, a large double barrel energy gun that emitted a reddish-orange glow at the end of the gun barrels, not seeing the cat in the hallway aiming at him.

"Any last words, organic? I've heard that your species sometimes like to say something before your lives are extinguished."

Olo struggled to sit up, a difficult task with his upper body throbbing the way that it was. He was finally able to sit up and, "Yeah, I do have something. Never turn your back on Batcat!!!"

The Ribiyar looked to the left and saw the cat aiming his mini machine guns toward him.

"Meow." Batcat said, deeply and forcefully speaking the sound, and Olo realized it wasn't his 'I want to play' meow. This was more like his 'I will destroy you now' meow. Arnold Schwarzenegger couldn't have said it better himself.

Batcat's arms lit up as his machine guns blasted into the Ribiyar, knocking him backwards into the wall. Batcat's bullets were thinner and pointer than normal bullets, Olo knew from reading his manual, and they managed to tear through the alien's armor and expose its inner circuitry. Batcat stopped firing, but as the smoke cleared, the Ribiyar still lived, and began aiming its rifle towards the cat. Olo thought they might have to make a run for it when Batcat's right paw flipped up and a small missile shot out of his arm. The missile shot into the Ribiyar's exposed chest, and he erupted in a small explosion. Batcat's machine guns went back into his arms and he went over to where Olo was.

I am definitely a cat fan now, he thought as he got up, after struggling for almost a minute to do so. After Olo was upright, he decided that, if the ship had already been boarded, then he needed to get to the armory, and properly prepare himself to repel the aliens from the ship. With his mind made, Olo slowly continued his trek to the armory, as Batcat scouted ahead of him in search of more Ribiyar to vent his wrath upon.

"Commander Jones, can you hear me? Commander!" Captain Whitefield yelled into his communicator. *Something must have happened on the bridge.* Whitefield lifted his hand to his head and it came back down with blood on it. When the first explosion hit the ship, he was thrown head first into a door he was about to open. When he regained consciousness a few minutes later, his head hurt like it had when he had been knocked out during a street fight in his younger days, and he figured the impact might have been enough to give him at least a minor concussion.

No time to worry about that now. His first priority was to head to the bridge, but he had to stop by the armory to arm himself, and help any of the crew he encountered. But before he did that, he had a trick up his sleeve that might buy the ship some time. He activated his communicator and interfaced with the ships computer.

COMPUTER READY: STANDING BY FOR ORDERS

"Computer, is the Laser Array on stand-by mode?" Captain Whitefield spoke to the computer through his communicator.

AFFIRMATIVE: NO TARGET HAS BEEN SELECTED

"Computer, access the targeting systems and open fire on the Ribiyar fighters orbiting the ship. Captain Override Code: Alpha79342, Gama1999, Omega8456."

OVERRIDE CODE ACCEPTED. WORKING... TARGETS IDENTIFIED. READY TO BEGIN FIRING ON YOUR ORDERS.

"Commence firing sequence."

ENGAGING...

Location: Aboard the lead fighter, orbiting around the *U.S.S. Ocean-Walker*.

"Ha! The organics scurry and flee like the insects that inhabit this world," One of the Ribiyar officers remarked.

"Don't underestimate them," Tau'Ka warned. "These organics always seem to have a 'trick up their sleeve', I believe their saying goes."

The officer was about to respond when he said, "Squad Commander, sensors are detecting a power build up aboard the organic's craft! Something is activating, and I believe it is some kind of weapon! Your orders!?"

Tau'Ka immediately responded, "Full power to weapons! Destroy the organics weapons before-"

On the *Ocean-Walker*, several large, bulky antennas, the fearsome weapon called the Laser Array, lifted upwards from their storage bays located across the hull, and they split open into X-shaped panels. The panels quickly lit up as power surged into their systems, and once they quickly adjusted their angle to face their targets, they produced a fiery red laser that soared towards Tau'Ka's fighter. The fighter was cut in half as the *Ocean-Walker*'s Laser Array sliced through it. The other fighters flying around the *Ocean-Walker* attempted to escape, or purge the Laser Array emitters, but they were too late. All the fighters in the air were shot down, bringing down a rain of scrapped metal into the ocean surface.

ALL HOSTILE AIRCRAFT DESTROYED.

DISENGAGING COMBAT ALERT AND POWERING DOWN LASER ARRAY.

Well, that takes care of that problem, Captain Whitefield thought as he watched the events unfold on the screen of his communicator. *But we are not out of the woods yet. Roughly 40 Ribiyar boarded the Ocean-Walker and they still have the fighters that have landed on the ship as well. We need to somehow stop them, and at the same time we need to secure their fighters as well.* Captain Whitefield continued to think of a plan as he made his journey to the armory to equip himself for the fight ahead.

Location: Onboard the Ribiyar Warship *Ji'Co*, in orbit of Earth.

"Tactical Analysist Cha'Hawk, I have news to report." Tel'Con Zan'Tar, an officer who wore a thin, sparkling red coating spread across the middle of his chest that identified him as one of Cha'Hawk's subordinates, along with his name, rank, and clan symbol, stood at the entrance of Cha'Hawk's work center. The room was a black colored, fairly large circular shaped area, with several upside-down pyramid shaped computer interfaces scattered around the room if a commander wanted several of his officers to work on something at one time. There were also holographic projections of several locations on earth shining on the surface of the wall, and most of the projections showed various cities throughout the world in ruins. Cha'Hawk was standing by the interface in the middle of the room. He ejected his data module from the interface and Cha'Hawk turned to Zan'Tar as it snaked back into his arm.

"Speak, Tel'Con Zan'Tar. What is it?"

Zan'Tar entered the room. "Squad Commander Tau'Ka's fighter has been completely destroyed, along with the majority of his fighter complement. It would appear that the organic's force that was targeted was more resilient than we anticipated. Scans show some of his warriors are still online, so his mission may yet succeed. Reinforcements are being gathered and will be deployed within one *Vel* (Ribiyar equivalent of an hour). I will inform you when the situation unfolds." His business completed, Zan'Tar left, knowing his superior preferred to be left alone when processing troubling news.

This does not bode well. Cha'Hawk thought. *Tau'Ka was the only high-ranking officer within my influence what wouldn't be highly curious or suspicious about searching for the Ra'Ta. Now what?* Cha'Hawk computed possible actions he could take, most of which ended in him being deactivated, taken apart and/or used for target practice, and it was then that the idea came to him. Don't take any action. Watch the events unfold. It was perfect. While it meant he would not be able to investigate the Ra'Ta, his instincts told him that it would appear soon enough, under enemy command. If these organics are as competent as 'High Order' Ki'Ra refuses to believe they are, they might be able to assist Cha'Hawk in his campaign to defeat Ki'Ra and end his rule.

If, the organic known as 'Captain Jack Vade' was as smart and resourceful as his instincts told him he was.

And his instincts had never failed him before.

Chapter 9

Date: July 9, 2132.
Location: Aboard the *U.S.S. Atlanta*, at the bottom of the Atlantic Ocean.

Lieutenant Commander Hayley nearly jumped out of her skin when she heard the captain first start to speak. He sounded so…different. Unnatural. It was like he was speaking through a vocal distorter used to disguise one's identity. She heavily battled two emotions inside her: one to tell the captain how grateful she was that he was still 'living', and the other to dissect him, the Genetic Modulator, and the entire computer mainframe and figure out what went wrong. Initially, she had waited to approach Captain Vade and Commander Rickman, so they could talk to each other for a few minutes, allowing Rick some time to help his captain with the initial shock of the transformation. But now, she had to intrude in the conversation, so she could examine his new body, so she could learn about how he operated and if his power systems had stabilized, and to see if she could find anything that might tell her what went wrong with the procedure.

"Captain?" He turned towards her, his body leaning against on the operating table he was on when the procedure started. She noticed that the restraints they had used to keep him held in place during the procedure had all been torn in half, a testament to how much Vade had grown and changed from the procedure.

"Before I begin, I am greatly relieved you are all right, sir. As you can see, me and the rest of the officers are examining everything related to the GM to determine what went wrong with the experiment. while they work, I need to examine you so we can ascertain how your body is functioning, and if there is enough of your genetic code left to change you back."

"Begin your scans, Lieutenant Commander," Vade replied, once again examining his hand to see the extent of his transformation. "Administer whatever test you can think of and get as much information out of them as possible." Nodding somberly to her commander's orders, Hayley grabbed an x-ray scanner that had been resting on one of the many tables in the room and stepped up to Captain Vade as she activated the device. Informing him to alert her if the radiation scans caused any side effects, she activated the scanner and slowly started to move the device over the captain. The screen connected to the scanner immediately began to show the data that was being collected, slowly constructed an internal map of his infrastructure.

"Forgive me if I'm prying, Captain, but if you don't mind my asking, how does this new body... feel? How is it different from how you were before?" She asked as she studied the data for anything that could indicate that any of his systems were destabilizing.

Captain Vade paused for a moment, and replied, "It is... difficult to put into words. I still sense objects with my normal senses like touch, but it also feels like I'm in a virtual program, controlling an artificial body. My vision is filled with a graphic overlay, supplying me with additional information my systems are collecting. It feels... surreal." Vade lifted his head up and turned toward her. "Lieutenant Commander, when the opportunity presents itself, I want you to bring me all the data relevant to the wreckage above us. With this body, it is possible I can free the *Atlanta* of her prison."

Stunned, she stopped moving the scanner as she asked, "How could you do that, sir?"

"I am made of a metallic composite that, as far as I know, does not exist on the periodic table. This material is strong enough that I believe it can even withstand the water pressure that exists this deep in the ocean," Captain Vade responded. "If I can get out of the sub, it is possible that I could move enough of the wreckage off the ship to allow us to ascend to the surface."

"Hold on, Captain. Slow down. How could you possibly know what material you're made of? My scanners aren't even close to figuring that out."

"It's... complicated. My mind is structured differently than it was before. I have access to my memories and experiences, but there is something else as well. Somehow, I have access to information stored within me that contains my... schematics. But even if I didn't have this information inside me, I also appear to have highly advanced scanning equipment that would be able to identify the metal."

Hayley deactivated her scanner. "Wait, do you think that your sensors could scan you to see if any of your genetic code is left in you? They would likely have a better chance of detecting it than our equipment, and your devices may not have the risk of irradiating the genetic material like these x-ray scanners do."

Vade cocked his head to the side as he thought, and then straightened it as he said, "I believe my scanners would be able to detect whatever organic material remains. Allow me a moment while I conduct the scan." Hayley stepped back as Captain Vade lifted his hands above his chest, and she was stunned when thin, aqua blue streams of light shone out from under his hands. The blue beams of light, likely scanning beams for the device, rapidly danced across his body for several moments, before they deactivated, and Vade lowered his hands to his sides.

Turning to Hayley, Vade said, "I am afraid, Lieutenant Commander Hayley, that I detect no genetic material left on my body, and only small traces of DNA samples left on my clothing. I doubt that alone would be sufficient to bring me back to my human form." He sat silently for a moment, inwardly confronting the now real possibility that he was stuck living his life as a machine. However, he quickly left his moment of thought, possibly to avoid facing his circumstances, and said, "I believe the best thing for you to do is to review my schematics and construction and see if I would survive an expedition outside the sub to remove the debris field above us." Before Hayley could ask how he would give her the information, Vade turned his head towards one of the computer displays in the room, and the screen suddenly began flashing with information and detailed computer graphics.

The data transfer continued for a few moments, and when it was finished, Vade looked back Hayley, who was slightly stunned from his action. "You even have an internal data transmitter?" She asked as she shook her head in disbelief. "If this was under different circumstances, I'm sure Chief Engineer Lexton would have a field day examining all the toys you have packed inside you." Taking on a more serious tone, she continued, "I'll look over the information you've sent, sir, and get back to you as soon as I can on whether you can withstand the water pressure. And though you say it's hopeless, I'm going to keep looking into the data we've collected and see if there is still a possibility of helping you."

"I appreciate your optimism, Lieutenant Commander. Though I doubt there is a way to bring me back to my previous form, the work you and the rest of the crew are doing is most appreciated."

Nodding in acknowledgement of Vade's words, Hayley then turned and walked to the Control Room, determined to do whatever she could to help her captain, and fix the mess that she put him in.

Commander Rickman started to approach the captain, but before he could, Ambassador Shaan walked up to Vade.

"I wanted you to know that my skills and services are available for your use in this matter, Captain Vade. Is there anything I can do for you?"

"There is, Ambassador. If you are willing, you can assist Commander Rickman and help him sort through all the data from the scans as we complete them. Do you have any skills with computers, Ambassador?"

"A great deal, Captain Vade. Before I become ambassador, I worked for CIA command and assisted with their program firewall and information protection." Seeing their confusion, he added, "It was years before Naee Aasha was born, and before I began to embrace the Indian traditions of my ancestors. I will endeavor to lend my skills in any way."

"Thank you, Ambassador." Turning his attention to Rick, he said, "Before you two assist the other officers to survey the information they've collected, Commander Rickman, I believe I have something to test out for you to see."

"And what would that be, sir?"

"If I'm correct, it seems that this body has a powerful array of weapons built within me."

Intrigued, Rick asked, "Really, sir? Do you think it would be possible to show us what they can do?"

"If you bring me something to shoot, I will decrease the intensity of the weapon to ensure it doesn't leave any permanent damage."

Rick retrieved a small empty metal crate and placed it onto a nearby table. "Are you ready, captain?" Rick asked as he walked clear of the blast zone.

"I believe so. Everyone, stand clear." Vade lifted his right arm up and aimed at the cups. The top on the middle of the captain's arm folded in, and a small black device appeared on his arm. The device was shaped like a rod, and then it split apart to make it V shaped, the point end facing the cups, with an energy emitter implanted on both side of the device. The emitter's shining brightly as powered was diverted into them, the device emitted a loud noise that sounded like a motorcycle engine revving, and then shot a blast of crimson orange at the crate. The blast soared towards the crate and sliced through it, bursting through the other side and striking the wall behind it. When the crew looked at the crate, they saw that it was mostly hollowed out, and reduced to a mostly-smoldering husk, and the blast had left a 4 feet-wide dent was left in the wall, sizzling from the heat of the blast.

The captain brought his arm down and the weapon folded back and retracted into his arm. Rick walked to the captain, keeping his eyes on the melted crate and the hole in the wall as he approached him. He turned to Vade and asked, "Was that supposed to happen, captain?"

"I apologize for the damage. I was not certain how powerful it would be at its current setting."

Glancing again at the wall, Rick asked, "What setting *did* you have it on?"

"The weapon was at 28% strength."

Rick was stunned. "It did *that* at only 28%!?"

"It did indeed, Commander."

"What other weapons do you have in there?"

"I believe we should wait until later to investigate my other tactical capabilities. I don't want to damage this place any more than I already have."

"Likely a wise decision, Captain Vade. I think it would be best to have a full report ready for the other senior staff in two hours. Would you be willing to let us run more tests to finish collecting the rest of the data we need?"

"Though I won't enjoy beginning poked and prodded like a lab rat, run whatever tests you need to. The sooner we find out what happened and examine the viability of my proposal to save the *Atlanta*, the sooner we may free the ship and get in touch with our superiors. We do still have an urgent food shortage to worry about, after all."

Location: Aboard the *U.S.S. Ocean-Walker*, on the border of the Atlantic Ocean.
Date July 17

Olo opened the hatch at the top of the ladder he was climbing, giving him an exit from the cramped vertical corridor he occupied. After climbing it for three levels, with Batcat riding on his back through the trip, it appears he finally made it to deck 7, and, according to the map the computer had given him, the armory should be located nearby on this level. Batcat jumped off his back and ran ahead to confirm the hallway was clear. After a few moments, he heard a meow, signaling that it was clear.

I can't believe I have a cat for a sidekick, Olo silently lamented to himself. Of all the macho leaders and soldiers he had heard about, he couldn't recall any of them left with a cat to watch their back. And then Olo's eyes widened as he asked himself, *With how powerful Batcat is, am I the* cat's *sidekick?* Shaking the thought out of his head, he hurried down the hallway and turned right and saw that the armory was just ahead. After reaching the door, he attempting to pull it open, but it was locked, and he had no idea what the code to the door could be.

"Lieutenant Oakland?" Startled, Olo jumped around to see Captain Whitefield walking up to him. The captains' uniform was torn in a few places, and a large bruise was on his head, though it didn't look like he was hindered by his injuries.

"It would appear we both had the same idea, lieutenant. I as well suspected that heading to the armory to better equip myself would be the best course of action."

"Exactly what I was thinking, sir. What do you suggest we-" Olo stopped talking as he noticed Batcat, was hunched down and growling at something down the hallway. He realized something was coming toward them; and it wasn't hard to guess what it was. Captain Whitefield hurried to the armory door and rapidly typed numbers into the keypad.

"Captain, is there any other exit from this hallway or the armory?"

Still typing, the captain said, "No. The elevators are shut down, and it looks like the

Ribiyar are coming from the ladders we took. We're trapped."

"I have an idea, sir. At the least, it can buy us some time to get a plan together." Olo then walked to Batcat and knelt to his height.

"Batcat, I need you to hold the Ribiyar off, at all costs. They can't be allowed to reach the armory. Do you understand?" Batcat meowed, signaling that he had received his orders. Olo stroked Batcat's fur and stood back up. Batcat meowed again, looked at Olo briefly, almost appearing sad to leave his side, and then leapt into the shadows of the hallway, disappearing from his sight.

"The door's unlocked, lieutenant!" Captain Whitefield said as the door buzzed and unlocked. Olo scrambled after the captain and helped him close the door. After relocking the door, he turned to survey his surroundings. The armory was twice as large as a person's living quarters on the ship, having three rows of fives gun racks, each containing different guns and the ammo to them.

"How long do you think that cat can keep them busy, lieutenant? I've heard of the might that E.V.A.N. units possess, but even they might not have the strength to survive the Ribiyar." Captain Whitefield said as he started to get some guns and attaching ammo packs to his belt. Olo went to some laser rifles and thought about what to pick.

"I don't know, Captain. Maybe, a few minutes at least." Olo put on some chest armor and started to get some battery packs, which was ammo for the laser rifles, when he heard Batcat's 'terminator' meow. The Ribiyar had arrived. Olo heard the Ribiyar shouting in their alien language, and then heard Batcat blasting into them with his machine guns. As he was linking his gun to a combat visor, a visor that went over the person's eyes that helped him see where he was aiming his gun, the armory floor shook beneath him and loud explosions sounded from the hallway. Olo feared that Batcat had been destroyed, but he still heard his machine guns blasting away, so he guessed that Batcat must have grenades stored somewhere on him. It was possible that Batcat had more weapons that he knew about; he hadn't been able to see the schematics of his weaponry before the attack began, so he didn't know what tricks Batcat had up his 'sleeves', or how many bullets he could store inside him for his machine guns. Just as Olo finished linking his guns to the visor, he heard a whooshing sound that he guessed was a flamethrower. How the designers fit that device into the cat, he didn't know.

The captain yelled above the gunfire, "Lieutenant, if we survive this mess, we need to head to the lower decks and get more crewmen to help us. Once we have regrouped, we need to get on the main deck and find a way disable their fighters without destroying them. Any technology we can gain from them could help us win this war."

Once he was done gather his materials, Olo asked, "Are you ready, sir?" He walked over to the captain, who was also wearing armor, had several guns and ammo clipped to him, and currently held a gun nicked named 'Quick-silver', a gun that had three machine gun nozzles, and had several clips stored into its main compartment, allowing it to store *a lot* of ammo. Because of the gun's weight, the user was required to wear a cast, a metallic robotic 'arm' that's wear on the user's arm that greatly increases the person's strength. Though the gun's weight meant the user had less maneuverability, it could fire 300 bullets a minute: earning the name 'quick' silver.

The captain was about to answer when he was knocked down as the ship shook beneath them from a large explosion, bigger than the ones that they heard earlier. As Olo helped the captain up, Olo realized that the gun firing had stopped. This could only mean one thing: Batcat had perished, and that the Ribiyar would be upon them in moments. The captain signaled Olo to stand by the door, which had been dented inwards slightly by the explosions outside. The captain punched in the code and threw the door open ... and then he froze. Olo jumped in front of the captain to sacrifice himself for him, when he saw why he had stopped. Outside the armory, the hallway was obliterated. Pieces of wall and ceiling platting where scattered everywhere, along with other pieces of the corridor, and several doors leading to rooms in the hallway had been blown open as well. If an object in the corridor wasn't on fire, destroyed by Batcat's grenades, or had bullet holes in it, parts of the Ribiyar were scattered on it.

And there was Batcat: sitting in front of the doorway, licking his paw.

"Lieutenant, how many Ribiyar do you see?" The captain asked as he tried to count.

Olo looked over the amount of the wreckage and replied, "It appears that there were... over 20 Ribiyar, captain."

Captain Whitefield turned to Olo and said, "How could this cat possibly destroy that many Ribiyar and not have taken any injuries?"

As Olo walked over the rubble to the ladders to travel to the lower decks, he replied, "It's simple, sir. He's Batcat."

Nuf said.

Chapter 10

Date: July 9, 2132.
Location: Aboard the *U.S.S. Atlanta*, at the bottom of the Atlantic Ocean.

"So, is there any hope to bringing Captain Vade back to normal?" Gabrielle Lexton, a woman with shoulder length black hair and a dark tan, who was the Chief Engineer of the *Atlanta*, asked. It had been two hours since the procedure had taken place, and Commander Rickman and Ambassador Shaan had worked hard studying scans, conducting tests with Vade, and looking over the data they collected from him as well. With all that data, he was as prepared as he could be to deliver his report to the other senior officers. All the officers were present in the briefing room except Captain Vade and Ambassador Shaan, the captain taking time to rest from his resent experiences, and the ambassador continued to work with other officers examining the data they had collected from Vade.

"I am going to be straight forward with you all." Rick took a deep breath and pressed forward. "There is *no* chance to bring the captain back." The room erupted in chaos as the officers began to shout their objections. After Rick got the room settled, Chief Lexton asked the question on everyone's mind.

"Commander Rickman, why in the world can't we bring the captain back? If we made him this way, can't we just reverse the process?"

"There are two reasons, Chief," Lieutenant Commander Hayley responded. "The first reason is that there is not enough of the captain's genetic material left, so there would be nothing to base our reversions on. The second reason is that, based on our analysis and computer simulations, the captain wouldn't survive the conversion back. It appears it just isn't possible to bring machinery to humanity, though it appears we can bring humanity to machines."

"In that case, Lieutenant Commander, do we know why the machine did this to him? I can't believe it did this because of something wrong with the programming, considering how closely we examined it. And that goes double for the Genetic Modulator itself."

"It is a difficult question to answer, Chief. We can't find a way to access the file the GM was set on, no matter how we try to get into the file. It doesn't appear that we'll ever be able to get in it, meaning we don't know the full extent of the transformation, even though we have the captain's schematics we downloaded from him. It is possible we will never find out how the settings where changed, or who did it."

"What about the security footage in the control room does it show anything?"

Lieutenant Kevin Nickland, a short man with crew cut red hair, who served as the *Atlanta*'s Chief Tactical officer, answered, "We have reviewed all of the footage in the control room and in the Research and Development room. There was no one in the control center when we believe the changes took place, and the computer display for the GM was on the wall, angled away from the security cameras. No one was in the room, but we can't see what was on the display. If we could've seen it, we might have been able to stop the events from happening in the first place."

After waiting a moment, Rick continued, "Though this situation is far from what we intended, Captain Vade has informed us that he believes, with this new body, he may have a chance of removing the wrecked ship above us."

"And how exactly is he going to do this task?" Chief Lexton asked. "No disrespect to the captain, but personally, I don't think that he alone can accomplish the task that the combined efforts of the crew couldn't complete."

"Under normal circumstances, I would agree with you, Chief. But from what we've studied of his schematics, Captain Vade has a powerful array of weaponry installed within him, and given enough time, the captain can cut through the wreckage of the ship and remove enough off the *Atlanta* to allow us to escape."

"And how long will it take to do that?" Lieutenant Commander Hayley asked. "We only have five days of food left, and the crew's morale is at an all-time low. I don't know how much longer we can go on like this, sir."

"I'm afraid we just have to make do with what we have, Lieutenant Commander, and keep pressing forward. The captain can't give us an exact estimate of how long it will take, but it is by far the best chance we've got so far."

"Commander Rickman," Chief Lexton spoke, "what if we use the Genetic Modulator to make more food and supplies? If the device created Captain Vade's new form, with all the advances in technology it had, couldn't we use it to synthesize food?

"I like your line of thinking, Chief Lexton," Rick replied, "But that is part of the problem with bringing Captain Vade back to normal. The GM apparently can only make inorganic material, like metal. The device isn't capable of making organic material, meaning we can't use it to make food."

"Does that mean that... if these changes to the captain's file hadn't been made, he wouldn't have survived?"

"It does, Chief. If we had returned the captain to his normal state, he would have been fine. The GM can bring back something that hasn't been altered. But you are correct. If the captain had been altered as we planned, he would never have survived." The room was silent as they realized that this unknown hacker had apparently saved the captains life. Lieutenant Commander Hayley was the first to break the silence. "How soon can the captain start working on the debris above us?"

"He said he is ready when the procedure is authorized by us."

"Why would he need our permission?" Lieutenant Nickland asked. "He is our superior officer; he can do whatever he thinks is best without needing our approval.

"That... is my last bit of news." Rick said cautiously. "The captain has officially resigned from command and designated me as the commanding officer of the *Atlanta*." The room once again erupted in argument and bewilderment over the news. When the room calmed down, Lieutenant Commander Hayley asked, "Why in the name of the seven seas would he do that?"

"Vade didn't feel that he was qualified to remain the captain with the recent events that have taken place. With his recent chance, he knew that our superiors back home were unlikely to allow him to retain his command and are likely to pull him away for study and examination. Also... should something happen to him while he's working on the wreckage, he wanted the transition of command already taken place so we wouldn't be without a leader to guide us forward." Looking at the faces of the officers in the room, Rick asked, "That being said, I think we should go ahead and decide. Does everyone agree that Vade should begin working on the wreckage?" When all the officers replied yes, Rick said, "If no one has anything to discus, this briefing is adjourned. I will inform Jack that he will begin within the hour." Leaving the other officers in the Briefing Room, Rick made his way to Vade's quarters to inform him of the decision and help him prepare for his undersea mission.

After traveling to Vade's room, still located at the captains quarters, as the change of command had only been made recently been made, and Rick didn't feel any desire to rush him out of the room, he raised his hand to knock on the door, but saw that it was cracked open. Slowly edging the door open, Rick peered into the room, and saw Vade sitting at his desk. He had removed the remains of his torn uniform, which Rick knew likely would have been unsettling for him as he had been extremely proud of his command attire and the position it accompanied, and was now clothed only by his metal armor, which made sense to Rick as he now possessed a purely mechanical body, like the Iron Man suit he had seen in comics and movies when he was younger. In his right hand, Vade held a picture from about ten years ago, showing Jack alongside a woman he didn't recognize, who had a light tan and red hair.

"Sir?" He asked, trying to respectfully grab his attention. Vade quickly put down the picture and turned towards him.

"Sorry, Commander- Captain Rickman," Vade said, correcting himself, "I was caught up in my thoughts and didn't hear you come in. And don't feel the need to address me formerly; there's no reason for you to do that anymore. Just call me Jack. It is my name, after all."

"All right, Jack," Rick said, trying to get used to the new title. "I wanted to tell you that, while everyone was understandably shocked by your resignation of command, we all agreed you should try out your plan to free the *Atlanta*, and that you can begin as soon as you're ready."

"Well, I'm as ready as I can be right now," Jack said as he got out of his chair. "I might as well go ahead and get out and started." Jack quickly deposited his picture in a desk draw and closed it, and followed Rick out of the room to the hatch Vade would use to exit the sub.

5 minutes later...

"*Are you ready, Jack?*" Chief Lexton asked over the communication channel, received silently into his internal transmitters. The docking hatch he stood in was a simple, small room that had the small flooring, wall, and ceiling plating as the other rooms of the ship, and all that the room held inside it was a circular docking port. The room was to be closed off and flooded, and then left open for Jack when he completed his task.

"I'm ready for departure Chief Lexton."

"*Acknowledged, Jack. We will stay in radio contact with you while you're out there and are standing by to provide whatever assistance we can.*" After a short pause, Lexton reported, *"Brace yourself, we are flooding the room now."*

Water immediately gushed from the circular docking port in the wall as it was lifted upwards into the ceiling above it. Jack maneuvered away from the geyser, and put his back against the wall. In minutes, the room was completely submerged.

Chief Lexton spoke through the comm, *"We've unlocked the hatch Jack, and you are clear to depart. Good luck."*

"Acknowledged. I'm opening the hatch now." Turning the wheel on the hatch, he lifted it upwards, and swam out of the compartment. Once he was in the ocean's water, he immediately felt the immense weight of all the water pressing down on him, but surprising it, his metallic structure so far seemed to be well withstanding the environment. Adapting to the darkness, his eyes activating a type of enhanced night-vision that allowed him to see in the dark. His scanning equipment also activated, without the use of the blue scanning beams, to provide him a rough visualized map beyond the reach of his eyes.

Swimming high enough to get a good look above the sub, he saw the crumpled and broken remains of the Korean battleship that laid over the *Atlanta*, but to his surprise, it was still mostly intact. From that realization, he knew that removing it from above the *Atlanta* would prove to be a more difficult task than he had anticipated.

"Jack, can you see out there? How bad is it?" Captain Rickman talked into the comm.

"It would be easier if I showed it to you, Captain Rickman." Jack began transmitting the visual and sensor information that he was receiving, so they would better understand what was happening. "It appears that it is worse than we thought, Captain. Though the hull integrity has most definitely been compromised, resulting in the death of everyone on board, most of the debris is still connected with each other, and collected mostly above the *Atlanta*."

"*How is the sub not being crushed?*" Chief Lexton asked. "*There's no way the* Atlanta *could support that much weight.*"

"It appears there are some rock formations around the sub that are acting like pillars to support the weight. It is going to be more difficult to complete this task than we had hoped."

"*So is there no chance to move the wreckage, Jack?*" Commander Hayley spoke through the comm. Because Rick had been promoted from commander to the captain of the *Atlanta*, he had decided to promote Hayley from lieutenant commander to commander, so there wouldn't be a lapse in the command structure.

"I didn't say that. But the odds are considerably lower than they were before."

"*Can you think of anything that you could do, no matter how unlikely it sounds? Even the most remote possibility could be the answer for our problem.*"

"Give me a moment to think." Jack was silent for a minute as he used all of his computing power to think of a workable solution to their problem. And then, after considering thousands of scenarios, a memory surfaced from a day before.

"Commander Hayley, yesterday you mentioned during a report that you gave to me that you thought that there might be a ship within the range of our communications, but was unresponsive when you tried to make contact?"

Hayley thought a moment and said, *"It is possible there is something out there. But, do you think it's wise to use the time to confirm it?"*

"If there is another ship down here, we need to get in contact with them and convince them to lend us aid. To be honest Captain Rickman, trying to find this ship is likely the best way to remove the wreckage from the *Atlanta*. There is just too much for me to move by myself."

After silently weighing his options, Rick replied, *"All right. Get over there as quick as you can and see if you can make contact with this vessel. Please hurry, Jack. There is no time to waste."*

"Don't worry, Captain, Rickman. I'll get over there in no time." Positing himself in the direction of the supposed ship, Jack activated another system he had been recently gifted with, a device similar to a jet pack. Two thin, 4 foot wings deployed from the middle of his back, and straightened out horizontally near his shoulders. In the exposed compartment where the wings had been located, a small, cone shaped engine raised outwards until it was out of his back. Activating it, Jack sped towards his destination, determined to save the crew he formally commanded. If he wasn't successful in freeing them, it was likely nothing else could save them from their fate.

Chapter 11

Date: July 9, 2132.
Location: Aboard the *U.S.S. Ocean-Walker*, on the border of the Atlantic Ocean.

"So, what's the plan, captain? Assuming, of course, that there is one." Olo said as he looked among the crew they had found. While scavenging the decks, Captain Whitefield and Olo had been able to find thirty crewmen fit to fight the Ribiyar. Whitefield had then ordered the wounded to remain in the mess hall and wait for them to return. The mess hall was a large room, with over a dozen tables occupying most of the space. Along the walls, serving lines and food trays were stationed for when the crew was receiving their meals. Because of all the injured crewman, all the tables in the room where serving as operating tables as field medics attempted to stabilize the wounded crew that lay on the tables, with many other officers laying on blankets scattered around the area.

"I do, but it is going to be difficult to pull off. Do you know if Batcat can reload his ammo by himself?"

"I don't know for sure, but we need to try anyway, sir. I would guess that he is getting low by now." While Olo and Captain Whitefield had been searching for other members of the crew, they had encountered roughly a dozen Ribiyar. Though they had defeated all of them, fortunately without taking any further casualties, Batcat had used much of his ammunition to secure their safety. Though the cat could apparently carry a surprisingly large amount of ammo, given how small his size would result in smaller space to store weapons, he knew Batcat was most likely very close to running out of bullets for his machine guns, which could be disastrous during the upcoming fight with the Ribiyar invaders.

"All right. Send him back to the armory with the code for the door. He'll have to find a way to open it himself. Tell him to load himself with as much ammunition he can carry and instruct him to then head to the main deck and wait for us to start fighting. We need him to provide cover fire for us while we make a break for the shuttles. We can't let them escape in them, or get in the air to attack us."

"Understood, Captain." Olo relayed the commands to Batcat, who immediately sped off into the hallway.

"Sir, couldn't we use the *Ocean-Walker*'s Laser Array to take the Ribiyar out?" Lieutenant Commander

Luke Fitzburg, a brawn, muscular officer with sandy blond hair, asked.

"I'm afraid we can't access it. The Ribiyar are blocking my commands, so they have either disabled the Array completely, or they have taken control of it. Regardless, the Laser Array can't target something that is on the decks of the ship, unfortunately."

"Is there any chance that another ship might come and help us with the Ribiyar?" Olo asked.

"I don't know. The *Ocean-Walker*'s records show that a distress message was sent, but I don't know if anyone was in range to receive it. Hopefully someone might notice we have been radio silent, but considering our mission, other ships might interpret the silence to sneak up on the Ribiyar. Unfortunately, we can't afford to wait for someone to help us." Captain Whitefield took a deep breath and continued. "Here's the plan. We need to travel to the upper deck, and make one final push against the Ribiyar there. The security camera's show that they are all up there, some of them in what's left of the bridge."

"Why would they risk leaving the camera's functional?" Lieutenant Commander Fitzburg asked. "Or, why would they leave the computer unlocked for us to access the security footage?"

"My guess is that they want us to confront them." Olo replied. "It would be easier to deal with all of us when were all in one place, out in the open. Or, they could be manipulating the video feed. For all we know, they could be on this deck, ready to pounce on us."

"We can't worry about that now." Captain Whitefield said. "Even if they know we are coming, we can't let that stop us from prevent their attempt to destroy the *Ocean-Walker*. When we get there, we need to split into two teams, one attacking the Ribiyar at the bridge, the rest securing the shuttles. If one group fails, the chances of success drop drastically, so coordinating our efforts will be essential to this plan. Are you all ready, officers?"

"Aye, Captain!" They all responded.

"Then let's, move out!!" Captain Whitefield led the way out of the room to the ladders they would take to deck two, right under the main deck.

Location: At the bottom of the Atlantic Ocean, aboard the *U.S.S. Atlanta*.

In the bridge of the *Atlanta*, Rick and the rest of the officers waited as patiently as they could under the circumstances as Jack made the journey to the unknown contact on their radar. The bridge was shaped ovular, with two doors leading into it, one on each side of the bottom half of the room. Various consoles were stationed around the room for the officers to send their orders to the other sections of the ship, or so the officers could access the ships systems, like radar or engine control, for their use. Two consoles were stationed in the middle of the oval, the helms control was the nearest to the wall, and the ships tactical console was stationed a few feet behind the console. Behind those two consoles lay the captain's chair, where the commanding officer could sit while he gave orders to his crew. To the left and right of the tactical console lay a stand that held a 6-foot-tall video screen that could show information from the computer, video footage from the *Atlanta*'s periscope, and other uses. The screen to the right of the captain's chair was currently active, displaying the video feed Jack continued to send to them as he traversed the ocean.

Sitting in his command chair as he waited, Rick felt foolish, partaking in what seemed to him like a wild goose chase, and let down after Jack had told him how unlikely it would be for him to move the wreckage off the ship. But all his other options for freeing the *Atlanta* had been exhausted, and he now had no other option than to hope Jack found some help so deep in the ocean.

After minutes of traveling through the ocean, Jack finally reported, "*Captain Rickman, I am getting close to the contact.*" On the floor of the ocean, there appeared to be a small canyon of some kind.

"Jack, is that canyon on the screen a natural formation?"

"*I don't believe so. It seems to be more similar to a crash trail of a ship. If so, the vessel would have to be a great size to create this big an impact.*" After a minute more of traveling, something large appeared on the screen, something that was clearly not part of the ocean. As Jack got closer, the video revealed sections of a ship hidden under sand and rocks from the ocean floor.

Though much of the ship was hidden, Rick could faintly make out several large engines at the rear of the vessel, and a large wing that was slanted upright out of the surface of the ocean floor. It appears that a ship was down here, just like they had hoped.

"Jack, do you have any idea what kind of ship that is? Or what nation it belongs to?"

After a moment of silence, Jack responded, "*I don't have a clue, Captain Rickman. It doesn't match anything I've ever seen before.*" As Jack continued closer to the ship, Rick began to see how big it was, at least a few city blocks in length and width, despite how much of the ship was buried under rock and sand.

"Jack, can you tell if the hull is still intact?"

"*I'm unable to determine that either. I don't know the designs of the ship, so I can't tell if something is damaged, or if it is meant to look that way. But, from what I can see... I believe the ship may be of alien origin.*"

"What!?" Captain Rickman exclaimed. "How can you be sure of this?"

"*As I said before, this ship does not match anything I have ever seen before, and from what I can see, it does not appear to be created using known methods of ship construction. The engines alone look far too advanced to be a ship of our design. Furthermore, from what I can see of the ship, it was meant to be a spacefaring vessel, and it would be immensely difficult for any nation on Earth to create a vessel this size without anyone discovering its presence. And you heard the same reports on the bridge that I did, reporting that alien ships were bombing their cities, and armies hunting down their citizens."* After a pause, Jack said, *"Captain, I want to try to board this vessel. If I can find a way to take control of it, I could try to use it to move the wreckage off the* Atlanta."

"Jack, if there are aliens on that ship, it wouldn't be safe for you to try to get in there. We just have to find another-"

"Respectfully, Captain Rickman," Jack interrupted, *"There isn't any other way. If there are aliens on that ship, and they fight me, I'll use every weapon I have to fight back. This is why I resigned my commission, so I could risk my life for my crew, without worrying if I would be able to make it back alive. Please, permit me to board the ship."*

Rick thought for a moment in silence and glanced at Commander Hayley. "Commander, what do you think?"

"Well... based on what Jack said, I agree it may be our only hope to getting out of here. I say you should go for it, sir." Rick thought a little more, and then made his decision.

"Jack, you have my permission. Do whatever you can to get in that ship."

"Thank you, Captain Rickman. I will require a moment to find an entry point. Stand by."

Moving closer towards the ship, Jack activated the scanning equipment on his hands, the blue light beams rapidly moving across the surface of the alien vessel. After traveling around some of the ship, he at last found an entry point on the underside of the ship.

Close enough to the ship to manage without his flight systems, he deactivated them and swam the rest of the way. Arriving within reach of the silver-colored hull of the vessel, he saw what looked like a docking hatch or an entry way of some kind. The housing of the hatch was circularly shaped, containing a similarly-shaped circular door within it. From what he could tell, the door appeared to break into smaller pieces when it opened, though he could not see an exterior control panel on the hull to open the hatch. When he could not find any external manual release mechanisms, Jack attempted to force it open with brute force. He pulled his arm back, rerouted additional power to his arm to increase his strength and punched the door with all his might. A loud clanging sound echoed in the water as the two metal surfaces collided. Though it appeared the port had bent in slightly, the door was otherwise unchanged.

Undaunted, Jack instead attempt to drill through the hatch with one of his new weapons. On the bottom of Jack's left arm, some of the metal folded apart. A black, cylindrical device, with a gun-like nozzle at the end, lowered out of his arm. The device, titled a Laser Cannon, revved up to full power, and activated, firing a continuous deep-red beam at the hatch. Reinforcing the Laser Cannon's energy cells with his own power core, he continued drilling for several minutes, until he finally made a hole barely big enough for him to squeeze through.

The inside of the hatch had little features in it, though many blacked-out, triangular screens lined the corridor. Fortunately, the alien ship had crashed so that it was tilted to the right. If the ship had landed flatly, water might have flooded the ship when after he broke through the door on the other side of the hatch, which would've considerably complicated his mission to take command of this vessel. The corridor was shaped circular, with the floor comprising most of the bottom of the circle. Another circular door was at the end of the hatch, but to Jack's surprise, and delight, he saw the door was slightly open, perhaps jarred loose during the crash. Like the outer hatch door, this door appeared to pull apart and separate as it was moved into the wall. Griping the small opening between the door plates, he used his all his strength to move them further apart into the wall, saving him the trouble of having to drill through it, as he did the other door.

Inside a hallway of some kind, Jack began walking through the vessel, alert for any of the crew that might ambush him, intent to find the bridge of the ship. The ceiling of the hallway was angling down toward the floor, like an up-side down V, leaving the corridor triangular, and the surface of the corridor was coated silver. Though the ship was completely dark, Jack's enhanced vision and sensor equipment allowed him to navigate through the vessel unhindered.

"*Jack, do you see any of the vessel's crew?*" Captain Rickman asked through the comm channel.

"Not from my current position, but I assure you that I will remain on alert for any of them. The ships power appears to be offline, but it's possible that the ship's systems managed to detect my entrance." Jack turned a corner and tripped over something on the floor. Jack quickly jumped to his feet and looked back to what he tripped on, and realized it was a body. Jack aimed his right V-shaped gun, also referred to as a V-gun, at the form, but it remained still on the floor.

"*Jack, is that one of the crew?*" Captain Rickman asked.

"It appears so, or at least a robotic drone of some kind. It appears to be unresponsive and may be deceased." Jack slowly walked closer to the body, and noted it's features, including its domed head, silver, metallic skin, it's four-fingered hand, and it's impressively strong-appearing structure. In its left hand, the alien held a rifle of some kind. The rifle was 5 feet long, somewhat resembling rifles that hunters used, but the gun had two-gun nozzles, one stacked on top of the other.

"*What is that thing?*" Commander Hayley spoke through the comm. "*Do you think they all look like this?*"

Jack continued down the hallway as he said, "It is impossible to tell, Commander. For all we know, only their warriors look that way, or he is simply one of a kind. There are just too many unknown variables."

"Jack, I recommend that you to head to their center of engineering. You may need to get the power back online, so that would be the best place to do so. Once you re-active the systems, you can try to access their computer systems."

Jack heard Chief Lexton speak to the captain, *"Sir, I don't know if that is the best course of action. If this ship has some sort of distress beacon, will reactivating the ship turn it on?"*

"We can't afford to miss this opportunity because we don't know what will happen," Captain Rickman responded. *"We have to risk the aliens being alerted to our presence."* Rick paused briefly, and asked, *"Chief, do you know why their power may be offline?"*

Lexton considered the possible reasons, and replied, *"Well... it's possible that the Korean battleship fired their EMP warhead at the alien vessel. We know the Korean's had it, since an EMP disabled our systems, causing are systems to get knocked out and trapped under their ship down here in the first place. I had just assumed that we had been the initial target, but it's possible we simply got caught in the pulse's blast. If that is true, the aliens must have been right on top of the Korean's ship. Otherwise, they wouldn't have risked being caught in their own weapon blast."*

Jack asked the Chief, "Then, is the power systems permanently damaged?"

"I wouldn't even be able to give you an educated guess. We are dealing with alien technology here. But, if the crew is all machines, they could have been all killed, leaving the ship defenseless. If I had to place a

bet, I would guess the ship's power is only disabled. The EMP would definitely fry something like you or those aliens, given how close to the pulse they were, but on a system as big as the ships? I would say there could be at least a small chance the power can be restored."

Jack considered this information, and replied, "Very well. I'll begin looking for the engineering center immediately." In order to search the ship at a much faster rate, he deployed Recon, a drone stored in his lower arm. The metal on the bottom of his arm opened, and a small, compact, football-shaped object lowered downward, held by small mechanical latches. The drone unfolded its wings, and the middle of the drone began to compress together with the wings no longer occupying the space. The front of the drone split open to reveal a camera-like lens, which served as the drone's eye. After the drone finished compressing together with their wings deployed, it was now shaped like an oval with two 9-inch long wings, and began humming softly as it's systems activated, and the engine on the back, similarly shaped to Jack's thruster, lit up as well.

Recon dropped from Jack's arm, and flew down the corridor, and began using its scanning equipment to map the ship's corridors, in the hopes that they would eventually stumble upon the engineering center. The storage bay on his arm closed, and in an effort to search the ship more quickly, he began constructing another drone within the arm within small emitters that acted similar to how the Genetic Modulator created materials from energy. While the new drone was begin created,

Jack jogged down the corridor in the opposite direction that Recon had traveled down, scanning the ship to find the engineering center.

Chapter 12

Date: July 9, 2132.
Location: Aboard the *U.S.S. Ocean-Walker* on the border of the Atlantic Ocean.

"Are you all ready?" Captain Whitefield whispered to the assembled officers. The crew had assembled at deck 2, just below the main deck. After debating who should go first, it was decided that Alpha group, the team going for the shuttle craft, should go first. They were the largest group and would be able to draw the Ribiyar's fire while the other group traveled up toward the bridge. Captain Whitefield would be leading Alpha team as they secured the alien shuttle craft, while Beta team, led by Lieutenant Commander Fitzburg, would secure the rear section of the main deck, including what was left of the bridge on the upper part of the deck.

After the officers replied that they were ready, Captain Whitefield whispered to Olo, "Lieutenant, do you know if the E.V.A.N. unit is in position yet?"

"I don't know, Captain. Batcat is fast, but it is possible he hasn't gotten up here yet."

"Unfortunately, we don't have time to wait for him. We can't risk the Ribiyar completing whatever they're working on up there, or give them any time to start boarding their fighters to use against us." Captain Whitefield turned to the crew and in a loud whisper he said, "All right, men. On my signal, Group Alpha is to start the raid. Fitzburg, you will decide when you will start, but be quick about it. Everyone understand?"

They all nodded and then the captain gave the signal to advance. Group Alpha quickly climbed up the two ladders to the top deck. A minute later, Olo heard the captain yell "Open Fire!!", and gun shots immediately followed, both from the crew's weapons and the Ribiyar's, as they fought back against the *Ocean-Walker*'s crew. Olo waited anxiously for Lieutenant Commander Fitzburg to give the order to advance, desperately wanting to help Captain Whitefield and the others fight for possession of the *Ocean-Walker*. Finally, Lieutenant Commander Fitzburg gave the order to advance, and Olo was one of the first officers to begin climbing the ladders to the main deck.

When Olo reached the deck, he was stunned by how damaged the main deck was. Several craters populated the deck from the Ribiyar's initial attack on the *Ocean-Walker*. Several large hulks of twisted metal were also spread along the deck's surface, presumably remains from cannons that had been in place along the ship. But the most gruesome sight was that several bodies, both human and Ribiyar, were also scattered along the decks surface.

As the remaining members of Beta team finished climbing the ladders to the main deck, the officers began attacking the Ribiyar positioned around the deck, and especially the aliens that had been pursuing Alpha team as they made their way through the large number of Ribiyar that guarded their oval-shaped fighters.

As the surrounded Ribiyar were shot down, Beta team slowly began making their way up one of the two stairways that led to where the bridge was, or rather, what was left of it. The roof of the bridge had been completely torn off, along with the equipment tower that had been stationed above the bridge, a drastic change from what he had seen the last time he had been above deck.

Beta team had made if halfway up the stairwell when Ribiyar on the main deck began firing at them from behind. Immediately, two officers were shot down as the rest of the team crouched down and returned fire at the Ribiyar. As the group began to take out the Ribiyar that were targeting them, Olo turned around and saw three Ribiyar appear at the top of the stairs, all three of them aiming their guns at the group. Before Olo could take them out or alert the other members of the group of the danger, an explosion flashed and thundered around the Ribiyar, and the remains of the aliens flew off the deck and into the ocean. Olo looked to the right and was surprised to see Batcat standing on the railing of the stairs on the other side of the deck, with a small cannon-like weapon, a box-shaped object with a long gun barrel on the front of it, protruding out of the left side of his back through a hole in his cape, apparently yet another weapon stored within the cat. Grateful for Batcat's timely rescue, Olo turned his attention to the Ribiyar attacking his fellow crew members. Moments later, they were successful in neutralizing the Ribiyar, and they continued their advance up the stairs.

They had nearly reached the top when more Ribiyar appeared, and additional Ribiyar also appeared above the other stairwell. Noticing the Ribiyar above him, Batcat turned and rapid-fired his cannons, deploying an additional out of the right side of his back, at the aliens. Acting quickly Olo forced himself to focus and he began attacking the Ribiyar at the top of his stairs as bright orange energy blasts struck his team members down, narrowing escaping injury himself multiple times. As Olo shot at the Ribiyar with his laser rifle, out of the corner of his eye he saw Batcat continue to hold back the Ribiyar with his relentless attacks as he jumped back and forth on the stairs in an effort to dodge the Ribiyar's attacks. Though a good deal of the Ribiyar were destroyed, along with a good portion of the deck plating with it, more Ribiyar continued to march forward toward Batcat from behind the bridge.

Beta team began making progress in fighting back the Ribiyar. The aliens at the top of the stairs were shot to pieces, and some of the officers leapt to the top of the stairs and fired at the Ribiyar that had been approaching the team, and the attack forced the Ribiyar to fall back and take cover in the bridge.

With the Ribiyar more or less dealt with for the moment, Olo turned his attention back to Batcat, when he saw the one of the Ribiyar manage to barely glace Batcat's leg while he was in midair during one of his jumps, not enough to damage him much, but the impact caused him to lose momentum and smack the side of the rail and fall to the ground. Batcat quickly scrambled to his feet and deployed his machine guns, but the Ribiyar laid down a massive barrage of energy blasts pummeled Batcat, burning a great number of burns in his fur. The final few shots knocked Batcat off his feet, and he tumbled down the stairs to the floor of the deck, where he landed in a heap of burnt fur and smoking machinery.

"Batcat!" Olo shouted as he and the other members of his team fired at the Ribiyar, neutralizing the aliens within moments. With the Ribiyar neutralized, Olo started to run down the stairs, but Lieutenant Commander Fitzburg stopped him by grabbing his arm.

"Lieutenant, we can't worry about him now. We need to eliminate the Ribiyar in the bridge, and help Alpha team secure the fighters. You can try to help him after the *Ocean-Walker* is ours again. Understood?"

Olo took a deep breath, still wanting deeply to help his odd companion, but knew the importance of the current situation and nodded. "Yes, sir. Let's finish this thing." Olo gave one final look at Batcat, who still hadn't moved from where he landed, and then continued up the stairs. With nearly half of their team remaining alive, the group managed to reach the top of the stairs and enter the bridge to engage the Ribiyar in the room. When the group had gathered at the stairs, they checked the door, and discovered that it was unlocked. After the count of three, they threw the door open and charged into the room, guns blazing. Only a handful of Ribiyar were hunkered in the bridge, and though they fought relentlessly, managing to take down two more of the remaining team members, the determined crew of the *Ocean-Walker* overwhelmed the alien soldiers. Once the bridge was secure, Lieutenant Commander Fitzburg assigned a small number of officers to deactivate the Ribiyar device and took the remaining nine officers with him to help Alpha team secure the alien fighters.

As Olo exited the bridge, he quickly searched the area to determine what he and the other officers were charging into. In total, there were eleven fighters clustered together in the front of the ship. The remaining 20 or so Ribiyar had retreated near the shuttle craft, somehow managing to block Alpha team from approaching by moving several hunks of metal, possibly the remains of the *Ocean-Walker*'s weapons, in front of the fighters, and from what Olo saw, it appeared the Ribiyar were going to board the fighters and take off, probably to attack the *Ocean-Walker*'s crew with the advantage of aerial supremacy.

Lieutenant Commander Fitzburg acted quickly and began giving his officers orders, "Men, fan out along the upper level and target the Ribiyar. The only chance of intercepting the Ribiyar in time is to shoot at them from here, were we have a better angle to attack them. Alpha team can't target the Ribiyar with them hiding behind the barricade, and they can't throw grenades without damaging the fighters. Use you aiming visors to improve your accuracy and fire when ready!" Olo quickly moved to the middle of the upper level, crouched down while aiming his rifle, and fired. The shot blew off the head of one of the Ribiyar that was boarding a fighter. The other officers in Beta team quickly fired several shots to keep the Ribiyar from boarding their ships, which gave Alpha team time to climb over the barricade and ambush the remaining aliens. In minutes, the Ribiyar were neutralized, returning control of the *Ocean-Walker* back to its crew.

With the *Ocean-Walker* under their control again, Lieutenant Commander Fitzburg left the group and met with Captain Whitefield, who had climbed back over the barricade, along with most of the members of the Alpha team. While the commanding officers conferred with each other, Olo left the few remaining officers of Beta team and traveled down the stairs and onto the deck to examine Batcat. When Olo reached him, he saw exposed wires and circuitry showing through burnt fur where the Ribiyar had hit him with their energy rifles. Several parts of him had crumpled inwards from the force of the blasts or torn open. Olo saw Batcat's eyes were still open, now devoid of their menacing glow, and staring listlessly back at him.

"Lieutenant!" Olo jumped up and stood at attention. Captain Whitefield and Lieutenant

Commander Fitzburg walked over to him, and Olo noticed that the captain was bleeding from several cuts along his right arm, though he didn't seem too concerned with his injuries. The captain's machine gun was clipped to his back, freeing him from having to carry it.

"At ease, Lieutenant Oakland," Captain Whitefield said as he approached, allowing Olo to adopt a more relaxed posture in front of the captain. "How badly is the E.V.A.N. unit damaged? Do you know if he can be repaired?"

Olo glanced at Batcat as he replied, "I haven't been able to examine him closely, but he looks pretty beaten up. It may take a while to repair him, but, with your permission, I want to try to fix him up. He proved himself invaluable during this incident, and we could definitely use him in future battles against the Ribiyar. And honestly, as weird as he is, I've grown fond of him."

Captain Whitefield nodded and replied, "Permission granted, Lieutenant. I'll try to arrange for you to get the parts to fix him, but don't count on the engineering teams to help you. With much of the crew dead or injured, we're going to be sorely shorthanded around here. But it's going to be a while before you get a chance to work on him, as I want you to help with the recovery efforts for the moment. Store him in your quarters and get back up here on the double."

Captain Whitefield turned to leave, when one of the officers in the bridge yelled, "Ribiyar fighters at nine O'clock!" Olo turned to see roughly 20 oval shaped ships rapidly approaching the *Ocean-Walker*.

"Lieutenant Commander Fitzburg, do we have control of the *Ocean-Walker*'s weapons yet?"

"I'm afraid not, sir. The Ribiyar have scrambled the ship's computers. We can't get anything online."

"We just can't get a break, can we? Men, stand ready for combat! If we're going down, we are going down fighting!" Captain Whitefield retrieved his machine gun from his back and opened fire at the approaching fighters, though it was difficult to hit them with how fast they were maneuvering around in the sky. As Olo heard the other officers start to fire, Olo grabbed his laser rifle, set it to its max setting, and fired several shots as the fighters continued to draw nearer to the *Ocean-Walker*. Olo managed to hit one of the fighter's engines, causing red smoke to leak out from it, but the damage was insufficient to cause the ship to fall out of the sky. As the *Ocean-Walker*'s crew continued firing at the alien fighters, managing to destroy a small number of the ships, the Ribiyar vessels finally got close enough to the ship and opened fire on the *Ocean-Walker*. Officers all over the deck were incinerated by the fighter's orange weapon blasts, dissolving into a gust of black dust-like material, including Lieutenant Commander Fitzburg, who pushed Captain Whitefield out of the way to save him from being incinerated as well. The fighters flew past the ship, and then flew up and did a half-loop, turning around to launch another barrage on the *Ocean-Walker*. The fighters fired down another salvo of energy blasts, leaving only a handful of officers left on the deck. The fighters again flew away from the ship, and then half-looped in the air, returning to deliver the final strike.

Olo felt someone grab his left arm, and he turned his head to see Captain Whitefield, still on the ground from when Lieutenant Commander Fitzburg had shoved him out of the way.

"Lieutenant, it has been an honor to fight by your side for this short time."

Olo smiled and said, "It has been an honor to serve under you, Captain Whitefield." Prepared to endure his eminent destruction, Olo turned his head forwards to look at the fighters, who were moments away from entering firing range once again. When the ships entered firing range, a blinding bright red flash completely filled his vision.

Incredible...

Date: July 9, 2132.
Location: Aboard the crashed alien ship, at the bottom of the Atlantic Ocean.

"Room scan is negative. Moving on to next corridor." Jack had been scanning the ship for over 2 hours now, and he still hadn't found anything that remotely resembled an engineering center. Over the course of his search of the alien vessel, Jack had fabricated (the term he had created for items made using the Genetic Modulator) a few dozen Recon Drones, all of them searching different parts of the ship. Though the increased number of drones to control did give him a measure of mental fatigue, Jack had lessened the strain by instructed the drones to act on their own and contact him only when they had news to report and when they had more scans to add to the growing map of the alien vessel. Though he now possessed a fairly detailed map of a portion of the ship, and had come across many more robotic alien's, all nonfunctional, he was apparently no closer to finding his goal.

Commander Hayley spoke on the line, her exhaustion apparent in her voice despite over a dozen cups of coffee he had heard her consume over the comm channel. *"Jack, is there any way you could speed up your search? With what we've seen of the ship's apparent size, you may not find the engineering center in time to save the Atlanta's crew."*

"I am doing the best that I can, Commander Hayley. The drones are already traveling at a speed high enough to make timely progress, but still provide a detailed scan for the map of the ship." Jack reached another room and scanned its interior, only to again find no engineering equipment of any significance inside the room. Determined to find the engineering center, Jack suppressed the impulse to get discouraged and continued down the hallway to scan the next room in the corridor.

"I'm sorry, Jack. I know you're doing everything you can to help us. I guess I'm just stressed with how quickly we're running out of time to free ourselves."

Jack was about to respond when he received a message from one of the drones scanning the ship.

RECON UNIT 25 REPORTING.

THIS UNIT HAS DETECTED A ROOM MATCHING SEARCH PARAMETERS.

TRANSMITTING LOCATION OF ROOM NOW.

After Jack retrieved the scans and reviewed the data, he agreed with the drone's assessment that the room was most likely the engineering center of the alien vessel, or at least a secondary hub of some kind. The drone's scans showed many power conduits leading to that part of the ship, and the door was comprised of a greatly reinforced metal, which would be logical if that room contained the alien vessel's power core.

"Commander Hayley, I believe one of the drones have found the engineering center. I am heading to confirm the finding now."

"*Understood, Jack. Good luck.*" Deciding not to activate his jetpack and risk damaging himself from flying at high speeds through the corridors, Jack took off jogging through the ship. Using the map he and the drones had made, Jack made his way through the alien vessel, gradually making his way up several levels of the ship, traveling up ramps that were sporadically placed around the ship that led to the level above or below the current one, and then proceeding to travel deeper into the ship's inner dwellings.

At last, Jack finally arrived at his destination, and he found himself in front of a large door that possibly contained the engineering center. The door was actually more of a large wall that had several creases in its structure where it would separate as it opened, or so Jack assumed as he examined it with his sensors. A single crease led from the all of the four corners of the door, and both sides joined in between each other in the middle of the structure, and the two creases merged together to make one crease in the middle of the wall. Nearly 20 Recon drones, which he had ordered to report here while he made the trip towards them, hovered around the door as they took detailed scans of the door and the surrounding walls to determine how to best force the door open.

After closely examining the door, he determined the best places to assign the drones to attempt to pry the door open. After he instructed the drones where to position themselves, they attached themselves to the door, and put their thrusters on full power. As the door slowly moved apart, Jack grabbed onto the growing space between the doors, and pushed them apart with all his strength. The door slowly inched opened, and finally, it was nearly completely open. Jack entered the room, and the Recon Drones detached themselves from the door and followed Jack into the chamber.

The room was colored silver, like the rest of the ship, and enormous in size, nearly five-story's tall. A multitude of different walkways and platforms were scattered at various heights above and throughout the chamber, many populated by 5 feet tall upside-down pyramid-like consoles that were spread around the room. In the center of the room was a huge giant pillar,

4 times the width of ancient Greece stone pillars. Two metallic rings hovered in place at the center of the pillar, where a large sphere was located, crossing together each other to make an X. Jack detected a magnetic signature in some of the material near the rings, suspending them in the air. Several power lanes ran from the ceiling and other places in the room into the two rings, and other cords connected from the sphere in the pillar to the rings. Jack guessed that the pillar was most likely the ship's power core: given how big the alien vessel was, it would take a power source of great caliber to supply energy to all its systems. He instructed the Recon Drones to scan the room and its equipment as he personally examined the power core, walking around the many deactivated aliens scattered around the place as he did so.

"Whoa! Is that thing the ship's power core!?!" Jack heard Chief Lexton shout into the comm.

"What else would it be, their cable antenna?" Commander Hayley remarked.

"Good work, Jack. I was starting to fear we would never find the engineering center," Captain Rick spoke.

"Don't thank me yet, captain. I still haven't turned this thing on yet, assuming that I can figure out how to operate this alien technology. Chief Lexton, how would you recommend I proceed?"

Chief Lexton though a moment before she replied, *"Well, I suppose the first step would be scanning the core. Maybe we might be able to figure out what is wrong with it and try to fix it. You could also try to activate on of the consoles in the room. Maybe you could use that to figure it out, assuming of course, you could interpret the alien's language. Could it be remotely possible that they happened to speak something similar to our languages on earth?"*

"With the luck we've been having, they probably won't have a language to interpret, just data and pictures," Jack replied as he reached one of the consoles close to the power core, and now that he was closer to the console, he could see it in more detail than before. The device was shaped like a pyramid, but upside-down, with the point on the bottom holding the structure up. There was also a small display on the flat side of the pyramid, and there was a small, circular port on the flat surface of the pyramid, and Jack assumed it allowed the aliens to connect to the console and receive direct access to the computer systems. He summoned two Recon Drones, and they attached themselves to the device, feeding power to it. The device flickered, and then activated, emitting an orange glow from several conduits that zig-zagged across the surface of the lower pyramid faces. The display on the top activated, projecting a holographic interface. Alien writing flashed on the image, and a picture that looked similar to the power core was in the center of the display, rapidly flashing red. Several low and high pitched beeps sounded from the console, further stressing the urgency of whatever it was reporting. On the other two sides of the pyramid, a display activated as well, reporting information about other devices that Jack didn't recognize.

"Chief Lexton, what do you suggest I do?"

"Is there any way you could connect to the console, perhaps through your drones? If you interfaced with their network, you might be able to find a better way to interpret the data. Do you know if their computer is operational?"

"If I had to guess, it's possible the computer is at least partially online, since the console is showing displays of different systems, and it has to get that information from somewhere. The drones could be channeling just enough power to reactivate the computer systems through the console."

"In that case, the best thing to do would be to take over their computer system."

To that, Jack asked, "Chief Lexton, do you have the experience to do that? I may be successful in connecting with the computer's systems, but interfacing with it and taking control of it are two different matters entirely."

"Personally, I wouldn't have the skills to take over the computer. But there are other officers with a great deal of computer experience that could do assist you in that task. Additionally, I believe I have something aboard the Atlanta *that might stand a chance of taking over the computer."* Lexton responded.

"What would that be, Chief Lexton?" Captain Rickman asked. *"To my knowledge, we don't have any computer equipment that would perform better than Jack' systems, and he's even admitted he may not be equipped to do it."*

"Remember that computer program, the Omega Virus, that the FBI confiscated from cyber-terrorists in

Texas a few months ago? There's a copy of the program aboard the ship."

"*WHAT!?!*" Captain Rickman exclaimed. "*Chief Lexton, do you have any idea how dangerous that program is? That program is powerful enough to hack* any *computer system, and slave its operating systems. They could then use their link to steal all the data they want from that computer.*"

"*What if someone on the* Atlanta *used that program to change the GM's settings?*" Commander Hayley said cautiously, aware that if what she said was true, one of her fellow crewmembers could have drastically altered Vade for their own purposes. "*That could be how they managed to do it so precisely and without our knowledge.*"

"*That isn't possible,*" Chief Lexton immediately responded. "*The program is loaded into a flash drive, locked in the ship's security vault, and it hasn't been opened since we've been down here.*"

"*Did anyone else know you've had this aboard, Chief Lexton?*" The captain asked.

"I did." Jack replied. "I had received orders to safeguard the copy while specialists analyzed it a mission to deliver it to Michigan for analysis. I had meant to inform you Rick, but it was right before this mess started, and I forgot about it since we've all been focused on freeing the *Atlanta*."

The captain sighed and said. "*Well, at least we have it with us now. This could just be the break we've been hoping for. Chief Lexton, how long will it take to begin downloading the virus?*"

"It will take a few minutes to load the program and configure our computer systems to focus solely on this task, so it performs as efficiently and quickly as possible. The download itself may take 10, 15 minutes at most. But, there is a complication. Jack will need to interface with the computer and 'distract' the computers security, causing it to focus solely on him. Once it is distracted, I can begin to download the program."

Commander Hayley asked, *"Will the alien's computer be able to detect the program?"*

"Most likely. Jack will need to protect the virus until it is strong enough to take control of the computer."

"What will keep the virus from going after Jack while it is downloading?"

"I can set the parameters for the virus, setting it only to go after the alien's computer. But even if it does go after Jack, I could just relinquish control of him after the task is complete. The virus takes control over computers; it doesn't destroy or alter them, like regular viruses."

"What if Jack is overwhelmed from the alien's computer security?" Captain Rickman asked.

"I don't know. It is possible that Jack's neural circuits could be destroyed, essentially killing him, if the computer system manages to defeat him while he is connected to it. I suppose it's even possible that the computer could take control of Jack, and reprogram him to attack us. To help prevent Jack from losing the battle against the computer, we do have a large arsenal

of normal computer viruses we can throw against it, though we would need to be cautious about infecting Jack's systems while we're using them. But Jack, I have to warn you that it is highly risky. Just from guessing, the alien's computer security will likely be heavily fortified. It is, frankly, highly doubtful this will work."

"*Then why do it at all? We have the ship; all we need to do is get it running, and we can get out of here,*" Commander Hayley said.

"*Because,*" Chief Lexton replied, "*it's likely that the computer may attempt to block us access from critical areas of the ships functions, including flight control. This is our best, and possibly our only chance, of getting complete control of the ship.*"

"I am willing to do it, Chief Lexton," Jack said. "This is the reason I resigned my command: I am more useful out in the field, where my skills can be used. Captain, do I have your permission to do this?"

The captain was silent, for several long moments, thinking hard about what to do. Finally, he said, reluctantly, "*Do it, Chief. Get whatever people you need. In fact, I want everyone with computer experience contributing to this.*" Commander Hayley hurried to the comm unit and informed the crew of their orders.

"Chief Lexton, how soon can you start the download of the Omega Virus?" Jack asked.

"*I will need at least ten minutes to retrieve the virus and load it into the computer and get it ready for deployment. Jack, if you position some of your drones correctly throughout the alien ship, we can get a stronger signal directed your way. This will give us the strongest connection we'll get under these circumstances. Do you think you can configure your drones to do that?"*

Jack computed the data, and replied, "I believe so, Chief Lexton. I will begin configuring the drones at once."

"*Great. Do whatever you need to do to get ready for this, Jack. I'll contact you when we're ready.*"

17 minutes later…

"Chief Lexton to R&D control room. Are you guys ready?" Chief Lexton asked as she spoke into her communicator as she stood on the bridge of the *Atlanta*, now ready to begin downloading the Omega Virus. Down below, she knew the control room of the R&D department was filled to the brim with officers manning the computers scattered around in the room. Because of the amount of computer consoles, this room was selected to be the headquarters of the group tasked to launching viruses at the alien's computer system. These viruses, though some deadly to even the most security protected computers on earth, would most likely have had little effect on their own against the firewall, so no one worried about the viruses disrupting the alien computer. Besides the officers tending to other duties on the ship, the remaining crew with any computer experience were split into two groups: one responsible for activating the Omega Virus and monitoring its condition, and the other group, which mostly consisted of the bridge crew, was tasked to keeping the connection to the computer stable, monitoring Jack Vade's neural circuits and his other systems, and giving instructions to the other two groups. The bridge crew would also be receiving information from Jack through the event, allowing them to keep track of the missions' progress.

"*Commander Hayley here,*" Chief Lexton heard on her comm. Though her position as commander would normally result in Hayley being present on the bridge during the operation, her computer experience led to her assignment as head of the officers in that area. "*We are ready to start whenever you are, Chief Lexton.*"

"Understood. Good luck down there. Lexton out." Chief Lexton stood on the bridge by the ships comm device. She checked with the other groups, and then told the captain, "All systems are ready, captain, and Jack has reported that all of the drones are in position and standing by. We're as ready as we're going to be, sir."

Captain Rickman took a deep breath and said, "All right, let's get this show on the road. Chief, divert all computing power to this operation. Use the back-up computer systems to regulate the *Atlanta's* other systems. Jack, are you ready over there?"

"*Yes, captain. The link between the Recon Drones is stable, and the alien computer appears to be as functional as these circumstances allow. I am ready to begin when you are.*"

"All right. Jack, begin the procedure."

"Right away, Captain Rickman. Initializing the computer link now."

In the alien ship, Jack still stood by the computer console, where he had waited as the Recon Drones positioned themselves throughout the alien vessel to optimize the efficiency of the Omega Virus delivery. The remaining drones had connected to other computer consoles, activating 11 in total, scattered near the power core to ensure the computer was as functional as it could be under the circumstances. While Jack focused solely on distracting the computers defenses, the Omega Virus would be deployed through the drones, as well as the other computer viruses, lessening the risks of Jack being affected by them. Jack had also opened a connection between himself and the *Atlanta*'s computer system, in the event the drones failed their function and he had to download the Virus.

Having received permission to commence the operation, Jack put his hands on the flat surface of the computer console and initiated the connection sequence. Across the middle of his hands and fingers, his metal plating separated, exposing small electrical interfaces stored within. Small energy bolts began leaping off the small interfaces and pulsed onto the console, connecting Jack and the interface together. A minute went by, and nothing happened. Jack began to fear that the connection was insufficient to link him to the computer, but it was then that he felt it. He felt his consciousness being drawn from his body and into the alien computer. Jack's vision blurred and grew dimmer, and dimmer, until there was nothing but darkness.

Chapter 13

Date: July 9, 2132.
Location: Unknown.

Jack opened his eyes, and he saw that he was no longer in the alien vessel's engineering center. From where he was standing, Jack couldn't see the ceiling, or any walls, and the floor was just an endless black surface that reflected his image at him. Rather than attempt to make any sense of his confusing environment, he reminded himself that he was inside the computer system and willed himself to focus on the main objective. He had to find a way to take over the computer core, without being neutralized by the mainframe's firewall. Jack surveyed his surroundings to find the alien computer, though he wasn't exactly sure what he should be looking for, when the room suddenly lit up behind him in a bright red glow.

"*Kon kar cho?*" Jack turned around to see an alien that had the body of those he had seen scattered around the alien ship, but this alien was different than the others. Its body appeared to be comprised of red light, and words and symbols from their alien language moved along its body, constantly shifting into different words and forms. Jack guessed that the alien was most likely some sort of physical manifestation of the alien's computer.

"*Par tu cho. Ko zepar.*" The alien lifted his left hand, and a red beam emitted from it, moved over Jack's body, most likely scanning him and attempting to determine what he was. Before Jack could stop the alien from scanning him, it suddenly stopped and lowered his hand.

"*Lak to grjar! Lak to grjar! Sep un tu qwar!*" At the alien's four-fingered right hand, a mass of energy extended outwards, until it stopped when it was 20-inches long. The energy morphed into a sword. The sword was comprised of two blades, which both curved outwards from the handle, before curving into each other to form a single tip.

"*Sep un tu qwar!!!*" The alien swung his sword at him, missing only by inches.

"Captain Rickman, if you can hear me, initiate the Omega Virus now! I don't believe I can hold him off for long!" Jack leapt backwards, dodging another sword strike. As he flipped through the air, he deployed both his V-guns, one on each arm, and began firing at the alien as he landed back on the ground. The alien was knocked back slightly from the attack, but it did little to injure it.

Captain Rickman spoke, *"We hear you Jack. We're watching what's happening through the computer connection between you and the* Atlanta. *Stand by for the first wave of viruses. We are deploying the Omega Virus now, but it will take a few minutes to fully download. We'll need you to buy as much time as you can give us."* Jack continued to fire at the alien as it slowly made its way towards him. Twirling the sword in his hand, the alien then threw it at Jack. He jumped to the side to step out of the swords path, but before he could turn back towards the computer, it knocked him to the ground, having rapidly advanced towards him. Keeping Jack pinned on the ground by placing his foot on his back, the alien raised his right arm upwards, another sword quickly materializing in its hand, and he positioned the sword downwards to plunge it through him and finish him off.

"Sep un tu qwar!" It started to swing the sword down, but the alien suddenly erupted in flames. Jack took advantage of the moment, wresting free from under the alien, and fired his V-gun at maximum power at the alien. Instead of the motor cycle revving he had heard at its lower setting, a sound similar to the booming during a thunderstorm sound, and massive blast shot at the alien. The blast rocked the alien backwards several feet, but the alien managed to maintain contact with the ground. The alien righted itself, and the fire over its body was suddenly extinguished.

"Captain Rickman, that fire on the alien, was that the Omega Virus?" Jack asked, slightly concerned. If that fire had been the Omega Virus, then their only hope of taking control of the alien computer had just been easily overpowered.

"*No, Jack. That was the effect of one of the viruses the crew had sent. You may see more random events like that as more viruses eat away at it.*" Rick paused briefly, possibly examining one of the displays or talking with one of the bridge crew. "*Jack, our computer reports that the Omega Virus is 30% downloaded. Have you seen any sign of it?*" Jack looked around, trying to find it before the computer started to attack it. Finally, Jack saw a small blue light about a dozen feet away from Jack and the alien. At first he couldn't make out what it was, and then he realized it was a small butterfly. The small insect was made of blue light, and words and information were rapidly moved over its body, like on the alien's body. On the butterflies' back, he could barely make out an Omega symbol (Ω) imprinted on it.

"*Jack, that has to be the Omega Virus. We've got the download going as fast as it can, but it is still going to be a few minutes. We had to triple the potency of the program if we had any chance of taking over this computer, which is slowing the download. We are sending your reinforcements now.*" Suddenly, dozens of thick vines appeared around the alien throughout the area, moving over the area and constraining him.

"*Ka! Olar co trifur.*" The alien swung his sword, quickly shredding through some of the vines restricting him. Jack continued firing his V-guns at the alien, but it did little to slow the alien down.

"*Car tu kritur!!!*" The alien finished freeing himself from the vines, and when he turned to face Jack, it was then that the computer discovered the Omega Virus, fluttering softly a distance away. Acting quickly, Jack launched Recon from his arm, and sent it to retrieve the Omega Virus before the computer could destroy it. Recon reached the virus, deploying four, small crane-like arms on the bottom of its body to grab it, and escorted it a safe distance from the fight.

"*Con fer to cara!*" The computer again threw his sword at Jack, and he though he dodged out of the way, the sword sliced through his right V-Gun, completely incapacitating the device.

"Captain, how far is the Omega Virus downloaded? I really can't hold this thing off much longer!" Jack deployed his Laser Cannon and fired it at a continual blast. The alien shielded himself with his arms, but the force of the weapon held him back. The alien again erupted into flames as another virus attacked it, but the fire almost instantly evaporated into steam. It appeared that the computer was gaining immunity from the viruses as they attacked them, rendering those viruses harmless against it.

"*The download is at 72%. Just hold off another minute!*"

The alien slowly adapted to the force of his Laser Cannon, and he again slowly approached him. "*Sep un tu qwar!*" Another sword materialized in the computer's left hand, and he sliced through the Laser

Cannon. Blasting the alien with his left V-Gun to slow him down, he deployed his final weapon system. On his back, two large metal plates lifted upwards, and moved onto the middle of his back. Two small energy-based machine guns lifted out form their storage spaces, moved by a mechanical arm attached to the devices, and the weapons attached to the sides of Jack's arms. He let loose with these weapons, but the alien was slowed little by them and the V-Gun. The alien suddenly rushed forward and managed to slam Jack on his back to the ground.

"*Jack!*" Captain Rickman spoke excitedly through the comm, "*The Omega Virus has been downloaded! You need to find a way to connect it to the alien, fast!*" The alien lunged his sword downward, but Jack managed to catch it with his hands. Using all his strength to hold it back, he quickly summoned Recon to return to him. Recon returned to him quickly, and when he was close, and the Omega Virus flew free off the drone's arms. But instead of going to the alien, the butterfly quickly fluttered to Jack, and in a flash, it turned into pure light, and flew inside him, and he immediately felt a sudden rush of energy as the Omega Virus integrated with his systems. The Omega symbol appeared on his chest, shining like a bright star. He suddenly knew that he had to maintain contact with the alien, and as he held the sword inches away from his chest, he was in exactly the position he needed to be in.

"Your species may have come to take control of this planet, but we are stronger than you think we are." Veins of blue energy quickly spread from the Omega symbol, traveled up his arms, and began to traverse the computer's sword. The alien tried to pull his weapon away from Jack, but he tightened his grip, and wouldn't let it go.

"*Lak ye tradar!*" The veins rushed up the sword and began spreading from the alien's right arm. The computer let go of his sword to get away from Jack, but he grabbed its leg, spreading the Virus in that area, and would not allow him to escape from his grasp.

"We will not lose our home without a fight, and it will take more than a computer to stop us from protecting our planet." The Virus continued spreading over the computer's body, looking similar to a complex root of a plant, and now almost completely covered it completely.

"You *will* obey my command!!! Yield to us!!!" Jack noticed a cluster of blue veins on the alien's chest forming together to form the Omega symbol, and now the veins completely covered the aliens body, altering its red surface to blue. The alien stood rigidly still for several moments, when the computer kneeled before Jack, it's sword vanishing in a burst of light.

"*Fon to conar. Kal don tor.*" Jack wasn't sure what his next action should be, when he heard the captain proclaim, "*Jack! It worked! We have full access to the computer files! It looks like the computer system is under our control!*" Before Jack could congratulate the crew on their efforts, his vison suddenly darkened, and he was quickly engulfed in a world of darkness. then lost all sight around him. As the world faded away, he heard his name being called several times in the darkness, but he couldn't find its source through the thick darkness that surrounded him.

"JJJAACCCKKKKK…"

"Jack…"

"Jack!!!"

Jack opened his eyes and was surprised to find himself back in the engineering center aboard the alien ship. Throughout the engineering center, the Recon Drones continued to hum softly as they continued to feed their power to the consoles, dimly lighting the room from the orange light the consoles produced.

"Jack! Can you hear me? Jack!!!" Commander Hayley yelled into the comm, but from the volume, it was like she was shouting in his ear right beside him.

"I'm here, Commander Hayley. I'm sorry for my delay in responding to you. I was disconnecting from the computer, and I was unable to respond while that process was ongoing."

"You've been doing that all this time? Jack, we gained access to the computer 5 hours ago. That's why I was shouting so hard. I thought we lost you."

"That is… unexpected. Connecting to the computer system must have affected my systems. I am initiating a diagnostic scan now to determine if any of my systems were corrupted."

"That's a good idea, considering how intense the process must have been for you. Who knows what your connection to the computer has done to your internal systems. But Jack, you should know that while you were unresponsive, we've been able to convert the alien computer to the English language. We found an entire

collection of Earth's languages in the computer! They have "

"Why would the aliens have our languages in their computer?"

"We haven't determined that yet. We have only been able to skim through a small percentage of the database so far. But now that we have control of the alien ship's computer, we can guide you through the repairs on the ship and get the power core operational again. We have already found what you need to do to get it working again, and I am sending instructions of what you need to do now." Moments later, Jack received detailed schematics of the engineering center's components, and other structures in the ship that needed to be repaired to restore functionality to the ship, along with instructions on how to repair them.

"I have received the information. I will begin my repairs to the core right away, and I will notify you when I have completed my work. Vade, out."

Chapter 14

Date: July 9, 2132.
Location: Aboard the *U.S.S. Ocean-Walker*, on the border of the Atlantic Ocean.

Olo cleared his eyes to make sure he was seeing clearly. A moment before, there had been a squadron of Ribiyar fighters soaring towards the *Ocean-Walker*, and then there had been a roaring flash of light, and now all that was left of the ships were debris falling into the ocean below. Olo grabbed Captain Whitefield's right hand and helped him to his feet.

"Lieutenant, do you know where that flash came from? It looks like it came from a Laser Array, but it couldn't have been from the *Ocean-Walker*. Our weapons are still offline." Off the deck of the *Ocean-Walker*, a huge waterblast suddenly shot up into the sky as a vessel flew out of the ocean. When the water fell back into the ocean, a ship was hovering close to the port side of the *Ocean-Walker*. The ship was fairly small, about big enough for four levels on the inside of the ship, and shaped like a triangle, with metallic, bird-like wings folded out along its sides. Length-wise, the ship was about a third the size of the *Ocean-Walker*, and there was an oval-shaped engine, spouting blue flames that kept the ship in the air, on the front and back of the side of the ship under the bird wings, and two additional engines were planted on top of the upper surface of the ship, giving the ship an additional source of speed to rely upon. The ship leveled down to the *Ocean-Walker*'s main deck, and a boarding ramp deployed from the side of the ship and lowered onto the *Ocean-Walker*'s deck. Olo reached for his gun, but Captain Whitefield stopped him.

"Easy, Lieutenant. I don't believe that they are our enemies. They did shoot down the Ribiyar after all. But be on your guard, just in case. We can never be too cautious these days." A gust of steam shot out of the ship, startling Olo as the vapor quickly formed a cloud around the ramp and the surrounding area. Through the steam, Olo could see people boarding the *Ocean-Walker*, hurrying into a defensive position. When the steam dissipated, Olo could see 15 officers spread near the ramp, all of them with their guns drawn at them. Then, three more officers stepped out of the ship; the lead officer, a muscular man with a Mediterranean tan and crew cut red hair, and the other two officers stood on each side of him, stopping 10 feet away from Olo and Whitefield. Several moments passed as both groups silently observed the other.

Finally, the lead officer broke the silence and said, "I believe I should be asking you for permission to come aboard, but under the circumstances, I believe I will skip the formalities and get to the matter at hand. I am Captain Jim Syvon, of the *U.S.S. Thunderfox*, and we are here to assist the *Ocean-Walker* in its attack against the Ribiyar forces in the Atlantic." It was then Olo recognized the *Thunderfox*. He remembered reporting that the *Thunderfox* had docked at Hawaii before he been reassigned to the *Ocean-Walker*. The *Thunderfox* was a class of ship known as the Firestorm: a prototype vessel that could function as a boat, but could also submerge under water, or deploy its wings and take to the air like an oversized fighter, with a top speed of Mach 8. The *Thunderfox* was the only ship of its class to be constructed before the invasion began, so it was extremely valuable to the survival of Earth.

"Your timing is impeccable, Captain Syvon. We wouldn't have survived if you hadn't shown up when you did."

"Indeed. Another Defender vessel intercepted your distress call, and reported it to Admiral Hofkins, and he sent me to try to rescue you, if the Ribiyar hadn't finished you off already. He has sent me to deliver a new mission to you as well. Satellite images show that one of the Ribiyar prison centers is located here, deep within the Atlantic Ocean. Our orders are to meet up with several other battleships that are gathering roughly 90 miles from this location, and then travel to the prison and free the people held there, or die trying." One of the soldiers standing by Captain Syvon cleared his throat. The soldier was a very muscular man with black hair, with a lock of hair that hung over his right eye that was dyed dark green, and had a scar that ran down his right cheek all the way to his chin.

"Oh, yes. Gentlemen, this is Victor Davidson, a mercenary that has been hired to assist in the fight against the Ribiyar." At the mentions of Davidson's name, Olo felt a strong flow of emotions burn through him as he realized who this man was. A little over 5 years ago, an unknown killer murdered his parents, and during the investigation of their death, Davidson's DNA was found at the murder scene. Victor was brought to court, but because of his team of elite lawyers, he was freed with minimal punishment. Olo had never forgotten how his parent's killers had escaped the reach of justice, and he swore he would not stop until justice prevailed, one way, or another. Victor recognized Olo as well and sneered at him.

"Well, well, well. Isn't this a small world? How ya doing, Ollie? I apologize for not attending your parent's funeral, but I was quite occupied with the trial. It sure is a shame about their… untimely demise." Olo was about to make a dash for Victor and punch his smug face, but Captain Syvon intervened.

"Victor, enough. We paid you more than what is necessary, given the circumstances. At least try to behave, will you?" Victor sneered again, but he made no other comment. "Victor has been hired because we need the most elite warriors on our side fighting the

Ribiyar. We can't afford to be fighting a war against the Ribiyar and be fighting amongst ourselves at the same time. Victor, since it doesn't appear your services are needed out here, get back to the *Thunderfox* and continue your training. You need to be properly prepared for the battle up ahead." Victor hesitated, but then made his way back in the *Thunderfox*.

"Captain Whitefield, considering the state of your vessel, I will assign engineering crews from the *Thunderfox* to help you get the *Ocean-Walker* prepared while we travel to our rendezvous with the ships. We need to leave in three hours to make our appointed time."

"Thank you, Captain Syvon. If you can, we could also use some medical teams to help with our wounded."

"Of course. I want you to meet my first officer, Commander Zhang Wei Ton. I have assigned him to coordinate crew placement among the two ships." The officer beside Captain Syvon, a very tall man who was bald and had notable Chinese ancestry, nodded toward the group.

Captain Whitefield took a deep breath and said, "Well, we better get to work. Captain Syvon, I have some matters that need to be discussed with you. Do you have anywhere we can talk, privately?"

"I do. Come with me, Captain." Captain Syvon walked to the ramp and entered the *Thunderfox*, with Captain Whitefield following behind him.

Once the captains had boarded the ship, Commander Ton immediately began giving orders to the officers who had rallied by the entrance to the *Thunderfox*. The few officers of the *Ocean-Walker* who weren't wounded guided the officers to where repairs were needed most, and other officers led medical teams from the *Thunderfox* down to the lower levels of the *Ocean-Walker* where the injured crew were located. Olo assisted the engineering crews, since he had a fair amount of engineering training, as they began repairs on the *Ocean-Walker*'s jet engines, an essential part of the ship to repair if they were to make the rendezvous with time to spare, until 20 minutes later, Commander Ton approached him.

"Are you Lieutenant Oakland, officer?"

"Yes, Commander, that's me," Olo replied as he crawled out from under the engine assembly and wiped the oil off his hands and onto his pant legs.

"Captain Syvon informed me that he wants to talk to you aboard the *Thunderfox*. I suggest you meet him right away. I will have an officer escort you to him."

"All right. I'll make my way over there now." Olo started to walk away, but Commander Ton stopped him.

"Lieutenant, I don't know much about you, but from what I observed earlier, it's obvious there is a great deal of some tension between you and Mr. Davidson. Do what you can to minimize it. Understood?"

"Understood, sir. Believe me, I'll stay away from him as much as possible."

"Good. I'll let you get to Captain Syvon." Ton walked away as he called an officer over to lead Olo to Captain Syvon and Whitefield in the *Thunderfox*. Olo hoped that the captain didn't have more bad news, but with the luck Earth's had since the war started, it probably was.

Date: July 9, 2132.
Location: Aboard the crashed alien ship, at the bottom of the Atlantic Ocean.

"All systems are ready. Standing by to begin power core reactivation sequence." Jack still remained in the engineering center on the alien ship, where he and several dozen other Recon Drones had been for the last 8 hours working on the power core of the ship. In addition to the drones that had worked in the engineering center, the other drones had traveled through the ship and repaired and/or replaced the necessary components that needed to be operational to reactivate the power core. Though the repairs had taken longer than Jack had expected, it allowed the crew in the *Atlanta* to dive deeper into the data from the alien's computer, and better understand the ship's functions. Though they also attempted to learn about the aliens and their plans for Earth, they had gathered little knowledge, other than they were a species known as the Ribiyar, as much of those files were heavily encrypted, and the computer was unable to decipher them as it wasn't yet fully operational.

Over the comm, Chief Lexton responded, "*All right, Jack. From what the computer tells us, we are as ready as we'll ever be to reactivate the core. Initiate power core startup sequence... now."* Jack gave the commands to the computer, and the system immediately began to reactivate the power core. After almost a minute of waiting, Jack was blinded when the power core reactivated and shined as bright as a star. Energy bolts surged outwards from the spherical center of the core and onto the two rings that surrounded it. From the rings, the energy pulsed into power conduits that were in the walls near the core, feeding power into the other systems of the ship. After a minute, the light from the core dimmed enough for Jack to see again. All around him, the room began to lighten up again as all the consoles in the room reactivated, and the lights in the engineering center ignited, casting the room in a bright silver light.

Jack accessed the computer console in front of him, the data now being translated into English. The display showed that all of the systems on the ship were slowly reactivating as power continued to work its way through the ship, and, to his great relief, the Omega Virus was fully active and integrated in the computer's operating systems, giving them full control of the alien vessel. Jack quickly began instructing the computer to hide the ship to keep the aliens from detecting its presence at the bottom of the ocean.

Computer, activate any equipment that will prevent the aliens that created the ship to detect it.

ACKNOWLEDGED. ACTIVATING SENOR DISPLACEMENT PROTOCOLS NOW.

DEACTIVATING HOMING BEACON.

"Jack to *Atlanta*. The repairs have successfully reactivated the ship's power core, and the vessel is slowly returning to an operational state. The computer has successfully deactivated the homing device on the alien vessel, and the ship has engaged its equipment to keep the ship hidden from the aliens. We should be safe from them, for now."

"*Great work, Jack,*" Captain Rickman responded. "*Do we have control of the ships flight systems yet?*" Jack accessed the computer and checked.

"We have control of the engines, but they are not yet online. Systems on the ship are still reactivating. From what the computer has told me, it also appears that the ship's course can only be plotted on the bridge. By the time I arrive there, power should be mostly restored."

"*All right. I want you to get to the bridge as quick as you can and fly the ship to the* Atlanta *as soon as the ship is ready to take off. Keep some of your drones down here to keep the engineering center in working order. You may want to give the computer control of them so it can direct them to what needs to be done.*"

"Understood. I'll get to it right away." Jack gave the computer control of the deployed Recon Drones and then departed the engineering center. Using the map of the ship that he had downloaded from the computer, he quickly made his way to a lift, an elevator-like vehicle, located a few corridors away from the engineering center, and instructed the lift to take him as close to the bridge as it could. The lift was ovular in shape, and had two curved, rectangular doors, one that functioned as the lifts door, which split open and slid across the interior of the lift, and another that also split open and swung outward into the corridor, which sealed the entrance once the lift had left the area. The interior of the lift, like the rest of the ship he had encountered, was colored silver, and several displays were mounted on the wall that showed status reports of various ship systems. The lift also had a big amount of space in its interior, with enough room to fit almost a dozen people.

As the lift moved towards its destination, it traveled both horizontally and vertically as the vehicle traversed the massive passage system within the ship. The computer moved other lifts out of Jack's path throughout the journey to give them the most direct route to the bridge. Finally, the lift stopped and the door opened on deck 13, the level the bridge was located. The bridge was located almost halfway between the front and the middle of the ship, so if the vessel was ever rammed, the bridge would be safer from harm than it would be it if was directly in the front of the ship. While Jack walked down the corridors, the lighting panels in the upside-down V support structures randomly powered up and began to produce silvery light through the corridor, leaving the hallway being unevenly lit in areas. After walking for a few minutes, Jack finally made it to where the bridge was located. The entrance to the bridge was triangular and contained a similarly triangular metal plate within it. When Jack approached the entrance, a small orange light appeared on the top point of the door, and a scanning beam shined over Jack.

After several seconds, the beam completed its examination and deactivated, and the door split into three smaller triangles, each section sliding into the wall. Jack entered the bridge, and was astonished by its size. The interior of the bridge was three levels high, and its length was over 50 feet long. The floor was partially made of a glass like material, so Jack could see all three levels, and he appeared to be on the middle level of the bridge. Unlike the rest of the ship, the materials that comprised the bridge had a golden-like color, replacing the silver color that seemed to cover all the other materials in the ship. Green and orange light was produced by lighting panels fixed onto the walls and support structures, and the glass-like flooring allowed all the lights in the room to work in tandem with each other, making the bridge a beautiful and mystical sight to behold.

Jack saw a cluster of consoles near the center of the bridge, a large, upside-down pyramid with serval holographic displays of the alien ship's systems dotted along its surface, surrounded by several other normal sized, upside-down triangular consoles, and jogged over to them. As he approached, a large hologram burst to life above the giant central console, displaying a model of the ship, and it was then that he saw the complete design of the ship. The vessel had an ovular design overall, and had a large, long wing that was placed on both sides of the ship. Surrounding the middle portion of the hull were two large ovular gaps in the vessel's construction, and in them lay several large cylindrical structures that ran the distance of the gap, which were used to store a vast amount of alien fighter craft.

Reaching the central console, Jack laid his hands on one of the smaller interfaces that surrounded it and activated the energy-connector system on his hands. His hands produced small energy bolts that leapt off his hand and onto the surface of the device, and a link to the computer was formed within moments. Once the connection was made, he was informed by the computer that the ship's systems were 83% operational and would soon be completely restored, and that the engines were now operational and on stand-by.

"Captain Rickman. The computer informs me that the engines are online and standing by to activate. Have the crew get the *Atlanta* ready for its ascendance. If all goes well, I will be there shortly to free the vessel."

"*Understood, Jack. We'll have the ship ready for you when you get here. Good luck.*"

As Jack activated the launch sequence, he also instructed the computer to seal off any areas of the ship that had been compromised during the crash, and the hatch that Jack had used when he had first entered the ship, so the ship wasn't flooded and receive any further damage.

Computer, initiate launch protocols and prepare to activate main engines. Set course for contact in sensor grid 942-719.

PROCESSING... TASK ACCEPTED.

LOADING FUEL CELLS INTO ENGINE CORES #1 THROUGH #8.

ACTIVATING LAUNCH THRUSTERS NOW.

Jack braced himself as he felt the ship rumble below him as the thrusters on the bottom of the ship activated and began to slowly lift off the ocean floor. The ship's progress was somewhat impaired because of the amount of sand covering the hull of the ship, and because several rock formations had piled onto the surface of the ship as well.

ATTENTION: STRESS ON HULL HAS INCREASED BY 32%.

WARNING: HULL BREACHES IN STRUCTURAL GRID 768-782.

EMERGENCY BULKHEADS DEPLOYED: SEALING COMPROMISED SECTIONS NOW.

"Come on, come on," Jack muttered to himself. He took action and gave the computer new commands.

Computer, use the ship's weapon systems to clear the rocks off the surface of the vessel.

TACTICAL SYSTEMS ACTIVATING; ROUTING POWER TO WING-PLATFORMS.

TARGETING MODULE ONLINE.

SCANNING... SPECIFIED TARGETS DETECTED AND MARKED FOR DESTRUCTION.

ENGAGING TARGETS NOW.

Jack used the visual sensors on the outside of the ship to watch as energy cannons along the ship's right wing activated. The base of the cannons was spherical, and the weapon had three long emitters that fired the energy. From the base sphere, the three emitters were placed equally along the side of it, and they spiraled off the sphere to form a single point where they all stood by each other. A surge of white energy pulsed through the emitters, the light shining through the structure, and raced to the adjoining point of the three devices. The white energy from the three emitters shot outwards towards the rocks and debris covering the ship. Accompanied by the other weapons on the wing, enough solid material was blasted apart to allow the safe ascendance of the alien ship.

ENGINE FUELING COMPLETE: PROPULSION SYSTEM ACTIVATION HAS BEGUN.

On the holographic display, the visual sensor showed the rear of the ship, and Jack saw the ships eight engines erupt to light as a blue fire burned in the reactor coils. Once the ship was a good distance off the ground, Jack put the alien vessel at a small fraction of its maximum speed, and the ship sped through the water to the *Atlanta*. In the front of the bridge, a holographic screen activated, showing a dark view of the ocean zooming by under the ship. Jack activated the ships forward light emitters, and the screen lit up considerably, now showing a clear, visible ocean floor.

"*Jack, how are we going to transport the* Atlanta?" Captain Rickman asked. "*With the damage she's taken, I don't know if she can manage a journey through the ocean on her own power.*"

"I plan to dock the *Atlanta* with the alien ship's hangar bay. Though the facilities are configured for their fighters, according to what I have learned from the computer, the docking equipment should be able to manage the *Atlanta*'s larger frame. If my calculations are correct, we will be able to fit the ship in it with room to spare." Jack then saw the Korean ship appear on the alien ship's video screen, and he felt the alien vessel automatically slow down and stop right above it. "I am launching the ship's towing cables now. I recommend you have the crew hold on to something. The *Atlanta* may be shaken up a bit when the Korean ship is removed from on top of its hull."

"*Understood. All hands, brace for impact!*" Though the alien ship didn't have a high-tech tractor beam system, the ship did possess long metal grappling cables with claw-like grapplers at the end. Twenty tow-cables fired from the bottom of the alien vessel, latching onto different parts of the Korean ship. So many cables were being used because the entire ship needed to be pulled off intact so sections of the ship didn't break off while pulling it off the *Atlanta*.

Jack activated the thrusters on the bottom of the alien vessel, and the ship immediately began to fly upward. He felt the ship below him abruptly stop as the tow cables tightened and kept the alien vessel in place as the Korean ship stubbornly clutched to the ocean floor, refusing to move off the *Atlanta*. After a few moments, the alien ship successfully yanked the Korean ship off the ocean floor. Once high enough from the *Atlanta,* Jack directed the alien ship a good distance away from the sub, and released the Korean ship, which quickly plummeted down below, and allowed it to rest on the bottom of the ocean once more.

"*You did it, Jack! Give us a moment, and we'll get the* Atlanta *high enough from the ocean floor to dock with the ship. Stand by.*" Jack steered the alien ship back to the *Atlanta* and magnified the video feed on the display so he could observe the sub's progress. The sub had activated its ascension systems, pushing water from its storage tanks and filling them with air, but even after all of the tanks were full of air, the sub still lacked the necessarily force to free itself from beneath the rock formations that surrounded it.

"Stand by, Captain Rickman. I am targeting the rocks around the *Atlanta*. I recommend you hold on to something." Jack decreased the intensity of the energy cannons, so he wouldn't critically damage the *Atlanta* by accident, and fired at the rocks that had fallen on the sub when the Korean ship had been moved, and the rock formations surrounding the *Atlanta*. After a minute, the ship stopped firing. Jack couldn't get a clear visual because of the dust cloud created from the rocks. Suddenly, the *Atlanta* burst through the dust cloud, and quickly continued to travel closer towards the surface of the water above. Jack began to move the alien vessel toward the *Atlanta*, but the ship continued to rise, which prevented him from docking with the sub.

"Captain Rickman, you need to slow your ascent so you can dock with the alien ship."

"*I'm afraid we're unable to do so, Jack.*" Captain Rickman responded, his voice slightly distorted with the *Atlanta*'s shaking as it flew upward. "*The air tubes are stuck closed. We can't get any water into them to slow us down. It also appears that our propellers were *broken off when we landed on the surface, we can't even move anywhere. Jack, you need to get us, before the* Atlanta *reaches the top of the ocean.*" It was then that he realized how much danger the *Atlanta* was in. If the sub surfaced the ocean with any Ribiyar ships around, it would be an easy target for them to take out.

"I am coming, Captain Rickman. I will attempt to position the alien ship so you will fly into the hanger."

"*Can you do that, Jack? I mean, can you do it without impacting with the* Atlanta?" His voice was even more distorted now, an effect of the sub rising even faster to the surface.

"In the time we have, there's only one way to find out." Jack rapidly gave the commands to the ship's computer, and activated the ship's auto pilot to allow the computer to make the complex and precise flight maneuvers needed in this situation.

TASK ACCEPTED. AUTONOMOUS FLIGHT SYSTEMS ENGAGED.

COMMENCING FLIGHT MANEUVERS REQUIRED TO INTERCEPT TARGET.

Jack was thrown across the bridge as the ship rapidly accelerated in a *very* short time. Jack slammed against a wall, making a body sized dent in the metal plating, and was held in place on the wall from the momentum of the maneuvers the ship was performing. Though his physical connection with the computer had been lost, he maintained contact through his transmitting and receiving equipment.

ATTENTION: 1000 *REZ* UNTIL TARGET REACHES LIQUID SURFACE.

Jack didn't know what a *rez* was, but from how fast the vessels were going he knew they wouldn't have much time to spare if this worked. From the data he was receiving, and from the visuals on the display, he saw on the screen that the alien ship had sped past the *Atlanta* and was moving itself above the sub. The ship then positioned itself so that the *Atlanta* would rise up to one of the docking lanes on the alien vessel. Jack had instructed the computer to place the *Atlanta* in the row on the left gap in the ship and the rightmost docking lane in that section, next to the main hull of the ship, so the sub would have the best cover possible if the alien ship was attacked.

ATTENTION: 500 *REZ* UNTIL TARGET REACHES LIQUID SURFACE.

When the *Atlanta* was within the docking lanes, four giant metal clamps emerged from their storage bays in the hull and grabbed onto the *Atlanta*, securing it in the docking lane. The ship then activated the thrusters positioned on top of the hull as it tried to stop before it reached the ocean's surface. Fortunately, Jack had programmed the computer to make a gentler stop, rather than the sudden burst of speed it had used when it chased after the *Atlanta*. If he hadn't, the *Atlanta*'s crew would've been killed as they were thrown against the sub's ceiling from the sudden speed decrease.

The alien ship stopped moving, and Jack finally managed to wrench himself from his seat in the wall, falling to his feet on the ground. Once he oriented himself, he quickly returned to the central computer console and placed his hands on the structure and analyzed the data to determine their current status. He was pleased as the ship's sensors informed him that the alien vessel had stopped ascending a fair distance from the ocean's surface. Acting quickly, Jack instructed the computer to quickly (but gently) return the ship to the bottom of the ocean. He then adjusted the visual display to show the *Atlanta*, and then he saw the sub, secure in-between the docking lane and the main hull of the alien vessel.

"Captain Rickman, is the crew all right? What is the status of the *Atlanta*?"

Jack heard something get brushed aside from the comm microphone, and then he heard Lieutenant Commander Hayley speak, "*I think we'll be fine, Jack. Captain Rickman was knocked unconscious when he fell against a computer console when the Atlanta docked. But don't worry, Doctor McGriffen has already examined him and he will be fine and should wake up soon. From the reports we received from the rest of the ship, there were no casualties, and only minor injuries have been reported.*"

"That's great news, Commander Hayley." After checking some more information from the computer, he continued, "Commander, I am going to activate the docking post that will extend a corridor to allow the crew to come aboard. It will have to drill through the *Atlanta*'s hull to get into the sub, so notify the crew in deck 4, section 9 to be ready for that. The docking structure will be tight enough in the *Atlanta* that it can drill through the hull without any water leaking in, though I do recommend that section be temporarily sealed off as a safety precaution."

"Jack, are you sure about that? If the sub un-docks from the ship, we'll still have that hole in our hull, and we don't exactly have the materials needed to repair it. It would keep us from traveling on our own power."

"Commander, I think the *Atlanta*'s sailing days are over. Its propellers have been cut off, and you can't descend into the water with your tubes stuck closed."

Hayley paused a moment as she thought, and replied, *"All right, Jack. Do it."*

"Right away, Commander. I am extending the boarding ramp now." Jack watched as a circular corridor, very similar in shape to the docking lanes, emerged from the hull of the ship and then connected with the *Atlanta*'s hull. Steam appeared around the boarding lane's endpoint as lasers at the end of the boarding lane drilled though the hull.

As the boarding ramp continued to drill through the hull of the *Atlanta*, Jack instructed the computer to begin pumping oxygen into the interior of the ship, since the alien ship had no air inside the ship, the result of being built by a robotic species that didn't need it to survive. Fortunately, the Ribiyar had installed atmospheric systems into the ship that could produce a wide variety of breathable air, supposedly if someone from outside their species was brought aboard, and luckily, the required chemicals needed to produce oxygen where part of the materials stored for the atmospheric system to use. As the oxygen was produced and spread through the ship's vent system, Jack directed the air to the bridge, the boarding ramp, the engineering center, and other areas the crew would be likely to use. Eventually, enough oxygen would be produced to support the entire ship, but until then, only certain sections of the vessel would be habitable by the crew. Jack also began heating the interior of the ship, as a specific temperature was not required the aliens and the ship had been exposed to an extremely cold environment for days, also to suit the needs of the *Atlanta*'s crew.

Soon after Jack had finished directing the airflow, the computer notified him that the boarding ramp had finished drilling a path into the *Atlanta*. The display then split into two video feeds, one showing the *Atlanta* in the docking lanes, and the other showing the inside of the docking port connected to the sub.

The hallway in the sub was slightly torn apart from the *Atlanta*'s rocky descent, and likely from the corridor drilling through the ship as well. A ceiling beam had come loose, one end touching the ground as the other end still held to the ceiling, and pieces of shattered wall plating covered the surface of the floor. The hallway was empty for a few moments, before a few of the *Atlanta*'s crew appeared on the screen, timidly approaching the hole in the ship and peering down into the boarding lane. Using the ship's communications system, many nearly jumping out of their skin in surprise to the unexpected communication, Jack informed the crew that he was sending drones to lead them to the bridge, the engineering center, and other points of the ship that needed to be operated. After he assigned the Recon Drones to their tasks, Jack quickly traveled toward the docking lane to board the *Atlanta*, and meet the bridge crew for a meeting in the briefing room to discuss their next plan of action. Assuming, of course, that there was one.

5 minutes later...

The *Atlanta*'s senior staff had gathered in the briefing room, with Jack present at the end of the table. Though he no longer officially a member of the *Atlanta*'s crew, the others felt he should be present at the meeting, considering his involvement in freeing the ship, and his ability to directly interface with the alien technology made him invaluable as the *Atlanta*'s crew struggled to control the unfamiliar equipment. Also, many had served under his command for over a year, and they knew that his insight and thoughts on the matters at hand would be well advised. Captain Rickman sat at the front of the table, a small bruise on the right side his forehead from his encounter with the computer console.

Commander Hayley got right to the point and asked, "What is our plan now, captain? Do we contact our superiors in the U.S. and inform them that we are still alive?"

Captain Rickman hesitated, and responded, "I don't think that is any longer possible. From the information I have reviewed from the alien's database, it appears that our military headquarters were one of the first sites that was attacked. I doubt that there is anything left of it. But, before we plan long term, we need to focus on our own needs first. We have only roughly a day's food left, and some of that is spoiled. Are there any islands we could go to and gather supplies?"

"There are, Captain Rickman. "Jack responded. "There is an uninhabited island about 60 miles west of our location. I suggest we take some of the alien fighters to the island to gather supplies. We should try to keep our possession of the ship a secret, until the time is right. We don't want to give up the element of surprise."

"How will we fly those ships? We don't exactly have time to learn how to do it," Chief Lexton asked.

"I can use my computer systems and pilot the shuttles myself. I recommend we have at least two Recon Drones aboard each shuttle for security on the island, and to strengthen my connection with the fighters' computer systems."

The captain was silent as he thought it over. After a few moments, he responded, "Alright. Jack, do what you have to do to pilot those shuttles. Chief Lexton, I want you to be the senior officer on this mission. Your engineering expertise may be required if any of the fighters suffer any mechanical failures, and it would be best if Jack didn't have to try to keep the ships together while trying to keep them flying through the sky. Assemble a team big enough for five shuttles, and set course for that island. Be back as soon as you can."

"Aye, captain." Chief Lexton responded.

"The rest of you, assign a skeleton crew to stay on the *Atlanta*. I want the rest of the crew to be on the alien ship. We are going to be spread pretty thin, but we need to personally supervise as much of the ship's operations as we can. Jack, program the rest of your drones to respond to our commands so we can use them to help maintain the ship."

Jack nodded. "Understood, captain. It won't take long to make the modifications."

"Good. If there is nothing else, you are all dismissed."

Date: July 9, 2132.
Location: Onboard the Ribiyar Warship *Ji'Co*, in orbit of Earth.

Tactical Analysist Cha'Hawk was busy reviewing battle plans in his work center for a raid on a base they had recently discovered on a land mass surrounded by a body of liquid the organics called the Pacific Ocean, when his monitors showed the brief appearance of a tracking signal, before it abruptly disappeared from the reach of the *Ji'Co*'s sensors. Cha'Hawk accessed the monitor, and reversed the display to the time where it had detected the tracking signal. The signal once again appeared on the monitor, and he froze the information on the display and studied it closely. There was no mistaking the signal: it was a homing beacon that clearly identified it as the *Ra'Ta*. Cha'Hawk immediately made his way to High Order Ki'Ra's chamber to deliver his mission report, and to personally give his knowledge of the *Ra'Ta* to his superior. He could not afford to give Ki'Ra any indication about his planned betrayal by delaying to reporting this development, for he did not yet have the plans in place to sever Ki'Ra from his rule.

Once Cha'Hawk arrived at the entrance to Ki'Ra's domain, Cha'Hawk inserted his data module into the port, which would send a message to Ki'Ra that he was at the door. After several minutes of waiting, a favorite tactic of the High Order's, for it clearly made it known who was in charge, the door split open, and a guard escorted Cha'Hawk to Ki'Ra. Ki'Ra's chambers was nearly as big as the Battle Coordination Hall and was covered in the same silver color that the High Order had demanded coat all of the ships in the fleet, both on the interior of the ship and on the exterior hull plating. The room was two levels high, though the second level was mostly a circle that loped around the ovular room. On the first floor, a glimmering stair case led to a chair that lay at the top of the structure. As Cha'Hawk moved through the room, it was hard for the soldier not to take notice of the handful of automatic gun turrets placed along the walls. Many would claim this was the most secure place on a Ribiyar battleship, for the room was located near the center of the ship, and it was also in close proximity to the security center, allowing reinforcements to be able to arrive in moments if needed. Cha'Hawk walked up the large stairway that led to the second level and waited while Ki'Ra finished talking with a squad commander that was reporting from another ship on the fleet.

Ki'Ra was seated on the command chair, though many thought of it as a throne. The seat was made from rare crystals they found on a planet years ago while traveling to Earth, and they discovered that the crystals glimmered even brighter when energy flowed through them. Because Ribiyar were powered by energy, the crystals would brightly shine whenever a Ribiyar sat on the throne. Moments later, the officer was dismissed, and Cha'Hawk approached Ki'Ra, and kneeled before him, as protocol demanded, though he hated bowing before the arrogant fool who somehow managed to remain in command of the Ribiyar forces laying claim to the planet known as earth, and all the other planets in the solar system.

"High Order Ki'Ra, I have news to report." Ki'Ra did not respond for a few moments, savoring the moment of having Cha'Hawk kneeling before him.

"Proceed with your report, Tactical Analysist Cha'Hawk."

Cha'Hawk rose and started his report. "High Order, the mission to destroy the organic's vessel, the *U.S.S. Ocean-Walker*, has failed. The initial team was destroyed, and the reinforcements were also neutralized. The organics may have had a ship hidden below them for support, but we had not detected it during the battle. I also have been contacted by holding facility Tri'La, informing us that they have progressed to 71% completion, and are now ready to receive the organics our warriors have captured to begin the experiments that you have ordered."

"Excellent. Begin rapid shipment to Tri'La at once. I want results from the organic studies within 2 *Qat*. How long until the Nexus has been constructed?" Ki'Ra asked.

"At their current rate, it will be operational within 8 *Qat*, and completed in 13."

"Excellent. The sooner a permanent presence of the Tora Cyrel (Ribiyar equivalent of an empire) is established, the better. What of the discovery of the organic's military base in the landmasses in what they call the Pacific Ocean. Are the preparations made to destroy the base, and then annihilate them?"

"I have been reviewing the proposed battle plans, and they appear to be soundly prepared. Once the troops have infiltrated the base and purged the organics inhabiting the landmass, they will download whatever information the base holds, then they will place bombs powerful enough to destroy the base, the island that holds it, and all the land masses near it as well. Though I do recommend simply bombarding the island with the cannons of the warships in orbit, you of course have the final decision." *Unfortunately*, Cha'Hawk silently added to himself. "The troops will be ready to strike within a *Qat*. I will leave it to their commanders to inform you their status.

"Very well. Is that all, Tactical Analyst Cha'Hawk?"

Cha'Hawk readied himself. "There is one more matter, High Order. It is possible that the *Ra'Ta* has been found and reactivated by the organics. It is only a matter of time before-"

Ki'Ra nearly jumped off his seat. "This *AGAIN!?!* I told you not to be concerned about that ship. It was destroyed during the invasion, and that is it! Are you so insecure in your position that you have to make up stories for you to receive the glory?!?"

"Ki'Ra, I assure you that I have not in any way inter-"

"IT IS *HIGH ORDER* KI'RA!!!" Ki'Ra was so enraged, Cha'Hawk could almost see steam coming off him from his anger and fury. "You are not to mention the *Ra'Ta* again! Am I clear about this Tactical Analysist Cha'Hawk? I will personally throw you in an Oblivion Chamber if I hear of this again! Guards, get this officer out of my sight!" A dozen Ribiyar officers emerged from their hideouts, and hurried to Cha'Hawk, grabbing him and pulling him out of the room.

Once they had dragged him to the lower level, Cha'Hawk managed to shake free of their hold, and he walked to the exit himself. Pausing as the door split open, Cha'Hawk turned to Ki'Ra and said, "You shall see, Ki'Ra. Your ignorance will be your downfall to us all. Do not underestimate the organics." Cha'Hawk then left the chamber before Ki'Ra could voice any more threats against him. This incident was the last mark. If Ki'Ra had listened about the *Ra'Ta*, Cha'Hawk might have reconsidered his rebellion against the High Order. But this development alone was proof of Ki'Ra's faulty leadership. It was time to take Ki'Ra down: once, and for all.

Chapter 15

Date: July 9, 2132.
Location: Aboard the *U.S.S. Thunderfox*, on the border of the Atlantic Ocean.

"The captains' quarters are at the end of this corridor, Lieutenant Oakland," Olo's escort announced. Inwardly, Olo cringed at the use of his name. Though he wished people wouldn't use his real name, he also understood that not everyone would be sensitive to his preferences. The hallway's he had traveled through where rectangular and colored a light tan, lit with florescent bulbs installed throughout the ceiling that bathed the corridors in a bright white light.

From what he had seen of the *Thunderfox*, the ship was more advanced than he had expected, even considering the ship's impressive flight equipment. The *Thunderfox* apparently had a computer system that was supposedly five times more advanced than the standard system for the other ships, and from its display of firepower in destroying the Ribiyar fighters, it obviously possessed enough power to match the *Ocean-Walker*'s considerable arsenal. But the most impressive feature of the ship was the *Thunderfox*'s propulsion. The ship used electromagnetic drives for propulsion, a type of engine that went into use for interstellar vessels in the early 2090's. The engines created propulsion from microwaves that were produced through the consumption of energy, which eliminated the need to store fuel onboard a ship.

Olo reached the end of the hallway, and as his escort returned to her post, Olo knocked on the door and awaited permission to enter. The door opened, and Captain Whitefield greeted him into the room. As he entered, he observed his surroundings and found it to be very cramped. The only furniture that populated the small room was a chair that was bolted to rails that were placed in front of a small table, which took up a good portion of the left side of the room, and a bed that inhabited a cubby hole in the wall of the right side of the room. The bed, which looked like a caged seat used in carnival rides, was a mattress with several blankets scattered on it, but it was contained in a wire-frame cage of some kind.

"If you're wondering about the bed," Captain Syvon said when he noticed Olo examining it, "it's custom built so a person sleeping on the bed isn't thrown across the room if the ship needs to make extreme flight maneuvers during combat."

"What happens if you are not in a bed?" Olo asked.

"You either need to be strapped into a seat harness, or wearing magnetic boots such as these," Captain Syvon said, pointing at the pair of red and gray boots he wore. He went on to explain, "Those boots magnetize you to the floor of the ship, which happens to be excessively metallic for that purpose. The engineers who built this ship needed the crew to survive flying in it."

Captain Whitefield cleared his throat. "If we could get to the matter at hand, Captain Syvon?"

"I apologize, Captain Whitefield," Syvon replied with a sly grin on his face. "It isn't often I get to give a tour of my ship. Lieutenant Olo, I understand that you have some field experience conducting search patrols through difficult terrain. Is this correct?"

Olo nodded. "Yes, sir, it is. Did you have a job in mind that would require that experience?"

"Yes, Lieutenant. I need you to lead a search party to scout the island we are to rendezvous at, and if you encounter any Ribiyar, you need to do your best to eliminate their presence there. Our forces can't afford to be ambushed before we even begin to try to free the people from the holding prison. Also, when you assemble the search party, I want Victor Davidson to be included in the group."

Olo hesitated. "Begging your pardon, sir, but may I ask why?"

"If there are Ribiyar on the island, you'll want Victor with you. He has acquired some powerful battle equipment that will make him a valuable asset for your team." Sensing Olo's reluctance, Captain Syvon asked, "Do you have something against Victor, Lieutenant?"

Olo took a deep breath and said, "I do, sir. 5 years ago, my parents were murdered while I was away on an assignment. I returned home to find my parents both dead in the living room. I called the authorities, and after going through the murder scene, they found Victor's DNA in the house, but when it went to court, Victor managed to get off free because of the team of lawyers he hired. It's an understatement to say that I'm not comfortable working with him."

Both captains were silent for a moment, and then Captain Syvon said, "I see. Personally, I myself greatly dislike being around the man, so I vaguely understand your... discomfort. I *am* truly sorry about what happened with your parents Oakland, and I wish I could do something to bring justice to their deaths. But unfortunately, there's nothing we can do to punish him at the moment. Like it or not he's vital in our fight against the Ribiyar, and I still need you to work by his side. Can you do this?"

"I'll do my best sir, and I will inform you if the situation gets out of hand between me and Victor."

Captain Syvon nodded. "Good. I know you can do it. I recommend that you go visit Davidson and see his equipment in use. That might help you form a strategy if you should fight the Ribiyar. I'll take the two of you to where he is training."

Captain Syvon led Captain Whitefield and Olo down to the third level of the *Thunderfox*, where a small training room was located. The training room was a medium sized room with a training mat in the middle, three punching bags near the metal plated back wall, and several lockers populated the two side walls to provide storage room for the officers' training in the room.

When the group arrived in the training room, the only person in the room was Victor, which wasn't surprising to Olo, considering Victor's current appearance, and his general attitude to everyone around him. Victor was wearing a suit of armor, but it was like nothing Olo had ever seen before. The armor was tan, with green serpent stripes along all of it. On Victor's back was a metallic, whip-like device, colored a mixture of tan and dark green, coiled into a lump, and the end of the whip trailed down to the back of Victor's waist. Two rectangular, blaster-like devices were attached to his arms, though Olo couldn't even guess what type of guns they were, and the ends of Victor's hands were razor sharp claws that looked like they could slice through a boulder. On Victor's head was a metal helmet, that had the appearance of a snake mask, a large, tan python like-head with dark, menacing green eyes that covered the top half of his face that hid his eyes and nose while leaving his mouth uncovered. The green eyes on the mask moved around the room as Victor practiced martial art moves, possibly following Victors' eye movements inside the mask. Lastly, Victor held a sword handle in his hand, a dark purple handle with blood-red wings at the top, though the device had no blade on the end of it. Victor noticed the group enter and walked over to them.

"So, you like my new duds?" Victor asked. "It was part of my payment for participating in the o-so-honorable fight for life, survival, freedom, and all that other junk."

"What happened to your sword?" Olo asked, trying to keep his voice even. Just being in the same room with the man made him want to grab the nearest gun and put Victor out of his misery. "You break one of your new toys already?"

"This?" Victor said, lifting the handle up in the air with admiration. "This, is the Phantom Blade. The last of the original Hydra-class weapons. And best of all, it's fully functional, and ready for a taste of those robotic aliens." Olo was skeptical of the weapons functionality. Early in 2115, the CIA got intel about a prototype energy blade, a class of weapon known as Hydra's because of their potential lethality, that were going to be auctioned off in the black market to the highest bidders. They intercepted the exchange with the buyers, and all but one of the blades were destroyed in the following firefight, the surviving one taken in by the CIA agents. After examining the device, they declared the blade non-functional, determining that the power core in the device apparently didn't possess enough power to project the energy blade, making the Phantom Blade worthless. After the CIA's intervention at the auction, no more of the Hydra weapons had been reported sold, or even made. As far as anyone knew, the knowledge of how to make the blade was lost when the sellers were killed in the firefight.

"So, you doubt my truthfulness?" Victor asked, seeing Olo's skepticism. "Very well." Victor pressed a button on the handle, the wings of the handle sparked and an energy bolt erupted in between the wings. The energy bolt expanded outward from the handle, eventually creating an energy form 12 inches long. The energy bolt sharpened into a solid form, resulting in a dark reddish-purple energy blade. Though Olo tried to hide his surprise of the device's functionality, he couldn't help a look of shock forming on his face. Captain Syvon was the most surprised of the blades functional state.

"How did you manage to get it working?" Captain Syvon asked surprise apparent in his voice. Clearly, he hadn't thought Victor would be able to activate the device when the CIA's best engineers had failed to do so.

"Magicians never reveal their tricks to outsiders, my dear Captain. Did you really think I'd ask for this as part of my payment if I couldn't make it work?"

"Ok, so it's a blade made of energy. So what?" Olo remarked, pretending not to be impressed with the Phantom Blade. Victor glared at Olo from behind the snake mask. Victor pressed another button on the handle, and swung the Phantom Blade. The sword flung off the handle, slicing through a chain that held a boxing bag up. The bag fell to the floor as the energy blade continued toward the wall of the room. The blade sliced into the wall, making a gash in the metal plating, and evaporated as the energy lost coherence. On the Phantom Blade handle, a new energy blade materialized.

"That, Ollie, is why the blade is so special." Victor remarked as he deactivated the blade and clipped the handle to his waist.

"Victor! Do you know how hard it is to replace those metal plates?" Captain Syvon exclaimed.

"Save your breath, Captain Syvon," Victor replied. "You paid me to be an asset to your rebellion against these aliens. 'Not breaking equipment' wasn't part of my contract." Olo could tell that Captain Syvon wanted to yell at Victor more, but the captain held his tongue. He guessed that Victor was right about him not having to go gentle with the Defenders' equipment, but that didn't mean Syvon had to like it. Syvon's communicator beeped, and he activated the wrist device and lifted it to his face to talk into the device.

"Captain Syvon here. What is it?"

"Commander Ton reporting, captain. Sir, the *Ocean-Walker* is ready for travel. We have been able to access their H-drive, and two of their engines are operational. We will be able to rendezvous with the fleet ahead of schedule."

"Good work, Commander. Have the repair crews remain on the *Ocean-Walker* to continue what repairs they can from inside the vessel. We're going to need to repair that ship as much as we can in the time that we have. Inform any other engineers we can spare aboard the *Thunderfox* to report to you on the *Ocean-Walker* soon. I want us to get underway within fifteen minutes, and we can't transfer officers while we travel there."

"Understood, sir. Commander Ton out."

"I should get back to my ship and oversee operations." Captain Whitefield said.

"Indeed. Lieutenant Olo, I want you to remain here to prepare for the mission. Is it alright if he transfers to my command, at least for the time being, Captain Whitefield?"

"It is, Captain Syvon. Lieutenant Oakland, you are to be under Captain Syvon's command for as long as he needs your services, understood?"

"Yes, sir. If I can make one request, Captain Whitefield, will you make sure that Batcat is returned to my quarters so I can try to repair him?"

"What is Batcat?" Captain Syvon asked.

"An E.V.A.N. unit Oakland has been charged with taking care of. Yes, Lieutenant, I will make sure it is moved to your quarters for you."

"An E.V.A.N. unit?" Victor said, suddenly interested in the conversation. "I should've put one of those on my payment list."

"Not now, Victor," Captain Syvon replied. "We have bigger things to worry about than your paycheck. Lieutenant Oakland, I will get you the roster for the officers available for this mission and let you get to work assembling your team."

"I'd better get back to the *Ocean-Walker* and get the ship ready for the trip to the rendezvous," Whitefield said as he moved toward the door. "Good luck with your search, Lieutenant," Whitefield said, glancing toward Victor, who had moved to one of the punching bags and was furiously unleashing his might into it. "You're going to need it."

Olo couldn't agree with Whitefield more, and hoped that he could keep his emotions in check, so Victor didn't experience an 'untimely demise' of his own.

Date: July 9, 2132.
Location: Aboard a fighter docked on the Ribiyar vessel, at the bottom of the Atlantic Ocean.

"Vade to Captain Rickman. We are ready to depart." Jack stood in one of the fighters that were docked on the alien ship. With some minor repairs, the fighters were soon restored from the ill effects caused by the electromagnetic pulse, and the landing party was now ready to head for the island to collect much needed food for the *Atlanta*'s crew. Along with Jacks fighter, there were six other fighters, and a total of 15 crewmen divided among the ships, that would be used for the mission, leaving the remaining 20 or so fighters behind if the *Atlanta*'s crew needed them. The ovular interior of the fighter was difficult at first for the crew members to adjust to, and as there were no seats to rest on during the flight, they were forced the occupants to hold onto the consoles for support during the journey. The holographic display activated as the ship awoke from its slumber, giving the crew a look at the alien vessel docking lanes, and the dark environment around them.

Among the eight members of the *Atlanta*'s crew who accompanied Jack in the fighter, Chief Lexton and Doctor Sadie McGriffen, a tall, brown haired woman who served as the *Atlanta*'s commanding medical officer, were standing by to relay commands to the other fighter crews, though Jack would be the one to do the flying from his computer connection with the fighters. Doctor McGriffen insisted on coming along to make sure that the crew didn't take back any food or plants that could be poisonous to the officers, and to provide medical assistance if they were attached on the island. Along with the crewman who rode in the fighters, two Recon Drones also accompanied them, attaching themselves to consoles in the ships, to improve the computer connection with Jack, and to provide additional firepower for the crew on the island, should they encounter the aliens as they searched for food.

"Understood, Jack," Captain Rickman responded. "You are cleared for takeoff. If possible, maintain radio silence, but you can contact us for support if you are attacked and it is absolutely necessary. If that happens, we will provide cover fire for you, but that would expose the ship and lose the element of surprise."

"Acknowledged. I will take care to keep the ship undetected. It would be an unnecessary risk to expose the ship's existence this early and put everyone at risk." As the docking clamps detached from the fighters and retracted back into the hull of the alien vessel, the primary power cores on the fighters activated, giving life to their engines and weapon systems. Jack gave commands to the fighters' computers, and the group sped through the ocean and made the journey towards the island. After over 20 minutes of travel, Jack took the fighters out of the ocean, bringing them into the bright illumination of the sun, which they hadn't encountered for what had felt like an eternity. As the fighters soared through the air, they quickly came to a decently sized island nearby. Towering trees populated the island's surface, and a large mountain-like hill sat near the center of the island.

"Jack, I think I see a good place to land in that clearing over there." Chief Lexton spoke, pointing toward a clearing in the palm trees that would just be big enough for their seven vessels to land in.

"I see it. Adjusting course now." Using the shuttles computers, Jack brought the fighters to the clearing, and after six landing stilts ejected from the hull and positioned themselves to support the craft, the fighters landed with a small thud on the ground. In the back of the interior of the fighters, a ramp lowered down so they could exit their craft. The Recon Drones emerged from the fighters first, scanning the area for any Ribiyar near the landing site, there blue scanning beams dancing across the area. Once the drones confirmed the site was safe, the crew exited their shuttles, enjoying their first exposure to the sun in many days. Around the fighters, there were many large coconut and palm trees, with green fruit hanging from many of them. There were also tall grass weeds that blocked a clear view of what laid beyond the trees.

Chief Lexton got to work at once. "All right, here is the plan. Lieutenant's Carter, Jessics, and Ensign Mathews, stay here and guard the fighters. Three drones will remain with you to ward off any attacks but be watchful for any aliens. We don't know how much they've spread through the planet, but we need to be careful. Understood?"

"Yes, sir," the officers responded.

"Jack, I want you to head to that hill over there." She said, pointing at a mound near the center of the island. "I want you to be our scout in the area, spot out food for us to gather, but be on the lookout for aliens as well. I need you to approach the hill on foot. I don't want the chance of them spotting you flying there, though admittedly, if they are here, they most likely already saw us when we approached the island in the fighters."

Jack nodded. "Understood, Chief Lexton."

"The rest of you, pair up in groups of three, and take a drone with you for some additional firepower and to function as a scanner to detect the aliens. Now, let's get some food so our crew doesn't starve while we're exploring this island!" Before they left the clearing, the crew made sure to grab weapons that the Ribiyar had stored on their vessel, which Jack had managed to repair and briefly instruct them how they worked. Now, most of the group carried the alien weapons with them, mostly the double-barreled rifle, providing them with stronger firepower than they would've had using their own guns. After gathering their gear, the group split up, and went into the depths of the forest of the island.

Jack quickly made his way through the thick trees and vegetation growing on the island, encountering a high number of fruit that he would report to the group once he reached his position above the mound near the middle of the island. But after running through the forest for only a few minutes, his enhanced hearing began to detect something moving through the trees, following him as he traveled on the island. Jack stopped in a thick patch of tall grass and scanned the area for anything that was following him, not using his beam scanners to conceal his location, but he didn't detect anything that looked threatening. Cautiously continuing his trek to the small mountain, he moved out from behind the grass, but a dark green bolt of energy struck him in the back, and the impact threw him against a tall tree, knocking some fruit perched on its branches to the ground around him.

Jack pushed himself off the tree and straightened himself, and scanned the area once again, this time using his hand-beam scanners to improve the resolution of the scan. Still finding nothing on his sensors, Jack used his sensor equipment to emit a low-frequency electromagnetic pulse. If anyone was using an advanced form of stealth technology to hide himself, the EMP would interfere with the equipment and expose their location, and Jack took care to make sure the pulse wasn't potent enough to damage his own circuitry in the process. Once the sensors were configured, Jack produced the electromagnetic pulse, and a distorted form of a person materialized on the upper branches of a tree near Jack. The person's form shimmered and sparked as the stealth technology concealing him started to malfunction, until finally the stealth field dissipated; revealing a person in armor, colored tan with green snake-like stripes, along with a menacing snake mask attached to his helmet in the trees. The snake-person jumped down from the tree, landing a few feet away in front of him.

Jack aimed the V-gun on his right arm at the stranger. "Identify yourself," Jack said to his stalker, who maintained a very calm and controlled appearance, despite the weapon aimed at him.

"Shouldn't you be doing the explaining?" The person replied. "Like how you just happen to travel in those Ribiyar fighters I saw as I got here, and how you just happen to be on the island where I'm supposed to exterminate any Ribiyar I find?"

"I am not a member of the Ribiyar species. It may be difficult to believe, and a complicated story, but I am Jack Vade, former captain of the *U.S.S. Atlanta*." Jack knew his argument was unlikely to convince him, but he had to at least try to come to a peaceful solution. He didn't want the mission to end in disaster because of him being attacked by a person who mistakenly thought that he was part of the robotic invaders, though it was admittedly understandable, given his appearance.

The snake-person chuckled. "It doesn't look that way to me, pal. And since you told me your name, I might as well let you in on mine. I, am the Dark Serpent: Ribiyar Slayer. Or at least they will call me that soon, after I finish off you, and the rest of your kind." The Dark Serpent grabbed a sword handle from his belt and pressed a button on the handle, and a dark reddish-purple energy blade surged to life on it. The Serpent swung the blade and Jack leaned backwards to dodge the attack. The blade flew over top of him, missing by inches. Jack straightened himself and fired his right V-gun, but the Serpent was nowhere in sight, and the blast shot through the empty air and onto a tree trunk, burning a hole deep into it.

"You cannot fight what you cannot see," Jack heard the Serpent's voice echo through the trees, staying out of sight. "This isn't my first rodeo, and I don't like losing, especially to aliens." Knowing the Dark Serpent may be too much for him to handle alone, he activated his internal radio and contacted the landing party.

"Jack to landing party. I am under attack and require immediate assistance. Do you read me?" The only response Jack received was ear-splitting static, meaning the Dark Serpent was probably jamming any communication signals that he might try to send out. As he visually searched the trees for any movement that could indicate the Serpent's whereabouts, he was suddenly barraged from behind by energy blasts coming from the tree tops, battering the armor on his back. Acting quickly, Jack jumped behind a tree as he fired back at where the energy blasts came from, but he was unable to score any hits on the Dark Serpent. Jack considered producing another EMP, but as his systems were still recalibrating from the last pulse, he thought it best not to risk crippling himself in an effort to find the Serpent. He instead launched the Recon stored in his arm, and the drone ascended into the tops of the tress, and began to rapidly fire laser beams through the trees, attempting to blindly hit the Serpent through his camouflage. Another dark green energy blast soared through the air and reduced Recon to pieces, but Jack managed to quickly fire at where the blast came from. Jack managed to hit the Dark Serpent, and his form materialized as the stealth device continued to try to conceal him.

With his cover blown, the Dark Serpent deactivated the stealth suit, aimed his arms at Jack, and fired the two blasters equipped on his arms. Jack jumped out from behind the tree, and as he moved to a new place to find cover, he quickly deployed and fired his Laser Cannon at the branch the Serpent stood on, slicing it in half. As the branch fell, the Dark Serpent jumped off the branch and landed on his feet at the base of the tree. As the Serpent straightened himself, a tan metallic tail with diamond-shaped green patterns on it, uncoiled off his back. The tail had three claw-like devices at the end of it, clasped together to make a very sharp, deadly spear to use against him.

Endurance

"Time to show you the sting of the Serpent!" The Dark Serpent grabbed the sword handle from his belt, and reactivated it, but the claws at the end of the tail opened, and he placed the sword in the claws. The claws latched onto the Phantom Blade, giving the tail a deadly enhancement. The Serpent jumped in the air and lunged at Jack. Jack jumped backwards right as the sword dived into the dirt that he had been standing on moments earlier.

The Serpent removed the sword out of the dirt and swung his tail-sword at Jack's direction. The energy blade flew off the handle and soared toward him. Jack dived right to dodge the blade, but the blade sliced the top of his right arm, leaving a 9-inch long gash in his armor and exposing the circuitry beneath. Jack aimed his right V-gun at the Dark Serpent, but when he tried to fire the weapon, it merely sparked and produced a small puff of smoke, having been sliced in half by the Phantom Blade. Jack deactivated it and stored it in his arm, while he deployed the V-gun in his left arm, and then fired it at the Dark Serpent. The V-gun produced its motorcycle engine revving sound right as the weapon discharged its energy, and the noise caused several birds nearby to flee the area. The Serpent dogged the blast, and then charged toward Jack, his tail-sword slinging more energy blades toward him. Jack jumped away from the path of the projectiles, but three of the blades sliced through his back as they flew past him, creating several deep gashes in his back. Struggling to maintain his balance in spite of his damaged systems, Jack turned to fire back at the Dark

Serpent, but he was no longer in front of him. A powerful energy blast from behind propelled him into the base of a palm tree, and the impact with the tree jarred his internal components which caused many of his systems to freeze, effectively paralyzing him as his systems readjusted. While Jack desperately tried to regain his motor functions, the Dark Serpent grabbed him and rested his back against the tree. Though his vison was blurred from the damage he had received, and the effects of the reboot in progress, he saw the Dark Serpent raise his tail-sword into the air and position it high above Jack's chest.

"You were a worthy adversary, alien. It's almost a shame to end our little event. But alas, this is where you meet your demise. And now, my Phantom Blade tastes the blood of its first kill." The tail-sword thrusted downward, the blade eager to finish off its prey.

Chapter 16

Date: July 9, 2132.
Location: Unnamed island in the Atlantic Ocean.

Just as the Phantom Blade was about to plunge into Jack, a voice echoed through the air, and the blade halted mere centimeters from Jack's chest.

"Victor, stop!" Jack slowly turned his head to see several of the *Atlanta*'s crew, among them Chief Lexton and Doctor McGriffen, along with a small group of officers he hadn't seen before, approach the two of them. The tail rested on the ground besides Jack, and then slithered toward the Serpent, whose real name was apparently Victor. While the tail recoiled on his back, Victor bent down, plucked the Phantom Blade from his tail, deactivated it, and attached the handle to his belt. The officer who had stopped Victor from killing Jack stepped close to the Serpent, clearly more than a little upset with him.

"Victor, I told you to stay with the group. What were you thinking, running into the woods like that?"

"Forgive me, 'sir', but we all saw those fighters land in the trees when we got on the island, and my equipment picked up his energy signature once we began moving through the trees," Victor said, pointing at Jack, who still hadn't moved from his spot by the tree, "and I thought that he might be a Ribiyar reporting us to his superiors. If I was correct, we could have been surrounded and captured by the Ribiyar by now. Which is why I didn't wait to get your permission before I left the group to engage him."

The officer exhaled deeply, still frustrated at Victor, but Jack saw that he found a small, yet rebellious, amount of wisdom in his actions. "All right. But from now on, I need you to report your findings and wait for my orders before you do something like that again. Understood?"

"Very well, 'sir'. What are your orders now, Lieutenant Oakland?" *Oakland.* The name echoed strongly through his battered memory as Jack who the officer was. Otlin Oakland, always insisting others call him by his preferred name Olo in place of his unusual given name, had served with Jack aboard the *U.S.S. Charger,* which he had been stationed on before he had risen to the rank of captain. Olo had been a remarkable officer aboard the *Charger*, and he and Jack had become close friends over the year they had served aboard the ship with each other. Though he had tried to keep in touch with Olo as much as he could while Jack progressed with his military career, he and Olo had fallen out of contact with each other as the years passed by, so it had been almost a year and a half since the last time Jack had talked to him. Though he wanted to reunite with his friend and tell Olo who he was, he needed to stay focused on the mission and wait for the proper time to inform him, as Jack's condition would be a great shock to Oakland and it would take time to adjust.

Olo turned toward the rest of the officers in his group. "We need to help these officers to get supplies for the crew on their ship," he said, addressing the *Atlanta*'s crew. "But first, we need to continue searching the island for any sign of Ribiyar, and we still have a lot more ground to cover." As Olo began to give instructions to the officers, Jack's systems finally succeeded in restoring his motor functions, and he gradually felt control of his arms and legs return. Slowly, Jack began to stand up, a somewhat difficult task as his systems still recalibrating from the impact with the tree and the damage received during the battle. Chief Lexton hurried over to Jack and helped steady him as he tried to stand.

"Jack, are you all right? You took quite a beating from the looks of it," Chief Lexton said as she moved under his left arm to help him stand, and as she glanced over the gashes in his armor.

"My condition is not optimal, Chief Lexton, but I can continue on with my task. My systems are bypassing damaged components, and I'll be able to function well enough until we get back to the ship." Jack moved his arm out of Lexton's support, and though he nearly fell, he managed to stay upright as Olo walked toward him.

"I apologize for Victor's actions, soldier," Olo said as he glanced toward Victor, who didn't look the least bit sorry for attacking Jack, with his smug grin on his face. "I didn't think anyone would be out here on this remote island, certainly not anyone wearing battle armor like yours."

Jack was about to respond when a small, triangular-shaped device fell from the sky in the middle of the group. The device had Ribiyar markings inscribed all over its surface, and like almost everything else seen by the species, the device was colored in a shiny silver coating. Jack immediately recognized the device from the information he had reviewed in the Ribiyar ship's computer, which identified it as a wide-radius explosive. Acting quickly, Jack deployed Recon from his right arm, which had automatically been fabricated when the other drone had been destroyed, and the drone latched onto the explosive device and soared high into the air as fast as its engines could manage. A large explosion erupted in the sky, destroying yet another of his drones, and the force of the blast threw many officers to the ground as they covered their ears. Jack, who had managed to remain standing, scanned the surrounding area for the Ribiyar who had thrown the explosive, when behind them, a Ribiyar jumped out of the trees and fired at them as he ran toward the group of officers. The alien quickly shot down three of the officers from Olo's ship, but before he could kill more, Victor grabbed his Phantom Blade, activated it, and flung several energy blades toward the alien, who was sliced into pieces and fell to the ground in a pile of sparking scrap metal.

"I am grateful you were not that aggressive when you faced me," Jack grimly remarked as he continued to scan the area, attempting different scanning methods as attempted to circumvent whatever techniques the Ribiyar were using to shield them from his sensors.

"I admit, I was toying with you for most of the fight," Victor said as he attached the Phantom Blade onto his tail. "It was my first time I could try out most of my toys in action."

Behind Jack, Doctor McGriffen feverously attempted to tend to the officers who had been shot by the Ribiyar. After a minute of performing emergency procedures to the officers, the doctor stood up and said, "I am sorry, Lieutenant Oakland, but their wounds were too severe. There was nothing I could do for them."

Olo grimaced, greatly pained that more people had been added to the long list of casualties in this war, and while they were under his watch. "They didn't deserve to die like this. Now that we now the Ribiyar are here, we have to send to signal the *Ocean-Walker* and then get off this island, before we're ambushed again." Olo quickly pulled a small trigger shaped device, removed a cap covering the top, and pressed the button within. A light on the trigger began blinking green, signaling the signal was beginning transmitted. Turning to Jack, he said, "Soldier, can you detect any more Ribiyar in the area?"

"My scans do not show any in the vicinity, but I was unable to detect him as well," Jack said, pointing at the remains of the Ribiyar attacker. "They are likely somehow masking themselves from my sensors. I am contacting the drones accompanying the officers from my ship and instructing them to perform a visual search of the area."

"What we need to do is to head back to our ship, the *Ocean-Walker*. We are too exposed out here, and we only have about ten minutes before they begin bombing the island." Olo turned his head to the thick vegetation surrounding them. "It's going to be a tough journey though, and it will be even more difficult if the Ribiyar find us and decide to shoot us down, which they probably will."

Chief Lexton stepped forward. "I may have a better plan, sir. We have several Ribiyar fighters that we used to get here. We can use them to travel to your ship. It would be a lot faster than trying to traverse through the island to get there. Jack, can you control the fighters from here?" He attempted to connect with the computer systems in the fighters, and though the connection was weakened from his distance from the ships, he was successfully able to gain control of all the fighters.

"I have established the connection with the shuttles. While I prepare the ships for takeoff, I will need you to inform the officers guarding them to come aboard as soon as possible." Chief Lexton contacted the officers stationed by the fighters, and a minute later, all the drones and personnel from that group were aboard. Lexton informed Jack that they were ready, and he sealed the fighters boarding ramps and activated their launch thrusters. Once they were in the air, the ships began flying toward them.

"Chief Lexton, there is a problem. The vegetation is too thick in this area. I cannot find a landing site for the fighters with all the trees around. We have to find somewhere where there is a big enough clearing for the ships to land."

"Should we go back to the clearing where we landed?" Doctor McGriffen asked.

"Negative." Jack reported. He had been monitoring the video footage the Recon Drones sent him as they searched through the island for Ribiyar, and many of the drones' footage showed a great number of Ribiyar warriors charging through the landing site, heading toward him and the others, right before the aliens shot the drones out of the sky. "There are Ribiyar traveling through our landing site, and they are currently heading our direction. The closest landing site that I can see is that hill." Jack said, pointing to the mound near the center of the island he had been traveling towards. "Chief Lexton, while I give the fighters their new heading, you need to inform the other search parties to make way to the hill as quickly as they can."

"I'm on it." Lexton grabbed her radio and contacted the remaining search party from the *Atlanta*'s crew. "Search party two, do you copy? You must head to the mountain at once! Repeat, head to the mountain as fast as you can!"

"Acknowledged, search party one," a male officer responded. "We are heading for-," on the radio, alien weapon blasters could be heard firing at the search party. "Search party one, we are under attack! Repeat, we are under-" The radio transmission cut off abruptly, followed by empty static. The other two search parties did not answer Lexton's calls, and Jack was unable to detect the Recon Drones that were assigned to the groups, which likely meant that both groups had been attacked, and subsequently killed, as well.

"Lieutenant Olo, do you have any other search parties in these woods?" Chief Lexton asked, stunned from the death of her crewmates. "They are likely in grave danger as well."

"No. My search party is, essentially, bait for the Ribiyar. In the event that they showed themselves, which they obviously have, and after I sent the signal of inhabitation, which I did a few moments ago, we were given only a few minutes to return to our ship before it launches a massive bombardment on the island to take the Ribiyar out. We have to get to the mountain, before the ship starts to open fire on this place."

"If you were planning to attack when you saw signs of Ribiyar inhabitation, why didn't your ship attack the island when you saw our fighters approach the island?" Jack asked after he finished giving the fighters their new landing site.

"We still wanted to see if you were alone on the island," Olo responded. "If you were, we wanted to attempt to overpower you and try to retrieve whatever technology we could from the fighters."

"Could we use the fighters to attack the Ribiyar?" One of the officers from Olo's group asked. "That might buy us some time as we make the run to the landing site."

"That... could work," Olo replied, sounding surprised that he hadn't thought of that himself. "Send enough to create a big enough commotion but leave us enough to travel without being packed in like a can of sardines." Jack quickly gave the fighters new instructions, again, and sent four of the seven fighters, who weren't inhabited by the *Atlanta*'s crew, to attack the Ribiyar chasing them across the island. "Come on, we need to get moving!" Olo said as he began to quickly run toward the mountain, with both his and the *Atlanta*'s search party following him. Jack ran alongside Chief Lexton and the other members in her search group as they quickly made their way to the landing site. As they traveled, Jack continued to give flight instructions to the fighters to dodge the Ribiyar's energy weapons, but the Ribiyar somehow still managed to shoot down the ships. One of the fighters had already been shot down, and he knew it wouldn't be long before the Ribiyar were able to destroy the other three. It was then that Jack made a decision, one that may save the rest of the officers, but may also cost him his life in the process. As he continued running by her, he said, "Chief Lexton, I am going to stay behind, and hold off the Ribiyar."

"What?" Chief Lexton asked as she stopped running, and looked at him. "Jack, you don't need to do that. We are all getting off this island, together."

"Chief Lexton, the fighters are not going to last against the Ribiyar forever, and not all of the aliens are being held back by the attack." With his enhanced hearing, Jack could hear the Ribiyar charging through vegetation as they raced after the officers, growing closer at every moment. "You're going to need a diversion if you all are going to get to the landing site, and you know that as well as I do. I may be the only one who has sufficient fire power to draw them away. When I have finished them off, I'll try to make my way to their ship, but you need to go. Now!"

Seeing that she couldn't convince Jack to change his mind, Chief Lexton started to continue her run, but turned back to look at him one last time. "Thank you, Jack. I won't forget what you did for us. None of us will." Chief Lexton took off running, hurrying to catch up with the group, who had just reached the foot of the hill. As Jack turned around to face the approaching Ribiyar, Jack instructed the Recon Drones in the fighters to program the fighters to take them to Olo's ship after the crew gave them the coordinates of its location, insuring they would make it if he didn't survive long enough to guide the ship's there. Activating all his weapon systems, along with the new Recon, functioning as a Laser Cannon as it hung from his arm, keeping only his damaged V-gun undeployed, he aimed into the tall grass, and fired relentlessly as the Ribiyar began to emerge from the thick vegetation of the island. Regardless of how many Ribiyar approached, Jack could not allow them to overwhelm him and kill the rest of the officers. No matter the cost.

Chapter 17

Date: July 9, 2132.
Location: Unnamed island in the Atlantic Ocean.

As Jack shot down more and more Ribiyar, more continued to emerge from through the weeds, trying to take him down and avenge their fallen brethren. His already-battered armor shielded him the best it could, but more and more of his structure was torn off by the force of the alien's firepower. To slow their advance, Jack used his Laser Cannon and sliced through the trunks of several palm trees nearby. The trees fell in the path of the aliens, momentarily blocking them from advancing further. The Ribiyar began to move around the pile of trees, but as Jack shot them down, several more Ribiyar climbed the pile and took aim at Jack. Before he could take them out, the Ribiyar were sliced in half as a barrage of energy blades cut through them.

Jack glanced behind him to see the Dark Serpent standing at the top of one of the trees, wildly swinging the Phantom Blade at the Ribiyar, slicing through more of the robotic aliens with deadly accuracy.

"You didn't think I'd let you have all the fun, did you?" Victor asked as he continued his attack. "How could I pass up a chance like this to rack up my kill count?" While the Dark Serpent fought off the warriors that continued to emerge from the tall grass, Jack attacked the increasing amount of Ribiyar that were appearing from the cluster of trees surrounding him. Though they struck down as many as they could, a large amount of Ribiyar arrived, and they found themselves utterly and hopelessly surrounded.

"Surrender, organics!" One of the Ribiyar officers shouted, "Or you will be purged!" Jack was about to declare he would never surrender, and prepare for the final moments of this battle, when Victor jumped down from the tree, landing besides Jack. Victor deactivated the Phantom Blade, attached the handle to his belt, and began slowly and casually walking towards the Ribiyar who had ordered them to surrender.

"What are you doing?" Jack whispered hastily to Victor.

"Trust me", Victor whispered back. The two words no one ever wanted to hear from a mercenary, especially one that only minutes ago tried relentlessly to kill you. Victor stopped walking when he was a few feet away from the lead officer of the alien warriors.

"Gentlemen, or whatever you are, as you may or may not know, I am a mercenary. If you don't have a translation for that word in your robot-alien-whatever language, it means that I fight for money, and whatever else that strikes my liking. In normal circumstances, this is where I would allow you to pay me off, and let you finish off this nuisance," He said, pointing at Jack. "But, these are far from normal circumstances, and if there is anything I hate more nuisances, its alien nuisances. Especially those who have the warp-brained notion that they can just pop out of nowhere and take this crummy planet without consulting my assistance. So, in response to your 'request', I have three words for you. Welcome to Earth!!!" Victor grabbed his Phantom Blade, activated it, and pressed a button on its handle below the activation button. The blade sparked to life, but it quickly grew to five times its normal length, measuring over 30 feet, in mere moments. Anticipating what the Serpent was about to do, Jack quickly readied his flight systems thruster for the coming attack.

"RRRAAAA!!!!" Victor swung around in a circle, and the Phantom Blade followed him as it cut through the aliens. As the blade came toward him, Jack rocketed up in the air right before he was shredded to pieces. The Ribiyar all collectively collapsed to the ground, cut in half by the Phantom Blade. Several trees surrounding the group also fell to the ground after being caught in the far reach of the Blade's wrath. Victor deactivated the Phantom Blade, and turned toward Jack, who had landed back on the ground.

"I told you that you could trust me. Come on, tin man. We need to getting moving before more of those aliens arrive," Victor said as he took off in the direction of the landing site. Reluctantly, Jack ran after Victor and grabbed ahold of him, fighting the strong urge to leave him to the Ribiyar, and used his jetpack to fly toward the landing site up on the hill.

"Keep moving! We're almost to the top!" Olo announced as he continued to lead the group to the landing site. Muffled sounds of energy-weapon fire echoed across the island as they continued to climb the dirt-bare hill to reach the fighters that had landed on the top of it. Chief Lexton was doing her best to keep the group moving, but it was difficult with her heavy conscious weighing her down, consumed with the death of her crewmates, many of whom she had been friends with, and that Jack had also decided to put his life in jeopardy in order to buy everyone else time to get to the landing point. Behind her, Lexton heard several trees collapse suddenly and loudly. She quickly noticed that a less than a minute later she could no longer hear any gun shots firing, meaning that either Jack had successfully held back and defeated the Ribiyar, though admittedly unlikely even with his impressive battle equipment, or the Ribiyar had managed to finish him off. If the Ribiyar had been able to defeat Jack, then the officers had preciously little time before the ruthless aliens caught up to them and eradicated them.

Just when the group reached the top of the hill, Olo suddenly stopped. "Wait a minute." Olo then looked around the area, feverishly looking for something. "Where is Victor!?" Though it took a moment, Chief Lexton quickly realized the danger they may be in. Victor could have turned back and given up their location to the Ribiyar, most likely in an attempt for them to spare him from death. Not that she expected them to keep whatever promise they made, unless it was for a brutal torture and eventual execution.

Chief Lexton was about to try to get the group moving again, when Doctor McGriffen yelled, "Incoming fighters at 7 o'clock! Take cover!" A little over a dozen oval-shaped fighters shot out of the water near the shore of the island and flew toward them at Mach speed, blasting at the group with their energy cannons. As Chief Lexton hunched close to the ground for cover, she saw Olo and the other members from his search party, apparently more willing to fight off the oncoming attackers, grabbed their laser rifles and fire at the fighters. Four of the fighters were heavily damaged by the attack, and they all plummeted to the ground across the island in fiery explosions. The other fighters continued firing their energy cannons, killing seven of the few remaining officers from the *Atlanta*'s and *Ocean-Walker*'s groups, leaving five officers, including Lexton, Oakland, and McGriffen, alive, not counting the three officers in their fighters on the hill. The alien fighters flew past them, and then flew upwards in a half-loop, quickly turning back toward them.

"Get your weapons ready! We may not survive another attack!" Olo yelled as he aimed his gun at the group of attackers. Lexton heard an engine of some kind activate somewhere on the island, and she glanced toward where the sound had come from as she aimed her energy gun, expecting to see more fighters heading toward them. But instead, she saw Jack emerge from the tops of the palm trees, holding Victor in his arms and flying toward the hill. Chief Lexton turned her attention back to the fighters and saw them adjusting their course away from the hill, apparently more interested in attacking Jack and Victor then finishing off the near-defenseless officers. Jack deactivated his flight systems and quickly descended to the ground as energy blasts soared past through where he had been moments before. Lexton forced herself to focus on getting to the fighters and escaping this island. As much as she hated it, there was nothing she could do to help Jack, not without risking the safety of the others.

As they fell to the ground, Jack hurriedly attempted to formulate some sort of plan or strategy that could help them survive the attack. There was no question that he had to divert the fighters from the group to give them more time to get aboard the fighters and fly to safety, but what he wasn't certain about was how much time he could provide them. He was already heavily damaged from his fight with Victor and the Ribiyar from the ground, so he was in no way in prime condition to take out the fighters. Holding tightly to Victor, he reactivated his flight systems right before they hit the ground and flew away as more energy blasts were fired from the fighters.

Jack quickly connected to the communications system in Victor's armor, allowing him to talk to the Serpent clearly "Victor, I need you to use your weapons and attach those ships while I dodge their attacks. I can't fight and fly at the same time, at least while I'm carrying you."

Victor hesitated, but then sighed in agreement, apparently not wanting to confront Jack while he was trying to save his life, despite their differences. "All right, but just because I'm helping doesn't mean we're pals now. Got it?"

"The feeling is more than mutual, Victor. Now, I recommend you begin your attack immediately. They are gaining on us." Jack struggled to maintain his hold on Victor as he reached for the Phantom Blade on his belt. Jack heard the blade spark to life, and the Serpent swung the sword, and though he couldn't see if it impacted its target, he heard a fighter crashing into the ground shortly afterwards. Jack tried to accelerate faster as the fighters continued to close the distance between them, but his flight systems was already pushing its limits by carrying Victor and maneuvering at these high-speed velocities. If pushed any harder, they could overload and shut down altogether, which would effectively condemn them to the Ribiyar's wrath.

"Victor, I cannot maintain this aerial attack much longer. I'm going to need to land. We should head near the landing site so we can form a defensive position around it."

The Dark Serpent continued his attack with the Phantom Blade as he replied, "Fine, but if you didn't notice metal head we will be extremely exposed by holding a defensive posture to protect the ships from these aliens. We, or at least you, may not survive the fight."

"I am aware of that Victor, and I never expected to when I stayed to hold off the Ribiyar. Hold on tight." Jack grabbed onto a tree with his right arm, holding Victor with his left, and made a sharp U-turn, the intense speeds maintained during the maneuver nearly ripping his arm off in the process. His on-board sensors showed that several muscles had been badly torn during the maneuver, which left his right in a near useless state with his V-gun out of commission, and with his arm at a fourth of its normal strength due to the injury.

Looking up ahead as he flew toward the hill, Jack saw the group had reached the top of the hill, and were beginning to board the fighters the *Atlanta*'s crew had ridden in. Jack just needed to buy them a little more time, and they would be safe. About a third of the way up the hill, Jack spotted a small ledge that was big enough to hold both him and Victor. Though they would be forced to maintain a near-standstill position due to the lack of maneuvering room, they had to make their stand and take down the Ribiyar fighters, before they managed to take them down first. Just as Victor took down a third fighter, leaving seven still in a functional state, Jack quickly slowed and managed to drop them roughly upon the ledge on the hill.

After Jack let go of Victor, he quickly turned around and fired his Laser Cannon at the fighters, while Victor attached his Phantom Blade to his tail. Victor began swinging it at the fighters, launching a barrage of energy blades as he simultaneously fired his arm blasters at the fighters. Working together, Jack managed to fire his weapons at the fighters and force them into the path of Victor's endless supply of Phantom Blades as they shot through the sky, hungry for more prey to sink into. Their assault resulted in the destruction of four of the remaining fighters. The other three were able to avoid a majority of the attacks, and looped high up into the air, and quickly begin to maneuver themselves back towards the hill, determined to finish off their adversaries. An idea sprang to life in Jack's mind, and he quickly turned to Victor, who was waiting for the moment that the fighters reentered firing range to resume his attack.

"Victor, I need to borrow your sword."

"Think again, Robocop. If you want a sword so bad, you can-"

"Victor, I need the sword, *now*. I will give it back after we survive this battle. It is your turn to trust me now." Victor sighed and grabbed the still activated sword off his tail and tossed it to him. Jack caught it with his right hand and activated his jet thruster, deployed his wings, and flew towards the quickly approaching fighters.

Time to end this. Jack readied the Phantom Blade for his attack, enlarging the blade to the same length that Victor had used when he had killed all the Ribiyar in the forest. The Ribiyar fighters moved close to each other, flying in a close triangle-like formation, they fired their energy cannons at Jack, determined to plow through him as they made their way back to the hill. Jack's armor was ripped apart even more as the energy blasts tore into him, and he struggled to maintain the systems that powered his flight systems as he rerouted power from other systems to support it. Refusing to be beaten down, Jack managed to maneuver himself right in the middle of the three fighters. Waiting for the right moment to strike, Jack continued to fly in the path of the space between the approaching fighters. The moment the ships reached him and began to fly past him, he felt almost as though time slowed down as he began his attack. Shouting a loud, warrior-like yell, Jack swung around in a circle, bringing the Phantom Blade in a circle with him. The Blade sliced through the armor of the fighters like they were made of tissue paper, and all three of the ships were cut in half and fell to the ground in chunks of scrap metal.

After watching satisfactorily as the remains of the fighters impacted with the ground near the shore of the island and erupt in fiery explosions, Jack began to travel back to the hill to continue to guard the fighters as the officers, now aboard them, were hastily preparing for departure, and to return the Phantom Blade to Victor, who awaited his return on the ledge. But, when he was halfway back to the hill, his thruster suddenly lost power, and Jack quickly started to plummet to the earth below. He attempted to restart his flight equipment, but it failed to respond, and his diagnostic reported that his thruster systems had suffered extensive damage and combined with the overexertion of the system, his thruster were broken beyond what he could fix in the little time he had left.

Jack launched Recon and instructed it to fly under him, attach itself to his chest (to provide a little measure of padding against the crash by landing on top of it), and do its best to slow his descent as much as possible. The drone flew under him and used its four crane-like arms to attach to his chest, and ramped up its engines to full thrust, but because of Jack's descent speed and his size, it had only a minimal effect on his downfall. Jack quickly tossed the Phantom Blade in Victor's direction, so the device wasn't damaged if his landing was as rough as he expected, and he braced himself for the imminent impact.

Flying 20 miles an hour, Jack slammed into the ground near the bottom of the hill, and his world went dark.

Chapter 18

Date: July 9, 2132.
Location: Onboard the Ribiyar Warship *Ji'Co*, in orbit of Earth.

Tactical Analysist Cha'Hawk watched as several fighters landed in the hangar bay. These fighters contained warriors who were being transferred to *Ji'Co* from other positions in the fleet, either because they were incapable of performing the required services, or their expertise was required elsewhere to optimize performance. Cha'Hawk was not unaware that one of these officers may soon lay claim to his post, if his opposition with High Order Ki'Ra got any worse. Fortunately, one of the officers was an old comrade of Cha'Hawk's, and he would rely heavily upon him for information and support if he was decommissioned, or worse, put in an Oblivion Chamber: a containment device used to restrain a Ribiyar convicted of a serious crime. Though the thought of being imprisoned in the device was unsettling, the Chamber was feared the most because of the effects it has on a Ribiyar's mind. Once a Ribiyar is admitted into an Oblivion Chamber, the device connects with the Ribiyar's data module, and imprints data into his mind. The data affects the Ribiyar's senses, creating the allusion that time goes by much slower than it really is, and also creates multitudes of vigorous visions and phantasms that are formed from the deepest regrets and mistakes from the officer's past. The effects of the Oblivion Chamber were so intense that many have gone mad from its affects, and fear of the Chamber has made many Ribiyar believe that death would be preferable to being imprisoned in the device. Though Cha'Hawk didn't share that belief, he wasn't exactly enthusiastic about being imprisoned in one either.

As the officers exited their craft, Cha'Hawk finally spotted Stealth Combatant Mi'Kel, who was coated in an inky-black coating that covered most of his body, signifying his rank and position as an experienced Stealth Combatant. Cha'Hawk had first fought with Mi'Kel at his side during the Third Fight of Mektar, a city on their world that had been overtaken with those that rejected the rule of Tael'Cyrel Tak'Tora, the current leader of the Ribiyar. During that battle, Mi'Kel had disobeyed Cha'Hawk's orders, who had stayed behind alone to give his squadron time to fall back, and returned to assist him. If it hadn't been for Mi'Kel, Cha'Hawk would have likely been overtaken by the advancing rebel troops. Ever since that battle, Cha'Hawk and Mi'Kel had slowly developed a strong trust between them, as they fought more and more battles together and protected each other throughout them. Mi'Kel spotted Cha'Hawk in the crowd, and he walked over to where he was waiting.

"Tactical Analyst Cha'Hawk. It has been too long since I have seen you."

"Too long indeed, Stealth Combatant Mi'Kel. I have missed having your distinguished experience to rely upon." Though both of them would have preferred addressing each other without having to include their lengthy titles of rank, protocol demanded that they do so, at least while they were in the presence of other officers. "These children just don't have the experience I'm used to working with." Even though Cha'Hawk and Mi'Kel were fairly young, only about 310 years old, it was common place to refer for Ribiyar under the age of 80 as 'children', considering members of the species can live well past 1000 years, and beyond. Unless, of course, the warrior is slain by his enemies in battle.

"I have noticed the majority of our attack force are among the younger generations of our people. But, Tactical Analyst Cha'Hawk, I know you didn't request that I transfer to this ship just so we can talk about the condition of the troops. What is really going on?"

Cha'Hawk began to walk to one of the entrances of the hanger, motioning to Mi'Kel to follow him. "Come, Stealth Combatant Mi'Kel. We have much to discuss."

Location: Unnamed Island in the Atlantic Ocean.

Standing on the boarding ramp of one of the fighters, Chief Lexton watched in horror as Jack slammed into the bottom of the hill, hitting it with enough force that she felt the ground shake from the impact. A cloud of dirt flew up into the air, blocking her view of the crash site.

"JACK!!!" Lexton yelled, but he didn't respond to her call one responded to her call. She began to make her way down the hill to retrieve Jack, when Olo grabbed her arm.

"Chief Lexton, we don't have time to retrieve him. We have to leave while we can."

Doctor McGriffen approached Lexton. "Chief, he's right. We have to go. He knew the risks when he stayed behind." Lexton was about to reply, when Ribiyar fighters began shooting out of the water near the shore of the beach. A *lot* of fighters, at least forty ships flying toward the hill, accompanied by an army of Ribiyar warriors now emerging from the waters and quickly moving across the sand and deeper into the island.

"Everyone, to the fighters! *Now*!" Olo yelled as he led Chief Lexton and Doctor McGriffen into the one of the three oval-shaped fighters. After they boarded the ship, the ramp automatically rose behind them, sealing the fighter shut.

"Ensign Mathews, can you get the fighter started?" Lexton asked as she moved around Olo and Doctor McGriffen, the only other officers aboard the fighter besides Ensign Mathews, and reached the front of the fighter. At both sides of Ensign Mathews was a Recon Drone that had attached themselves to the fighter's computer, their mechanisms purring softly as the ensign feverously tried to get the fighter moving.

"I don't know, sir." Mathews responded. "I have given the drones the location of the *Ocean-Walker* supplied by Lieutenant Oakland, and they should be programming the fighter to take us to your ship, but it is taking longer than anticipated." Though the officers could manually pilot the fighters themselves as the holographic interfaces had been translated into an English language, there had not been enough time for anyone to learn how to control the ships during flight, which left Jack and the Recon Drones as the only ones who could effectively control the ships. "It is possible that Jack's… injuries may have disrupted the drone's computer systems." She said cautiously, not yet wanting to give up hope on Jack's survival, however unlikely that was.

"We don't have much time to wait for the drones to get these ships moving," Olo said. "But there might be a way to buy a little more time." Bringing his wrist communicator to his face, he spoke, "Captain Syvon, this is Lieutenant Oakland. I am surrounded by Ribiyar on the hill in the middle of the island and have boarded three Ribiyar fighters with my team and some other officers we found here. I'll explain that later, but I need you to buy us some time to fly to safety. Please, help us, sir."

Lexton began cautiously but hurriedly reviewing the ship's controls, trying to figure out how she could fly the ship, but the controls were just too alien for her to safely guess how it worked.

"The Ribiyar will be here in approximately... 10 seconds!" Mathews reported after quickly checking the ships sensors. Lexton found it odd that it was taking the Ribiyar so long to arrive, considering they could have been here moments after emerging from the ocean, but she realized the Ribiyar were likely toying with them, and allowing them to experience as much fear and ill-conceived hope as possible before violently ending their lives.

"Sirs!" Ensign loudly exclaimed when one of the consoles began rapidly flashing red, "A large number of incoming projectiles are coming our way!" Now Lexton knew for certain that the Ribiyar were simply making a big show of the event, considering only a few shots from their energy cannons were likely all that was needed to destroy the fighters. One of the computer consoles displayed the data collected from the visual sensors, and showed small silver spherical objects deploying from the fighters' armor. The sphere's shape quickly reconfigured itself as three wings deployed, and the sphere smoothed out and elongated to create the form of a sleek, deadly missile.

A swarm of over 20 missiles sped toward the fighters on the hill, intent on reducing their prey to ashes. Just before the projectiles reached the fighters on the hill, the crimson-red fury of a Laser Array destroyed the missiles in a fiery explosion. A ship with bird-like wings suspended on its sides suddenly appeared and positioned itself in front of the fighters on the hill, absorbing the Ribiyar fighters' energy blasts with its metal hull plating covering the ship and shooting down more Ribiyar missiles with its machine guns placed around the surface of the ship. The sky once again lit up in crimson-red as the ship attacked the fighters with an enormous barrage of laser fire, instantly shredding many of the fighters to pieces.

"*This is Captain Syvon of the* U.S.S. Thunderfox," the captain's voice produced through Olo's wrist communicator and echoing sternly through the fighter. "*We will hold off the Ribiyar for as long as we can, but be warned that the* U.S.S. Ocean-Walker *will soon begin its barrage on the island. You have three minutes to get out of there while you can. Captain Syvon, out.*" The channel closed, leaving the ship noiseless, besides the commotion of the battle taking place outside the fighter.

"Chief Lexton, have you had any luck trying to find the helm controls on this thing?" Olo asked as he moved to the front of the fighter to examine the consoles that lay before the Chief.

"I believe I have found the console that controls the ships flight, but I can't give you any kind of guess on how to fly the ship. We're more likely to crash into the side of the hill than getting anywhere near this ship of yours." Just before Olo was able to respond, the Recon Drones produced several chirping noises, startling the officers, and moments later, the fighter's engines began to roar to life as they activated, and the location of the *Ocean-Walker* appeared on the flight console. It appeared that the drones had finally roused from their slumber and were finally taking command of the fighter's flight controls.

"Lieutenant Oakland," Chief Lexton said after she recovered from the surprise of the drones' timely assistance, "I want you to inform Captain Syvon about our officer stranded near the bottom of the hill. Ask them if they can locate and retrieve him."

"What about Victor?" Doctor McGriffen asked as Olo transmitted the message to the *Thunderfox*. "We can't just leave him here."

"As much as it pains me, you're right," Olo said after a moment of thought. "I'll Captain Syvon to try to contact Victor and tell him to try to reach your friend and get aboard the *Thunderfox*. I'll also inform the *Ocean-Walker* that we're traveling in these Ribiyar fighters. We don't want them to think that we're Ribiyar trying to attack the ship." Olo turned to Chief Lexton. "Chief, I never did get the name of that officer that stayed behind to buy us time to escape. Who is he?"

Lexton took a deep breath as she quickly tried to think of something to say, but, deciding that lying wouldn't benefit anything, she told him the truth, as unbelievable as it was. "That man is Jack Vade, my former captain of the *U.S.S Atlanta*. And that wasn't a military combat suit he was wearing. That *is* him."

"Wait...*what*!?" Olo exclaimed. "How can that be Jack!?" Olo said as he grabbed on a computer console to stabilize himself as they began to lift off.

"I'll try to explain it to you later," Lexton replied as she grabbed onto one of the computer displays on the wall. "It's a long, and complicated story."

As the world exploded above and around him, Victor was left with a difficult choice. He had just retrieved the Phantom Blade, which had landed 12 feet below his perch on the hill, when he heard the sounds of an armada of fighters approaching the island, and the roar as dozens of projectiles were launched at the fighters on the hill. Victor had been debating running away from the hill and into the island's thick vegetation, with the hope that the vegetation, combined with his armor's stealth capabilities, would keep those blasted alien's from finding him, when none other than his employer, Captain Syvon, had appeared in his mighty battleship and engaged the Ribiyar forces. Victor had been about to make his way aboard the ship when Syvon contacted him, ordering him to retrieve Jack, the one person so far during this journey that had actually given Victor a challenge. Sure, fighting of dozens of aliens, while dogging un-relenting barrages of weapon fire, could be challenging to anyone, but Jack had been able to take Victor on all by himself, a task that few people would dare try, and even fewer able to live to brag about it.

And, as Victor saw it, he had three options. First, he could go with his original plan and flee into the thick vegetation of the island, hoping that the Ribiyar wouldn't find him, though, admittedly, it probably wouldn't work out for him, since either the Ribiyar forces would find him, or he would be wiped out by the imminent bombardment from the *Ocean-Walker*. His second option was to return to the *U.S.S. Thunderfox* without trying to retrieve Jack, but if he did that, it was likely that Captain Syvon would lock him away for insubordination, no matter how important he was in the fight against the Ribiyar. His last option, was to follow his orders and retrieve Vade, and leave the business of repairing him to the people who actually cared about his wellbeing.

Sighing heavily, Victor jumped down from his perch to the crater of Jack's crash site. Using his Dark Serpent armor's sensors, he was able to pinpoint Jack's exact location, several feet below the rock and dirt. Victor activated the Phantom Blade, and with the precision of a skilled surgeon, cut through the rock and dirt around him, exposing the majority of Jack's beaten body. Victor deployed his tail, and sent it slithering across the ground and latching it onto a nearby tree as he climbed into the hole that he had cut out, and grabbed onto Jack. The Dark Serpent's tail began slithering up the tree, and slowly pulled Victor, reluctantly holding Jack in his arms, out of the crater. As Victor let go off him, letting him fall to the ground, he could tell that Jack had taken heavy damage in the crash, and that it would take a lot of work to repair him, if he was repairable at all.

Though tempted to finish Jack off for good while he was in his weakened state, Victor decided against it, for now, and contacted the *Thunderfox*. "Dark Serpent to Captain Syvon. I have retrieved him. Now, I need you to get us out of here, sooner rather than later."

"*We hear you, Victor.*" Captain Syvon responded through his comm system. "*Stand by. We are attempting to position the ship over you now, but it may take a moment. It is difficult to maneuver with all these fighters buzzing around us.*" Above Victor, the sky continued to explode as the *Thunderfox* continued to attack the fighters with its Laser Array and the other weaponry that it possessed. Slowly, the ship began to maneuver above Victor. Once the ship was above him, a hatch opened in the bottom of the ship, and three ropes were dropped with to the ground. Victor tied two of the ropes to Jack, and he grabbed the last one for himself.

The ropes began to lift them up toward the ship, but when they were half-way to the ship, several Ribiyar troops emerged from the islands vegetation and opened fire on Victor, blasting several dents in his armor. Refusing to allow himself to be beaten by the invaders, Victor activated the Phantom Blade and launched several energy blades at a fighter that was attacking the *Thunderfox*. With the precision of a lightning strike, the blades sunk into the craft's hull, cutting it into several pieces. The fighter fell to the ground on top of the Ribiyar warriors, erupting in a blazing fireball. Grinning with satisfaction, Victor deactivated the Phantom Blade and placed it on his belt as he and Jack were lifted into the bottom of the *Thunderfox*.

"Sir! Both officers have been retrieved, and the search party has successfully returned to the *Ocean-Walker*," Commander Ton reported to Captain Syvon from his station on the bridge. The bridge was shaped like a triangle, and on the base of the triangle was a window that gave the crew-members a view of the front of the ship. To protect bridge personnel during combat, metal plating automatically lowers down in front of the glass when the ship entered combat status, and a projector would then activate to show the events occurring in front of the ship. Captain Syvon, wearing the magnetic boots that would keep him attached to the floor while the *Thunderfox* made its various flight maneuvers, sat in the center of the bridge, where the captain's chair was positioned.

"About time," Captain Syvon muttered as he began to give out new orders. "Commander, inform the *U.S.S. Ocean-Walker* to begin their barrage at once. Helm, take us out of here, maximum speed. Reroute power from the Laser Array if necessary. Tactical, cease fire, all weapons. Let's save whatever ammunition we can."

"Aye, sir!" The officers reported as they scrambled to fulfil their orders. Syvon gripped the edge of his seat as the ship raced forward, intent on getting away from the island before the *Ocean-Walker* began its assault with its barrage of explosives. The remaining fighters resumed their attack as they chased the *Thunderfox* while it traveled across the island to where the *Ocean-Walker* was anchored. On the display in the front of the bridge, the image magnified the main deck of the *Ocean-Walker,* showing the cannons on the ship aiming toward the island, the Ribiyar forces encamped beneath the water, and the fighters that were pursuing the *Thunderfox*.

"Helm, execute maneuver Syvon Alpha-5! *Now*!" Syvon felt his stomach travel down to his feet as the *Thunderfox* veered upwards, traveling out of the line of fire of the *Ocean-Walker*'s cannons. Seconds later, the *Ocean-Walker* opened fire on the Ribiyar forces, gradually obliterating the Ribiyar fighters, and whatever troops that may have been stationed on the island, or in the surrounding ocean water. The bridge crew cheered as the Ribiyar fighters were blow out of the sky, though the mood did somber as they watched the island burn in flames. Though regrettable, the cost of the wildlife and resources on the island was preferable to what would have happened if the Ribiyar had been able to ambush the fleet as the other ships arrived.

As the barrage began to cease, Lieutenant Lucy Kael, a short, redheaded officer that served as the communications officer, reported, "Sir, the *Ocean-Walker* is requesting further instructions."

"Inform Captain Whitefield to remain on watch for our allies' arrival, and that further instructions will be relayed once the fleet arrives," Captain Syvon ordered. "Also, instruct Lieutenant Oakland and the other officers involved in the search that I want a briefing aboard the *Thunderfox* as soon as possible. And tell Victor to get to my quarters immediately. I want to know what happened down there." Captain Syvon then stood up from the captains' chair, left the bridge, and traveled to his quarters to await Victor's explanation of recent events.

Location: Onboard the Ribiyar Warship *Ji'Co*, in orbit of Earth.

"Do you now understand why Ki'Ra must be stopped?" Cha'Hawk and Mi'Kel had returned to Cha'Hawk's work center, and quickly locked down the room, sealing the door, ensuring that they would have total privacy as they discussed his plans. Cha'Hawk had used his data module and inserted it into a port in Mi'Kel's right arm, which their minds together and allowed Cha'Hawk to show Mi'Kel everything that he had experienced since the invasion had begun within mere seconds; everything from discovering the *Ra'Ta*'s survival, Ki'Ra's refusal to listen to Cha'Hawk's report, and the apparent reactivation of the *Ra'Ta*'s systems by the organic lifeforms of the planet.

"While I may not completely agree with the extreme measures you intend to implement," Mi'Kel responded, "I do agree that something must be done about the High Order. We have the warriors needed to wipe out these organics swiftly, and we could have done so the very day that we arrived at this world, and yet High Order Ki'Ra has restrained our forces to attack only in small, meaningless skirmishes. And all the while, the organics continue to grow bolder, and stronger. They are adapting to our attack strategies, finding weaknesses in our defenses, and apparently now possess one of our *Ax* class cruisers. The organics must be purged from this planet now, before they do more damage than they already have." The communication system in the work room emitted a paging sound, startling the warriors into drawing their weapons from their holsters. Two energy pistols, small spherical objects that produce rapid-fire energy pulses from an emitter on the surface of the spheres, ejected from storage compartments in Mi'Kel's arms and Cha'Hawk grabbed a battle staff from his back, which was an 8-ft long pole that could perform well in a verity of different battle scenarios, whether by deploying three blades along the two sides on the pole, or by utilizing the ordinance launcher at the end of the pole that fired small explosives loaded into the staff.

"Tactical Analyst Cha'Hawk, I have urgent news that needs to be delivered immediately." Cha'Hawk recognized the voice as Tel'Con Zan'Tar, one of his subordinates. Cha'Hawk motioned for Mi'Kel to put away his weapon, and Cha'Hawk also holstered the weapon on his back as he walked to the computer interface by the entrance and un-locked the door. The door immediately split open and Zan'Tar quickly walked through.

"Speak quickly, Tel'Con Zan'Tar," Cha'Hawk said in a menacing tone. Though he was not actually angry at Zan'Tar, he had to give the impression that he was. High ranking Ribiyar did not welcome interruptions while conducting private discussions, especially by lowly assistants such as Zan'Tar. "What news do you bring that is so vital that you needed to disrupt important matters of the Tora Cyrel?" Though Cha'Hawk knew he hadn't been technically discussing future plans for the Tora Cyrel, he knew that if Zan'Tar thought that, then he would be more likely to deliver his news and depart as quickly as possible.

"I beg forgiveness, Tactical Analysist Cha'Hawk," Zan'Tar spoke, slightly bowing before Cha'Hawk as a show of respect, "but our forces stationed on one of the land masses in the 'Atlantic Ocean' have been attacked."

"How many warriors were slain, Tel'Con Zan'Tar? Were they able to destroy their attackers?"

Zan'Tar braced for any punishment he may receive. The phrase, 'don't kill the messenger', was not an expression known among the Ribiyar, and it would not be the first time an officer was slain because of the information he brought with him. "Tactical Analysist

Cha'Hawk, all of the warriors stationed on and near the island have been destroyed by the organics."

"*What*!?!" Though Cha'Hawk did not harm Zan'Tar, it was clear from Cha'Hawk's tone that this news did not set well with him. "Why were reinforcements not deployed? Were the organics disrupting their communications?

Zan'Tar hesitated, but he then replied, "More troops were requested, Tactical Analysist Cha'Hawk, and their transmission was received, but High Order Ki'Ra did not see fit to send warriors to their aid."

"Why would the High Order do such a thing like that?" Mi'Kel demanded as he stepped toward Zan'Tar.

Zan'Tar turned toward Mi'Kel and responded, "I believe High Order Ki'Ra had said 'If those warriors cannot defeat a handful of organics that have barely a third of the physical strength we possess, then they do not deserve assistance from the Tora Cyrel'." Seeing the fury in both of the officers, Zan'Tar quickly said, "I will report when I have more information, Tactical Analysist Cha'Hawk", and then fled the room before Cha'Hawk and Mi'Kel could release their fury upon him.

After Cha'Hawk re-sealed the room, he turned to Mi'Kel and said, "Now do you understand why Ki'Ra must be stopped? We must not allow him to continue to waste more of our kind to pay for his incompetence.

"Cha'Hawk, you do realize that you can't just walk into the command center and purge Ki'Ra. He may be ignorant, as you claim, but that doesn't mean he is stupid. Am I wrong to assume that he has installed automatic weapon turrets, posted guard's and surveillance systems in the chamber, and upgraded the door to make the room impenetrable?" When Cha'Hawk did not respond, Mi'Kel continued. "Even if you do make it in the room undetected, you would never leave it alive. The warriors would eliminate you before you even take a step out of the chamber."

"I *do* have a plan, Mi'Kel. I have given this much consideration, and I believe that I can take down High Order Ki'Ra, and then lead this invasion to decisive victory. If, and only if, I have you by my side. Will you trust my instincts, as you have done many times before?"

Mi'Kel remained silent, and he walked to one of the consoles and inserted his data module into the console, establishing a connection between him and *Ji'Co*'s computer. Cha'Hawk watched silently as data and video images appeared on the visual display on the wall and rapidly passed by as more information replaced it, reviewing all of what has happened since the invasion began. Though Cha'Hawk wanted desperately to renew his discussion and continue to speak his mind, he knew that now he could only wait and hope that Mi'Kel would side with him against Ki'Ra, and not report his planned mutiny to the officers on the ship. When Mi'Kel reached the end of the information, the screen returning to its previous setting of showing current sensor data, he turned toward Cha'Hawk, his decision made.

"You have my full trust and support, Cha'Hawk. Now, tell me more of your plan to bring an end to High Order Ki'Ra."

Chapter 19

Date: July 9, 2132.
Location: Aboard the *U.S.S. Ocean-Walker*, anchored near an unnamed island in the Atlantic Ocean.

> UNIT IS ONLINE.
> RUNNING DIAGNOSTIC CYCLE:
> MEMORY: OPERATIONAL.
> ATTENTION; DAMAGE TO SYSTEMS IMPEDING FULL FUNCTIONALITY.
> CURRENT OPERATING STATUS; 89%.
> WEAPON SYSTEMS:
> DAMAGE DETECTED IN R. V-GUN.
> STATUS: OFFLINE, DAMAGED BEYOND QUICK REPAIR.

MINOR DAMAGE AND WEAR FROM USAGE DETECTED IN REMAINING WEAPON SYSTEMS.

WEAPON SYSTEMS FUNCTIONALITY: 59%.

MOTOR FUNCTIONS:

OPERATIONAL CAPACITY AT 43%.

SEVERE DAMAGE IN SEVERAL COMPONENTS AND STRUCTURAL BEARINGS IN R. ARM DETECTED.

REPAIRS RECOMMENDED BEFORE FURTHER PHYSICAL ACTIVITY IS INITIATED.

OPTIC, AUDIO, SENSORY RECEPTORS: PARTIALLY OFFLINE.

CAUSE; DAMAGE DETECTED IN CEREBELLAR SYSTEMS.

OPTIC RECEPTORS ARE CURRENTLY OFFLINE AND WILL NOT BE FUNCTIONAL UNTIL DAMAGE TO CEREBELLAR SYSTEMS ARE REPAIRED.

WARNING: MENTAL FUNCTIONS WILL DETERIORATE IF REPAIRS ARE NOT INITIATED WITHIN 71 HOURS.

UNIT OVERALL POWER LEVELS ARE AT 49%.

RECHARGE IN PROGRESS.

ESTIMATED TIME OF RECHARGE COMPLETION: 3HRS, 19MINS.

SCANNING... UNIT FUNCTIONALITY IS AT 51%

WARNING: REPAIR IS VITAL FOR UNIT SURVIVAL.

THIS UNIT MUST SURVIVE.

INITIALIZING RECON DRONE CONNECTION.

DISCONTINUING ALL OTHER OBJECTIVES.

REROUTING RECON DRONES TO UNIT LOCATION.

OBJECTIVE: REPAIR UNIT TO FUNCTIONAL STATUS.

ACTIVATING UNIT GENETIC MODULATOR TO CONSTRUCT PARTS FOR REPAIRS.

ENGAGING...

As the setting sun shone brilliantly, the fighters landed upon the deck of the *Ocean-Walker*, and once the bombardment of the Ribiyar forces came to an end, the officers in the fighters exited their craft, and found themselves confronted by a flurry of questions by the *Ocean-Walker*'s staff. Though they knew a report needed to be presented to the commanders of the *Ocean-Walker* and *Thunderfox,* the officers from the

Atlanta were able to convince them to hold off the briefing temporarily while they bring Jack aboard the *Ocean-Walker* and have him examined. Jack had just been transferred from the *Thunderfox*'s cargo hold and onto the main deck of the *Ocean-Walker* when all the Recon Drones suddenly bolted from the Ribiyar fighters and swarmed over Jack. The drones deployed their crane-like arms and then began to grab tools that were left over from the *Ocean-Walker*'s repair crews. They then went back to Jack and started to repair him, prying off broken metal plates, adjusting his systems, and repairing broken parts by replacing them with materials that were slowly produced by a compartment on the bottom of Jack's right arm, where his Recon Drone was normally stored.

"Have you seen this happen to him before?" Lieutenant Olo asked as he walked toward Jack, with Chief Lexton leading the way.

"No, but he has only been like this for a day. For all we know, this could be a normal occurrence for him."

Olo was quiet for a minute before he finally asked, "How did Captain Vade get like this? Did the Ribiyar do this to him?" Olo asked, worried of the atrocities the robotic species could have inflicted on countless other lives.

"It wasn't the Ribiyar." Lexton took a deep breath. "It was us who did this to him."

Olo was shocked and viewed Lexton suspiciously. "Why would you do this to him? He was you own captain!"

"Lieutenant, we didn't in any way force Jack to go through with the procedure that changed him into this. In fact, his senior staff aboard the *Atlanta*, myself included, warned him of the dangers of the device, and advised against anyone, especially the captain, to use the device. But, our ship was, and still is, running out of food and other supplies, and the captain thought he should volunteer in case the device could somehow lead to the ship being liberated from its prison on the bottom of the ocean. And somehow, he was able to free the *Atlanta* because of his transformation."

Olo was silent as he let this information sink in. He was about to respond when Jack's eyes suddenly opened, startling both of the officers. His pupils enlarged and then shrunk, and continued to rapidly switch between each as they tried to make sense of what they were seeing. Jack opened his mouth to speak, but all that came out was some garbled sounds. His head jerked to the left, and he looked forward again and tried to speak.

"Where am I? Is anyone there?"

Lexton maneuvered around the Recon Drones repairing Jack and knelt down next to him. "Jack, its Chief Lexton. I'm right here beside you. Can you see me?"

"I... I cannot," Jack said, looking toward her direction, his eyes continuing their re-adjustments, the sight unnerving Lexton slightly. "Some of the circuitry compromising my visual cortex has been completely crushed, leaving my optic receptors... my eyes I mean, non-functional." Jack turned his head to the right, and she saw a portion of the lower half of his head had been crushed inwards, and she remembered that area was around were the brain maintained processed information from the eyes. As he was talking, a Recon Drone began to pry off the bent metal plating on his head, and she began to see a large mass of high-tech circuity beneath. She averted her eyes from the bizarre scene of her former captain's head being pried open, fearing it would be too much for her to take. "Chief Lexton, I believe it is best to meet with the leading officers of the forces here and inform them about what we found in the ocean, and to learn what we can about what has happened since the invasion began. Who is the commanding officer around here?"

"That would be me," a voice behind the group announced. Lexton turned to an officer walking towards the group.

"Captain Whitefield," Olo said, standing suddenly in surprise.

"John. I... didn't expect to find you out here," Jack said as he looked towards Whitefield, still unable to see.

"I am equally surprised to find you all the way out here, in the middle of nowhere and anyway from the *Atlanta*. I guess it is true what they say. It's a small world that we live on."

"Captain Whitefield, you know Jack?" Olo asked, surprised.

"We have a long history together," Captain Whitefield replied. "I have been trying to sail the seas without the shadow of my family over me, but it appears I will never escape from my family's legacy."

Lexton looked at Jack, and then again at Captain Whitefield. "But, that still doesn't explain how you know of each other."

"It's quite simple, actually." Captain Whitefield took a deep breath before he added, "Jack and I, are brothers."

Chapter 20

Date: July 9, 2132.
Location: Aboard the *U.S.S. Ocean-Walker*, anchored near an unnamed island in the Atlantic Ocean.

    Jack said nothing to Whitefield's revelation, reacting only by looking away from him.
    Chief Lexton, however, did not remain silent. "You're his brother?!" She blurted out in surprise, her attempts of holding in the outburst unable to contain her reaction.
    "Why would you want to hide being related to Jack?" Olo asked, trying to keep a firmer grip on his reaction. Though it was apparent he was stunned from the news, he glanced from Whitefield to Vade, Jack saw Olo was beginning to see the physical resemblance between the two. Before he turned into a machine, of course.

Captain Whitefield sighed. "Jack had always done better than me in every aspect in life, everything from sports to school and military training. When I was old enough, I decided to change my name, so I could serve in the military without having the shadow of my family's reputation over my head. And... we have other reasons to stay away from each other as well." He added, and then went silent, not divulging any further information.

The Recon Drones removed a mangled piece of gray circuitry from Jack's head, and inserted an undamaged replacement, produced from the genetic modulator in his arm, and his eyes finally stopped their frenzied movement and were at last able to process the world around him. "Captain Whitefield," Jack said, adopting a more formal tone of voice and skipping over having any civil discussion between them, "I need to give you a report about recent events, and I would like to take part in further operations to fight back the Ribiyar. I don't plan on letting them take our planet without giving them a fight they won't soon forget."

Whitefield, despite himself, smiled at Jack's commitment to the mission, even while being as injured as he was. "I admire your willingness to fight. On that matter, Captain Syvon of the *U.S.S. Thunderfox* has requested a debriefing with the commanding officers that were involved with what happened on the island, including you. Do you think you can make it there?"

Jack thought a moment, and then responded, "If you give me about 12 minutes, I will be well enough to attend the debriefing."

"Very well," Captain Whitefield responded. "I will inform Captain Syvon that he can start in about half an hour. Lieutenant Olo, I want you and the officers attending the briefing to help Jack get to the briefing room to the *Thunderfox*, where the meeting will be taking place. Once you're aboard, the *Thunderfox*'s crew can show you where to go."

Whitefield turned to leave, but before he left, he turned back to Jack and said, "It was good to see you again, Jack. I'm... so sorry about what happened to you." He looked like he wished to say more, but he stayed silent. "Stay safe out there," he said finally, and left the officers and conversed with several crewmen on the main deck.

"Good to see you as well, brother," Jack spoke softly, a small amount of anger slipping into his voice, but he talked quietly enough so the officers around him didn't hear him. Looking toward the other officers, Jack said, "When the time comes, I would appreciate your assistance in boarding the *Thunderfox* for the briefing. For now, however, I need to power down to allow the drones to preform necessary repairs on my systems. I will reactivate once it is time to board the ship." Not giving the officers any chance to ask about the tension between Jack and his brother, not even taking time to acknowledge his old friend Olo, he closed his eyes and quickly powered down his systems, allowing the Recon Drones to begin administering the needed repairs.

30 minutes later...

Location: Aboard the *U.S.S. Thunderfox*, near an unnamed island in the Atlantic Ocean.

"So, let me get this straight," Captain Syvon spoke after a period of silence. Aboard the *Thunderfox*, in the ship's briefing room, many of the officers that were on the island when the Ribiyar attacked. In addition to Lieutenant Olo, Jack, Chief Lexton, and Doctor McGriffen were seated around the table in the briefing room. The briefing room was small, with the rectangular table taking up a large portion of the room. Most of the surfaces on the grey, metal-plated walls were covered with various computer displays, showing the status of the ship, layouts of the surrounding land near the ship, and there were a few displays that were black to allow the officers to display data, or look up information from the *Thunderfox*'s computer. On the wall that was closest to the outside of the ship, a large window dominated much of its surface, showing a large portion of the *Ocean-Walker*'s main deck, and the bright horizon behind it as the sun continued its descent.

Standing in front of the window, taking in the view outside the ship, Captain Syvon continued to try to piece together recent events. Though they had already given a thorough recount of what had happened on the island, Syvon was now interested in learning what had happened to Jack, and the events that led up to him and the other officers arriving on the island. "Jack, you were the captain of the nuclear submarine *Atlanta*, up till recently trapped under the remains of a Korean battleship, and when an experimental device turned your body into machinery, you resigned your commission, and eventually gained control of a disabled Ribiyar vessel crashed a distance from the *Atlanta*. You then used that ship to free the *Atlanta*, and you later took part in an expedition to retrieve supplies for your ship. Once you left the alien ship, you proceeded to the island, were attacked by Victor, managed to survive, barely, and up with join Lieutenant Oakland's search party, and you were then ambushed by the Ribiyar on the island. Is this what happened, Mr. Vade?"

Jack nodded. "That is correct, Captain Syvon. But I would like to add one thing. It is imperative that me and the remaining officers from our landing party return to the *Atlanta* and deliver food to them immediately. Their food stores are either completely depleted, or they soon will be. After the briefing is completed, I request that we be allowed to the *Atlanta* and deliver the food and the other resources they need."

"Request granted, Mr. Vade," Captain Syvon responded. Syvon quickly contacted Commander Ton, and instructed him to load the fighters with food and medical supplies from the *Thunderfox*. Ending the transmission, Captain Syvon turned back toward the group. "Is there anything anyone would like to add?"

"I have a question, captain," Lieutenant Olo asked "Are the ships assigned to the task force still going to rendezvous in this location? Would it not be wise to meet somewhere else?"

"I appreciate your concern, Lieutenant, but I don't believe that it will be necessary to change the location of our rendezvous." Captain Syvon replied. "With the *Ocean-Walker*'s bombardment on the island, I believe we have destroyed any Ribiyar that were stationed in the area. Besides, the ships are scheduled to arrive within a few hours, and we need to start our mission before the Ribiyar have the chance to launch another attack on us." Syvon paused a moment to take a good look at the officers before him. "I have to be honest with you. The odds of us successfully completing this mission are slim, and the probability of surviving it is even slimmer. But we must make some sort of stand for ourselves if we are to fight against the Ribiyar. This war can't be won with small skirmishes and random attacks. We must attack the installations so important that the whole invasion force will feel the effects of it. Will you stand with me, and the rest of the soldiers coming on those ships?"

When everyone replied yes, Captain Syvon said, "Then this meeting is adjourned. Jack, I want you and your fellow officers to head back to the *Atlanta* on the double and deliver the supplies they need. Inform Captain Rickman that he, his crew, and the captured Ribiyar battleship will be required for this mission. Afterwards, have Rickman head back to the surface and attend the briefing that we will be conducting with the other captains once they arrive. It is then we will plan for our mission, and devise a way to strike at the Ribiyar like never before. You are all dismissed."

Location: Aboard a Ribiyar fighter stationed on the main deck of the *U.S.S. Ocean-Walker*.

"All systems are online and fully operational. Course has been plotted, and engines are on standby. Requesting clearance to take off." Jack stood at the command console in one of the three fighters assigned to the *Atlanta*'s search party. In addition to their three fighters, Jack had taken control, with some assistance from the Recon Drones, of the eleven other fighters the crew of the *Ocean-Walker* had taken from the Ribiyar that attacked the ship, as the crew of the Atlanta would have better luck making use of them with the hacked computer assisting there efforts of mastering the alien technology, and so the presence of the fighters aboard the *Ocean-Walker* wouldn't attract the attention of the Ribiyar. The crews of the *Ocean-Walker* and the *Thunderfox* had graciously donated a large amount of food and other supplies that the people of the *Atlanta* desperately needed, and were now safely stored in the empty fighters for transport. Though Jack had not had near enough time to allow the drones to complete the repairs on himself, they had completed enough of the critical repairs that his condition was, for the moment, stabile enough to allow him to perform his needed services.

After receiving clearance to depart from the *Ocean-Walker*'s crew, Jack activated the fighters' engines, and the 14 fighters gently rose off the *Ocean-Walker*'s main deck. When the fighters had risen several feet above the *Ocean-Walker*, the fighters' engines hummed softly as they accelerated away from the island. After breaching the surface of the water, and traveling roughly 15 minutes through the ocean, they were finally able to get a visual of the alien ship, which was currently landed on a large span of sand near a large coral reef.

"Captain Rickman, this is the search party. We have returned with supplies for the crew and are requesting permission to dock with the alien ship. Captain Rickman, can you read me?"

After several moments of silence, the face of Captain Rickman appeared on one of the computer displays, with the layout of the bridge of the alien ship shining brightly behind him. From what Jack could see, Captain Rickman was using the central console in the middle of the bridge to communicate with him, and the console's display allowed both of them to see each other. The captain looked a little pale and weak from lack of food and sunlight, and Jack could only hope that none of the crew had died from starvation while they had been away. "Affirmative, Jack. We hear you loud and clear. It's good to see you again. Permission to dock is granted, and I request that you dock close to the *Atlanta* to reduce the distance the crew needs to travel to recover the supplies? Wait a minute," Rick said as he studied the visual display on the front of the bridge, which likely showed a readout of the approaching fighters. The captains pause was most likely caused by his realization that Jack had more fighters than he did when he left the ship. "Jack, your flying with more fighters than you took with you. You didn't encounter the Ribiyar, did you?"

"Unfortunately, we did, Captain Rickman, and I am afraid to report that the majority of our group was killed during the conflict with the Ribiyar." Jack paused to allow the captain a moment to process this information. Though he briefly looked like he was going to weep over the loss of his officers, the strain of recent events so overwhelming, he was able to regain control of his emotions and bury his feelings inside him. Jack knew all too well what Rick was going through, as he had lost several crewmen during his time in command as well, and the feeling of dread never completely left those in command, even after many years have passed by. "A report of recent events is in order, Captain Rickman, but there are more pressing matters to attend to. Once we dock aboard the ship, we need to begin distributing the food among the crew immediately." Jack could tell that Rick wanted him to discuss what had happened, but the captain was also acutely aware of the need to get the crew fed before discussing recent events.

"You are correct, Jack. We need to get the crew taken care of first. But I do want to get the briefing done as soon as possible." After Rickman turned away from the camera briefly and gave an order to someone on the bridge, he turned and said, "The crew is being informed the crew of your arrival, and people should be there soon to receive you and help unload the supplies."

"Understood, Captain Rickman. I am bringing the fighters in now. Signing off."

One hour later...
Location: Aboard the *U.S.S. Atlanta*, at the bottom of Atlantic Ocean and docked aboard the Ribiyar vessel.

"Are you sure this is the best course of action?" Commander Hayley asked. After the crew had finally been fed, the senior officers, including Jack and Ambassador Shaan, had gathered around the table in the briefing room on the *Atlanta*. Though the crew was anxious to determine what they would do now, especially if it meant participating in an attack on the alien forces, some of the officers were concerned that the mission that Captain Syvon had proposed was too risky to take part in.

"Commander Hayley," Jack responded, "I believe this may be our *only* course of action that we can take. If we restrict our attacks to random skirmishes on the Ribiyar's forces, we may never be able to inflict any lasting damage against the invasion force. To be truly effective, we must coordinate our attacks with our allies, and combine our forces to strike hard against these aliens." After a moment of silence, Jack turned to Captain Rickman, who had been silent ever since the briefing started. "Captain Rickman, the decision is, of course, ultimately yours. What do you think that we should do?"

Slowly, the captain took a deep breath, and responded, "I think that Captain Syvon's plan, though full of risks, is the best possible option available to us. We must take up arms alongside our allies, and fight for our planet." Captain Rickman looked at Jack. "Jack, I want you to head back to the surface and attend the mission briefing. Your job will be to represent the *Atlanta* and Ribiyar ship in my place. I would go myself, but I need to be here and supervise the crew as we attempt to figure out how this Ribiyar ship works. Besides, you have already been in contact with some of the chief commanders there, and you'll know them better than I would if I attended the briefing." Though Jack felt the urge to object with working with his brother, knowing the possible conflict that may ensure, he kept his mouth shut, and could only hope that he and his brother could maintain a professional air and focus and the task at hand. "I trust your decision making, but if you do need my input on a decision, you can always contact me, though I wouldn't advise it, in the interest of keeping the Ribiyar ship as hidden as possible."

Jack nodded and said, "Understood, Captain Rickman. I will do my best to make the best plan of attack, and increase the odds of success as much as possible."

Captain Rickman looked at the rest of the officers. "Is there anything else anyone wants to add?"

"I have something to say," Doctor McGriffen announced. "I think it best that you should be informed of the status of the crew. Without taking into consideration that the crew had been operating for a long period of time without any time to rest and recharge from work, most of the officers aboard are suffering from the effects of food deprivation, and that may take a while to subside. Many are also weak from a lack of energy, sunlight, and sleep, and are also suffering from a lack of focus, caused by those effects. It isn't advisable to push the crew any harder. Bringing them into a combat scenario, especially one with the odds of survival as low as they are, may cause irreparable damage to their physical and mental wellbeing."

"I understand, and appreciate your concern, Doctor," Captain Rickman responded, "But we simply can't refrain from taking action against our aggressors. This mission may be tough on the crew, but it can, and will be, even harder on them if we allow our fears and concerns to keep us at the bottom of this ocean. We can't just stay down here and hope the aliens don't find us. We must take a stand against the Ribiyar, and fight for our claim on Earth." Captain Rickman again looked at the rest of the officers. "Anyone have other concerns that need to be addressed?"

Ambassador Shaan stood from his chair, focusing his attention to Jack. "I do have concerns to voice, Captain Rickman. But it is not about the wellbeing of your crew. It is the wellbeing of you, Vade."

"Me?" Jack asked, puzzled by the ambassador's concern "What do you mean, Ambassador Shaan?"

"You have only been in your mechanical body for only a few short days. You require training to fully understand your capabilities, to learn the limits of your functions, and to adapt your current fighting techniques to become truly effective in combat. I want to train you to become the warrior that you can become with your new form."

"Ambassador," Jack replied, "I do appreciate your concern, but I don't think we have the time for you to train me. And, with all due respect, I don't know how effective you would be in training me on improving performance of my flight systems, or how to better regulate the power distribution throughout my motor systems.

"I myself may not be able to train you, but I could create computer scenarios that would challenge you with your various problems, whether on combat situations, effective deployment of your drones, and so on."

Jack considered this, and realized the benefit he could have from a program the ambassador was proposing. "I would welcome any help you could provide, ambassador. Once you have finished it, I'll try it out and see what I can learn and improve from it."

"If you would like, Jack," Chief Lexton added, "I could look over your schematics, and your system regulation programs, to see if I can find anything that can improve your performance. I could also do what I can to help Ambassador Shaan with the program."

"If you can find the time," Jack responded, "I would appreciate any help you can provide."

When no one else voiced any other concerns or objections, Captain Rickman said, "I believe that this concludes our meeting. I will be in my quarters if anyone needs me. You are dismissed."

20 minutes later...

"Captain, do you have a minute to talk?" Jack stood outside the doorway of the captain's quarters, now officially Rickman's residence. Captain Rickman sat at the desk in the room, and was currently studying information accessed from the Ribiyar vessel.

"Yeah, come on in, Jack. I was just reviewing the weapon capacity of the Ribiyar ship, so I know how much damage we can inflict during the assault. I have to say, the Ribiyar definitely know how to make efficient and powerful weapons. I've never seen anything like them." Jack walked into the room and stood by the desk.

"Captain, I would like to request that Chief Lexton and the engineering crews install several modified Genetic Modulators aboard the Ribiyar vessel."

Captain Rickman deactivated the computer screen and turned toward Jack, surprised by his request. "Why would you want to do that? We both know that the GM can't do what it was built to do. What would the purpose be to install them on the ship?"

"As I have found, the Genetic Modulator can be used for more than altering genetic code. I was equipped with a miniature, modified GM during my transformation, and I have successfully used the device to create replacement parts to repair my damaged systems. What I am proposing, is that we use the

Genetic Modulators to create a large store of Recon Drones to use in the assault on the Ribiyar base."

Captain Rickman thought a moment, and responded, "How many drones are you thinking about constructing?"

"To be effective in the assault, we would need hundreds of Recon Drones to be constructed."

Captain Rickman jumped to his feet in surprise. "Hundreds!? How are we supposed to store that many drones?"

"The drones are not that large, Captain Rickman. I have calculated the available space in the Ribiyar vessel's storage bays, and we will have more than enough room to store the amount of drones proposed. Once we are ready to deploy the drones, we can instruct them to report to the hatches around the ship, and we can simply open the hatches, and allow them to exit the ship through them."

Siting back down in his chair, Captain Rickman asked, "How many Genetic Modulators would we need to facilitate that size of production?"

"To create them in a timely manner, it is likely we will need at least ten constructed."

The captain sighed and said, "Very well. I will have Chief Lexton assign teams to begin working on the devices. Do you foresee any difficulties for their construction and installation?"

"I do not, Captain Rickman. To be safe, I will remain on the ship long enough for the crew to have the foundations of the device prepared. I will also alter the Genetic Modulator's operating programs so there will be no risk of the crew being changed or altered by accident, and program the devices' programming into the computer so you can operate them efficiently."

Captain Rickman nodded. "I would appreciate that, Jack. Thank you for taking the time to do that."

"You're welcome, Captain." Jack turned to leave, but he turned back toward the Captain and said, "Captain, could I ask a favor of you?"

"Go ahead, Jack. What do you want?"

"If you can find the time, could you give the Ribiyar vessel a name more fitting to its new mission under our command, so we don't have to call it by the title its creators had given it?" Jack had found the Ribiyar vessel's official designation while he had been connected to its computer, the *Ra'Ta*, and he knew he wasn't the only one aboard that wished for the vessel to be rechristened under a new name.

Captain Rickman smiled and replied, "I'll get right on it, Jack. I have a few ideas for the name, and I should have one by the time you get done with the mission briefing."

"Thank you, captain. If you need me, I will be on the other ship assisting the engineering crews build the Genetic Modulators, before I leave the vessel to meet with the other captains."

"Understood. I will be here if you need me. Safe travels." Jack saluted the Captain, and then traveled to the engineering center of the alien ship.

Chapter 21

Date: July 10, 2132.
Location: Aboard the *U.S.S. Ironclad*, traveling through the Atlantic Ocean.

"So, does anyone have any bright ideas that can get us through this death trap of an assault mission?" Captain Saria Conner, a tall, tanned woman with fiery red hair, who was the commander of the *U.S.S. Ironclad*, remarked. An hour after Jack arrived from the Ribiyar vessel, during the time he had finally finished the rest of the repairs on himself, the other allied battleships began to arrive at the island. The ships assigned to the fleet for this mission were some of the few remaining ships with Laser Array's, one of the few of humanity's weapons that had had an impressive impact against the Ribiyar craft, and two of the ships also possessed EMP projectiles, devices that would bring any Ribiyar caught in their wake to their death.

When the attack fleet's flagship, the *U.S.S. Ironclad* finally arrived, the captains of the other ships, plus Jack, representing the *Atlanta* and the Ribiyar vessel, boarded the *Ironclad* and met in the ships' mess hall, the only room big enough to hold the group, after a Ribiyar attack had destroyed the ship's briefing room. After the officers boarded the *Ironclad*, the ships in the fleet immediately began their lengthy journey to the Ribiyar stronghold. The mess hall was a rectangular room, with grey metal plating comprising the surface of the walls, floor, and the ceiling. The room was populated with several tables for the crew to eat on, a large serving counter for the cooks to place prepared food, and a large window on one of the wall's that ran the length of the room, giving a bright view of the noon sun shining upon the main deck of the *Ironclad*, and the ocean surrounding the ship. The officers in the mess hall consisted of Captain Whitefield, Captain Syvon, Captain Conner, Jack, Captain Max River of the *Tsunami*, a civilian ship that had been covertly equipped with several weapons to sell as a destroyer, Captain Carley Lace of the *U.S.S. Pocahontas*, Captain Grace Gold of the *U.S.S. Un-Holstered*, Captain Lucy Picket of the *U.S.S. Blaze-of-Fury*, and Admiral Samuel Tinel, who was the lead officer of the operation. The officers were seated around two tables that had been moved together, and some of the officers were also eating their meals as they participated in the meeting.

"Would the Ribiyar vessel be part of the force dealing with the defenses on the stronghold?" Jack asked, in an attempt to answer Captain Conner's question. Jack had briefed the captains about the commandeered Ribiyar ship, and they had been enthusiastic to have its massive array of weapons at their disposal during the assault.

"Not at first," Admiral Tinel said from the head of the table. "We need to keep the Ribiyar vessel on reserve for when the fighters and other starships retaliate against us. When they commence their attack, then we will launch the ship into battle. In addition to the alien ship, I also want the *Thunderfox* to wait until the fighters and starships attack before they join the battle."

"What about the attack on the stronghold itself, Admiral?" Captain Lace, a woman with white skin and chocolate-brown hair, asked. "If the mission is to capture the base, won't we need to send invading parties to breach the perimeter?"

"That is a good point, Captain Lace," Admiral Tinel responded. "We will need to send in a lot of officers to secure the facility, but I believe that we should send in an elite team to take command of the strongholds control center."

"How should we decide who is assigned to this elite team?" Captain Whitefield asked.

Admiral Tinel thought a moment, and replied, "I believe that the captains of the fleet should each choose the best fighter from their ship. That should give the team enough strength and experience to seize the control center. Mr. Vade, do you know if the schematics of the stronghold in the alien ship's database? We only have a short aerial visual, taken by a small surveillance drone right before it was shot down."

Jack nodded. "The schematics are indeed on the Ribiyar vessel's computer, and I have them with me now, Admiral. With your permission, I will display the information on the projector."

Admiral Tinel nodded. "Permission granted, Mr. Vade. Let's see what we're going to be up against." Jack promptly left the table and walked to the computer interface on the wall. Jack pressed his hand on the interface and connected to the *Ironclad*'s computer to speed up preparations. "The mission's likelihood of success will increase if we know the layout of the stronghold. Using the schematics of the stronghold, we may learn the best points of entry, weak points in the security perimeter, and the best route for the assault team to take in order to reach the control center."

Jack accessed the controls for the equipment in the mess hall, and activated the projector, which was positioned on the ceiling above the tables the officers occupied. As the projector powered up, Jack lowered the blast screens, metal plates that shield the glass during combat, over the windows in the mess hall, and lowered the lighting in the room to create a better resolution for the projectors image. As the blast screens closed, the projector activated, projecting an image that covered a large portion of the wall.

When the officers saw the stronghold, or the Holding Facility, as it was officially called by the

Ribiyar, many of them were shocked to see how huge its size was, even the ones who had seen visual footage from the drone. The installation was somewhat similar to a medieval castle; a large wall surrounded the outer complex, with large turret towers along the wall that contained formidable-looking energy cannons on the top of them. The cannons were shaped like a triangle, with the point facing outward containing three antennas that appeared to project the energy from the weapon at a target.

Within the wall, large 12-story tall dome-like buildings were placed close together throughout the large area within the wall. According to the data contained in the schematic file, the domed buildings were where the prisoners were being held, and being experimented on to aid the Ribiyar in their quest to purge the organic life on Earth. But the most formidable looking-structure of the stronghold was the tower positioned in the middle of the stronghold. A huge 60-story building stood tall over the rest of the instillation, with a multitude of passageways and access tunnels connecting the tower with the domed buildings surrounding it, and the wall containing them. The tower itself had different shapes contributing to its make-up; a pyramid-like base supporting the foundation, with several elevator tubes visible running up from the base to higher up the tower. The upper part of the tower was cylindrically shaped, with various outcroppings protruding from the tower, and they appeared to be extensions of workrooms, landing pads for fighters, or various type of antennas or energy cannons dotting the outside of the tower.

"How in the world are we supposed to attack this thing, much less take control of it?" Captain Gold, a woman with long, gold color hair, exclaimed.

"We need to examine the facility's layout more closely," Admiral Tinel observed, "to see if this thing has any structural weaknesses we can exploit." Tinel turned toward Jack, who was still near the computer interface and connected to the *Ironclad*'s computer system. "Mr. Vade, can you analyze the design for any flaws in its construction?"

Jack nodded. "I can indeed, Admiral. Commencing analysis now." The officers observed as the projector image zoomed in on various parts of the holding facility, and then zooming back as it focused on others as it rapidly moved around the Holding Facility. After several minutes of near nauseating motion sickness, the image zoomed out and reverted to its original viewpoint, once again giving an outlook of the whole facility.

"Admiral, I am afraid there are no major design flaws in the Holding Facility's construction," Jack responded. "There are a few points I could recommend for attack, but it would by no means cripple the Facility."

The officers were silent as they waited to find a new course of action. After a few moments of silence, Captain River, a muscular man with a handle bar mustache, asked, "Mr. Vade, do you have any information about their troop deployments throughout the holding facility? Specifically, the tower in the middle of complex?"

Jack cocked his head to the side as he searched the data file for any information related to the troops on the station. The image on the projector zoomed in on the tower, and the image was immediately covered with red dots throughout the corridors in the interior. "I am afraid I do not have specific intel on their troop placements, as this is simply the layout of the Facility, and not an actual display of the current status of the installation. But the locations highlighted would appear to be, at the least, standard or suggested postings for the troops." Jack pointed to the image. "The small dots represent Ribiyar troops, and those larger dots appear to represent…," Jack paused as he accessed the datafile to find more information. Finding his information, Jack continued, "The larger dots represent vehicles known as Enforcer Pods."

Several of the commanders let out a collective gasp/groan, for some of them had heard rumors of the destructiveness of those vehicles, rumors that were difficult to confirm as few had survived an encounter with them. Enforcer Pods were sphere-shaped vehicles that a Ribiyar officer would occupy and control. The Enforcer's roll at high speeds towards their targets, and when they reached their destination, it releases four claw-spear legs to walk upon. Once the Pod has deployed its legs, the Enforcer could release its deadly arsenal, six large, high-powered energy cannons that could rain continuous fire-power upon their targets. In addition to those cannons, the Enforcer Pods possessed a large amount of spherical devices, the same type equipped on the Ribiyar fighters, that form into sleek missiles, which are unleashed on large groups of hostile targets.

After the officers settled down, Jack continued with his report. "It would appear that the Enforcer Pods are posted near the entrances of all the shuttle docking pads on the tower, which will obviously add difficulty for any attempt to breach these locations. The Pods are also positioned near the command center of the Holding Facility, which is located near the top of the tower, guarding it from anyone who would attempt to commandeer it."

"Mr. Vade, can you determine why the Control Center is so important?" Captain Syvon asked, hoping they had found the Holding Facility's Achilles' Heel.

Jack again cocked his head to the side as he searched the datafile. "The Control Center is where the commanders of the facility give the other Ribiyar officers of the station their orders. But it seems the control center is more important than that. It appears that the control center is the only place in the complex that allows direct access to the stations computer cores."

"Why is that so important to the station?" Captain Picket, a woman with crew cut black hair, asked. "Are their computer files that important?"

Jack was surprised the captains didn't recognize the important of the computer system. "Captain Picket, in one form or another, many of the systems of the station are controlled by the computer. And, one of those systems in particular is the Holding Facility's weapon systems."

Captain Picket immediately straightened in her chair. "Do you mean that if we can take their Control Center, and then their computer core, we can deactivate the station's attack against our forces?" The other officers were also charged with excitement with the discovery of their possible winning strategy.

"Affirmative, Captain Picket. But I need to caution you not to get too excited. It will be extremely difficult to break through the computer's firewall and take control of the computer core."

"Mr. Vade," Admiral Tinel began, "is there any way you can take control of that computer, if we can get you to the Control Center?"

Jack hesitated, and then replied, "There *is* a way, admiral. It is the same way we were able to take control of the alien ship's computer system. The Omega Virus." The officers did not ask what the Omega Virus was, so he assumed they had already heard of it. "But it was extremely difficult to take control of, and it very nearly resulted in failure, which would have likely lead to the destabilization of my neural circuits, essentially killing me. In addition to the difficulty we faced, the Holding Facility has a much greater firewall protected computer core. Doing it by myself, the possibility of overcoming the computer's encryption is unlikely, at best."

The officers were silent as Admiral Tinel asked, "Is there any way we can improve our odds, and make the computer takeover more likely to succeed?"

"It is possible we can use the Ribiyar vessel's computer to administer the Omega Virus. The ship's computer is by far more advanced than my own processors, and would have a much better chance of overpowering the Holding Facility's computer, in theory. If we are able to grant the Ribiyar vessel access to the computer core, which can only be done from the Holding Facility's Control Center, we would be free to release the Omega Virus into the computer. If we can do that, I believe that would increase the odds of overpowering the Holding Facility's computer immensely. However, it will be very difficult to reach the Control Center, I cannot compute any other successful plans of assault on the Holding Facility. As low as the odds of success are, this is likely the best course of action available to us."

Admiral Tinel lowered his head and stroked his chin with his hand, concentrating on the matter at hand. After a minute of thought, Admiral Tinel had his response. "Mr. Vade, will you be able to make whatever adjustments needed to the Ribiyar ship's computer, and prepare it to take control of the Holding Centers computer?"

"I believe I can, Admiral Tinel," Jack announced. "I calculate an 89% chance that the computer can be configured for this purpose."

"In that case," Admiral Tinel responded, looking to the other captain's in the room, "Do the rest of you agree that raiding the stronghold and taking command of the Control Center, and using the Ribiyar vessel to gain access to the computer, is a workable plan?"

After the captains thought, Captain Syvon was the first to reply. "Sir, I don't know if I speak for the rest of these officers, but I think that even if this plan is unsuccessful, it will do well to bring down as many Ribiyar as possible. Let us light a fire that will scar the Ribiyar for years to come!" The other captains cheered their agreement of opinion.

Admiral Tinel agreeing with that statement, he agreed to use the proposed attack, and began to fine-tune the strategy and actions to be used for the rest of the assault. For the next two hours, the officers and Jack worked to iron out the best attack strategy, what to do when the Ribiyar ships respond, and how the boarding squad would infiltrate the tower and arrive at the control center.

At the end of the two hours, the captains made their way to their ship's as their vessels momentarily stopped to allow the captains to board.

And then the vessels resumed their course; determined to enact vengeance upon the Ribiyar invaders.

Location: Onboard the Ribiyar Warship *Ji'Co*, in orbit of Earth.

With the meeting nearing its end, Tactical Analyst Cha'Hawk was about to connect himself to his podium, ready to commence his plan that would lead to the end of High Order Ki'Ra, when his assistant Tel'Con Zan'Tar, rushed into the Battle Coordination Hall and hurried to High Order Ki'Ra, who was positioned in his podium on the upper level. Cha'Hawk glanced at Stealth Combatant Mi'Kel, who stood watch behind him, and returned his attention to Zan'Tar, who had reached Ki'Ra by his podium.

Zan'Tar kneeled before Ki'Ra. "High Order Ki'Ra, I have an urgent report to deliver. With your permission, may I connect with the display and show the report?"

"Do so, and be quick with your task." Zan'Tar stood in front of the podium, and lifted his right arm above the podium. Zan'Tar's data module snaked its way into the port on the podium, linking him to the equipment in the Hall. Zan'Tar projected a holographic display in the gap on the middle of the second level, allowing all the gathered officers to see what he needed to show them. The image magnified, and showed a clear image of several of the organic's battleships traveling through one of the large liquid surfaces scattered around their planet.

"High Order, this image shows several of the organics sea vessels traveling toward Holding Facility Tri'La, positioned deep in the Atlantic Ocean, and it is reasonable to assume that they mean to assault the facility. I recommend that we send a taskforce to intercept the attack force, before they reach their destination."

Ki'Ra computed the data, and then replied, "I do not believe that will be necessary, Tel'Con Zan'Tar.

The troops at Tri'La are well armed and trained, are they not?"

"They have been trained to repel any invaders that attack them, High Order," Zan'Tar responded.

"Then it will serve no purpose to waste the time and effort to intercept them, when they already travel toward their destruction. There forces are of no concern to us. We shall await the report from Tri'La once the battle has concluded, and-"

"*ENOUGH!*" Cha'Hawk thundered. The entire hall quieted from Cha'Hawk's unexpected outburst. Nearly all the officers were stunned by his interruption. All but Ki'Ra, who seemed to grow more infuriated by the second.

"*YOU DARE TO INTERUPT ME!?*"

"I do, 'High Order'."

"I have had enough of your insubordination, Tactical Analysist Cha'Hawk."

"And I, have had enough of your incompetence as our leader, Ki'Ra." The officers were so stunned that few moved, and the ones who did move where slowly reaching for their weapons, if the need for them arouse. "We could have conquered this planet in a matter of *Vels* after our arrival, but you have insisted that we instead enslave the survivors of our assault and imprison them in our installations that take hundreds of our warriors away from combat so the Holding Facilities can be constructed and maintained." Cha'Hawk looked at the other commanders in the room, many of which he had fought beside in numerous past battles. "It is time that we make a change in our leadership, and crush the inhabitants beneath us until they are no more. Who stands with me?"

None of the officers voiced their agreement, and even more continued to draw their weapons from their holsters. Even Mi'Kel stood silently behind him, not voicing any support for Cha'Hawk's leadership.

After a minute of silence, Ki'Ra let loose a short laugh. "Did you really think that these warriors would turn upon me? They know who leads this invasion, and they also know when a misguided fool would lead them down the path of destruction." Ki'Ra pointed at Cha'Hawk and ordered, "Apprehend this fool at once, and bring him to me!"

With his options exhausted, Cha'Hawk reached to his back to grab his battle staff, when Mi'Kel swiftly moved toward him and slammed him down to the ground. Grabbing one of Cha'Hawk's legs, Mi'Kel began to drag him toward a flight of stairs that led to the upper level. Though he tried to resist Mi'Kel, two other officers rushed to Mi'Kel's aid and restrained him, leaving him unable to resist against his oppression.

"Mi'Kel," Cha'Hawk hastily shouted as he was dragged up to the third level, "What are you doing!? This is not part of our plan!"

In a menacing tone Cha'Hawk had never heard Mi'Kel use before, he answered, "Your plan was going to end this way, regardless of my intervention. I have merely reduced the time required for it to reach its conclusion." Mi'Kel tossed Cha'Hawk to Ki'Ra's feet, and before Cha'Hawk could fight back, the two officers that had restrained him, in addition to Zan'Tar, who had apparently quickly thrown away his loyalty to Cha'Hawk, held him down while Ki'Ra walked to him. When he reached Cha'Hawk, he bent over to face him and casually examined him as if he were a piece of outdated computer equipment.

"You never should have opposed me, *former* Tactical Analyst Cha'Hawk. Because of your actions, the clan of Hawk may never recover from your disgrace as a warrior of the Tora Cyrel." Members of the Ribiyar species were partially named after their clan. For example, two of Cha'Hawk's other clan members (only a total of fifteen members of each clan are constructed and online at one time) were Tho'Hawk and Ply'Hawk. The actions of earlier clan members greatly influence how other Ribiyar viewed a clan, and though Cha'Hawk was already considered a disgrace of the clan of Hawk, which was partially the reason he had been assigned to the invasion force as a Tactical Analyst, reduced to merely analyzing battle plans instead of fighting the enemy, he knew his actions would exponentially lower the view of his clan. It is possible that the Tora Cyrel might just exterminate them outright, as a response to his dishonorable service.

It is just as well, Cha'Hawk mused to himself. *I never liked those miserable excuses for Ribiyar anyway.*

"To ensure your rebellion ends here, it is time to put you out of your misery, here and now." Ki'Ra reached for his small, pyramid shaped gun on his lower left leg, but Mi'Kel stopped him. "High Order Ki'Ra, if I may interrupt, I recommend a different course of action. I believe that an execution is too quick and easy for an insurrectionist like him. I suggest that we keep him in an Oblivion Chamber, until the invasion has been won, and we return to Ribiyar space. Then, we can make an example of him, and show the rest of the Tora Cyrel the mistake of acting against their leaders." Cha'Hawk saw that this proposal pleased Ki'Ra, most likely because he believed that he would receive all the glory of the outcomes that action would bring.

"Very well. Take him to the Oblivion Chamber on the lower levels and inform the operator to set it on its highest setting." Many Ribiyar had been mentally damaged from the Oblivion Chamber just from its lowest effects; the most powerful setting usually left the Ribiyar either mentally insane, or the Ribiyar's mental core simply deteriorated, bringing a slow and excruciating execution.

As they dragged Cha'Hawk away, Mi'Kel spoke, "It is time to truly see how powerful your mind is Cha'Hawk. I look forward to seeing the results." Though Cha'Hawk struggled against his handlers, they dragged him out of the room.

And as the door closed, the last thing he saw was Ki'Ra's look of satisfaction for silencing the strongest oppressor against his rule.

Chapter 22

Date: July 10, 2132.
Location: Aboard the *U.S.S. Ocean-Walker*, traveling through the Atlantic Ocean.

"So, do you think you can fix him?" Olo asked as Jack examined Batcat. Jack and Olo stood in crew quarters that no one had been assigned to and were attempting to determine whether repairing Batcat was a lost cause. The beds in the room were filled with spare parts for Batcat, and a small table had been brought in and the E.V.A.N. had been placed on it, giving Jack and Olo room to maneuver around him to administer repairs. While the captains considered who to assign to the elite squad that would assault the Control Center, Captain Whitefield requested Olo be reassigned back to the *Ocean-Walker*, so he could operate Batcat and supervise him through the assault on the base. While

Olo lacked much of the proper training and skills that would qualify him for this sort of mission, he had the most experience with Batcat, and had the best chance of retaining control of him. Though Jack might have a chance of taking control of Batcat's computer systems, he wouldn't be able to control him once he connected to the Holding Facility's computer, since all of his computing power would be diverted to overcome the computer core's defenses, which would be extremely hazardous for the assault team if the E.V.A.N. went out of control during that time.

"I'm not sure," Jack replied as he scanned Batcat with the sensor beams on his hands, walking around him so he could get a complete scan. "Though he has taken a great deal of structural damage, I believe it should be repairable." Jack leaned down so he was right next to Batcat to get a closer look at his systems. From his scans, he determined that several of Batcat's circuity components had been destroyed or damaged during the fight, resulting in his unresponsive state. Jack fetched new parts for the damaged ones, and after he and Olo replaced them, he reactivated Batcat's power systems. Batcat's limbs began to twitch, and his crimson-red eyes sprang open. Batcat jumped to his feet, surveying his surroundings, when he focused on Jack.

"Meow." At once, Batcat jumped to his feet, deployed mini-machine guns on his front arms, and fired at Jack. Not wanting to harm Batcat, Jack attempted to dodge what bullets he could, which was difficult with so little room to maneuver in, and tried to shield himself with his arms. Bullets bounced off of Jack, flying all around the room, one bullet striking the wall only a few inches from Olo, who was frantically looking through a pile of spare parts.

"Meow." Batcat stopped firing, and jumped high into the air to tackle Jack, releasing thick, long razor-sharp claws from his paws, but he suddenly deactivated, his eyes turned dark and lifeless, and he thumped harmlessly against Jack, and fell to the floor.

"I found Batcat's off switch," Olo said as he held up a small transceiver. "It looks like he thought you were a Ribiyar, and considering his programing, I guess that could be understandable, given your appearance. I may need your help to reprogram his identification systems, among other things," Olo said as he and Jack lifted Batcat back up to the table to continue working on him.

"I will stay to assist in the reprograming, but I will need to report elsewhere eventually. There is much to prepare for before the assault on the Holding Center begins." Jack connected with Batcat's computer systems and began to adjust his settings so Batcat wouldn't attack him, and, as much as he would enjoy it, Victor when he was in his Dark Serpent armor.

"Jack," Olo said after working for a few minutes, "I know we haven't had time to talk since we first saw each other again, but I did want to tell you that I'm relieved to see you are doing well, all things considered."

Though he continued to work, Jack smiled and said, "It is good to see you as well. I am glad to see you are progressing well through your career. I must apologize for not staying in touch after I was transferred from the *Charger*. My life became extremely busy once I was given command of the *Atlanta*, and..." Jack paused, trying to find the right words, but found himself at a loss for them.

"It's fine, Jack. I suppose I also could have tried harder to stay in contact with you."

Wanting to catch up with his old friend, Jack said, "It is going to take a little time to complete Batcat's alterations to his systems, but I would like to make some upgrades to his weapons to make him more effective against the Ribiyar. If you don't mind me asking, could you tell me what's happened to you after I transferred from the *Charger*?"

"I would be glad to share some stories with you, but don't think you can get away without filling me in on what you've been up to." For the next hour, Jack and Olo worked hard on Batcat, completing the adjustments to his computer systems, and also working to upgrade Batcat's weapons and enhancing some of his other components, such as his agility in movement and his targeting sensors. And while they worked, Jack and Olo were also able to learn about each other's past few years, using what little time they had to resume their friendship.

1 hour and 30 minutes later...

"Chief Lexton, can you and the engineering crew complete these tasks, based on the data that I've sent you?" Jack stood in the *Ocean-Walker*'s communication center, now located in the lower decks after the destruction of the bridge. His hands were pressed against one of the control console's for the communication equipment, energy lancing off them and onto the device, linking him to it, allowing Jack to silently partake in the conversation as his voice was transmitted directly into the equipment, and Chief Lexton's response routed into his systems.

"*I believe so, Jack. It may be difficult, with how busy all the officers aboard this ship are, but I can either reassign some officers, or have Captain Rickman have some of the other senior officers assist with the computer adjustments. And Jack, Ambassador Shaan and I have finished that training program he talked to you about is ready for you to use. Do you think you will have time to make use of it?*"

"I should be able to find the time to run them after I perform my duties. Can you download the information to this ship for me?"

"*I believe I can, Jack, but I will need to sign off for the data to be sent. But before I do, Captain Rickman wanted me to tell you that he has chosen a new name for the Ribiyar ship; the* Defender, *named after our resistance, for it will be one of our greatest assets in our fight against the Ribiyar.*"

"I think it's a perfect fit, Chief. Good luck out there, we're all going to need it. Vade, out."

After his many duties were completed, Jack was finally able to make his way to the training deck below the *Ocean-Walker*, where the selected officers from the other ships had met. The training room covered a large area of space, and possessed a two-story tall ceiling to support a rock climbing wall, and several targets were spaced around one side of the room, either hanging from the ceiling, or standing on stands near the wall. In addition to the targets, there were also some punching bags and martial arts equipment to allow the officers to improve their karate or other self-defense practices. Along with practicing with their gear and equipment, the group was instructed to prepare a mission strategy for their assault, and become acquainted with each other before they went into battle. In total, there were nine crew, counting Olo, chosen for this mission. Those chosen were Jack, Batcat, Olo, Colonel Vern Brown, who was designated as the leader for the mission, Major Buck Aru, Larry "Beef" Rogers, his nickname originating from his endless love of beef jerky, Lieutenant Johnny Fairchild, Lieutenant Commander Simon Owen Stone (or SOS, as his friends had nicknamed him, for his ferociousness in battle), and Victor Davidson, in his Dark Serpent armor, of course.

When Jack entered the room, he immediately got the impression that he was dealing with highly trained professionals. Most of the people in the room were either firing at targets placed around the room, practicing martial arts with self-defense mannequins, or huddled by tables in the far corner performing maintenance and adjustments to their weapons and equipment.

Jack decided to first meet the officers firing at the targets, and he walked over as they fired at the targets until they emptied their weapons. One of the officers, Colonel Brown, a tall, extremely muscular man with long brown hair that fell to his shoulders, turned to Jack as he inserted more ammo into his modified AK-47 rifle. From a visual inspection, the rifle appeared to have been modified to provide a more powerful shot, and the ammo was configured specifically to penetrate metallic material; a necessary improvement if the gun had any chance to breach the Ribiyar's metal skin.

When Jack arrived at the group, Colonel Brown tossed his rifle toward him. Jack caught the gun with his right hand, and before he could question why Colonel Brown had given him the gun, the major said in a heavy New York accent, "Hey tinman, I hear that you're supposed to be some advanced machine-guy, possessing super smarts, targeting, and other mechanical stuff like that. This true?"

Jack nodded. "It is. My transformation has greatly increased many of my functions, including-"

"Don't bore me with the details," Brown interrupted. "I don't care about all that techno-specifics stuff. What I do care about is what you can do with a gun, particularly, how good you are at aiming. I know we don't have moving targets, but those bulls-eye's over there are good enough." Brown took a step back from Jack and leaned against a cabinet containing equipment. "Go ahead, mechanical man. Show me what ya got."

Now, the rest of the officers that had been shooting at the targets were closely watching him, observing him to see what skills he possessed. Refusing to be embarrassed mere moments after meeting his team, Jack cocked a round into the chamber, aimed his rifle, and fired at a target directly in front of him. The bullet scored a direct bulls-eye. Wanting to show the others what he was truly capable of, Jack fired at the targets, making a total of 11 bulls-eyes. To really impresses the group, Jack surveyed the room around him, measuring a multitude of angles necessary to make this super-shot. Jack retuned his focus to his selected target, a circular target that had fallen off its stand and laid flat on the ground. Without looking behind him, Jack aimed the rifle behind him, knowing the bullet's flight path was away from the officers in the training room, and fired. The bullet bounced off the wall behind him, ricocheted off the ceiling, and struck another perfect bulls-eye on the fallen target. The other officers, Beef Rogers, a fit man with crew cut black hair, who was chomping on a strip of beef jerky, and Johnny Fairchild, a young-looking officer with silvery-blond hair, were astonished by the display. Brown approached Jack, clapping as he walked.

"Very good, mechanical man. At least we know that we can trust you not to hit us by accident in a firefight with the metal heads. Now, go test out your hand-to-hand combat on those sparring dummies over there," Brown said as he pointed to the punching bags and martial art mannequin's. "You two," the major then said, talking to Beef and Fairchild, "I want you two to keep working on your aim. If you can't hit non-moving fake targets, you aren't likely to hit real, moving targets either." Sighing, they reluctantly complied and grabbed their weapons. Beef carried a flame-thrower that shot out white-hot fire at his opponents and a laser rifle for when his flame-thrower ran out of fuel, and Fairchild carried a Quicksilver, a machine-gun that possessed three bullet nozzles.

As they resumed their target practice, Jack walked over to the martial arts part of the training room, where Major Aru, a muscular man with short, black hair who had the insignia of the Marines tattooed on his right arm, and Lieutenant Commander Stone, a dark tanned officer with combed, brown hair, practiced their moves on each other. Deciding he would most likely hurt one or both of them if he joined in their moves, and considering that he could punch a hole through the punching bags without breaking a sweat, Jack decided to run on the programs Ambassador Shaan had made that would prepare him for the upcoming combat. Jack walked to a corner, where he was far enough to not hit anyone or anything if he accidently preformed his moves outside of his mental simulation, he closed his eyes and activated the martial arts training program.

PROGRAM 'NINJA SKILZ' UPLOADED AND ACTIVATING IN FIVE SECONDS.

DEACTIVATING MOTOR SYSTEMS AND REROUTING MENTAL FUNCTIONS TO PROGRAM.

ENGAGING...

Jack opened his eyes to find that he was in a training dojo. The room he was in was a large, two-story facility with no windows on the walls, and the light in the room was produced from strobe lights chained to the ceiling. On the floor of the dojo, a large training mat covered the entire floor of the room, with Jack positioned in the exact center of the mat.

"Greetings, Vade." Jack turned to find Ambassador Shaan, dressed in a sensei-like robe, standing behind him. "I see that you have taken the time to activate one of my training programs. Good. In the short time you have left before your biggest trial begins, you must learn to fight at your maximum strength, and know the limits of your abilities. While you may see training for your guns and flying more important than fighting with your fists and legs, you must realize that our ancestors fought with their hands before swords, spears, arrows, and guns were invented. If your devices fail you in battle, you must use your available assets to continue fighting against our aggressors. So, this program is designed to test your fighting strengths using only limbs, not any of your fancy weaponry. But be warned, these opponents are designed to adapt to your moves as you progress, challenging you as you grow stronger. Let us begin."

The second he spoke those words, Ambassador Shaan vanished, leaving a black-robed ninja in his place. The ninja possessed spiked gauntlets on his hands, showing that he was capable of piercing Jack's metal skin. The ninja launched at Jack, leaping high into the air. Jack jumped to the left just as the ninja struck his metal claw into the ground where he had been standing. While the ninja was stuck on the ground, Jack kicked the ninja with his right leg, sending the ninja flying into the wall with his gauntlet still stuck in the ground. The ninja slammed into the wall, and erupted in a puff of smoke, and the gauntlet evaporated in a cloud of black smoke as well.

"Just thought I should let you know," Ambassador Shaan said, reappearing behind Jack, "The opponents are programed to evaporate when you inflict a blow that would have knocked them unconscious. So, a good rule to follow, is if they are still in the training program, fight on." Shaan again vanished, but this time leaving three ninjas in his place. The middle ninja leaped into the air, the other two charging toward Jack on the ground. Jack lunged for the ninja in the air, but the ninjas on the ground grabbed him and threw him to the ground. Just as Jack landed on the mat, the ninja that had been in the air landed on him, shoving a gauntlet into Vade's right shoulder. Though the blow didn't pierce all the way through his armor, it went deep enough to sever some of the circuitry that allowed him to send commands to his right arm, causing him to lose control of the arm, and it fell uselessly to the floor. Refusing to give up, Jack grabbed the ninja with his left arm and used him like a club against the other two ninjas, causing them to slam into the wall and erupt into smoke. Several more ninjas appeared in their place, doubling the number of the last group, and Jack felt control of his right arm return to him. Boldly facing the enemy, and still holding the ninja in his hands, Jack fought against the group, and continued to fight against more and more ninjas, when the program suddenly ended and brought him back to reality.

"Hey mechanical man, can you hear me in there?" Jack opened his eyes to find Colonel Brown waving his hand in front of his face.

Jack cleared his thoughts and said, "I apologize, sir. I was running training programs to improve my hand-to-hand combat, as you suggested."

"Well, I don't remember telling you to go all technical about training, but hey, whatever gets you into fighting condition is fine with me. Come on, we need to get our little group together and formalize our plan to trash this Ribiyar base we're heading to." Brown led Jack back to the group, and after everyone had gathered together, the major led them to the *Ocean-Walker*'s briefing room, and finalized their approach to the Ribiyar Holding Facility, their plan of attack and route to take once they were in the base, and the possible defensive positions and attack methods they would use while they guarded Jack as took control of the Holding Facility's computer.

Five hours before they were to arrive at the base, they were finally ready to bring destruction to the Ribiyar invaders. Now all they had to do was get some rest, and wait for their attack on the Holding Facility to commence.

Michael Mishoe

Chapter 23

Date: July 11, 2132.
Location: Aboard the *U.S.S. Ironclad*, near the Ribiyar Holding Facility positioned in the Atlantic Ocean.

"Admiral Tinel, we are on the outskirts of the Ribiyar Holding Facility, and awaiting your orders, sir," Captain Conner reported. The bridge of the *Ironclad* was very similar to the one of the *Ocean-Walker*, except that a display table, a virtual screen with a circular gap in the information to allow the captain to see the front of the ship clearly, had been installed in the space between the captain's chair and the massive window in the front of the bridge.

Just about an hour before the sun would begin to rise, the fleet finally arrived at their destination. Directly in front of the *Ironclad*, was the island that held the infamous Ribiyar Holding Facility. Nearly all of the trees that had populated the island had been destroyed, leaving a desolate land surrounding the Holding Facility that lay in the center of the island. All around the island, several octagon-shaped metal surfaces dotted the land, marking the Ribiyar fighter bays that lay hidden underneath. Since the invasion had begun, no one had attempted an assault on these fortresses, and for good reason. The Holding Facility had a powerful array of energy weapons to unleash upon any who dared to attack it. In addition, four Ribiyar cruisers, the huge-oval shaped vessels that had large fighter storage lanes on the sides of their hull, the same type of ship as the *Defender*, hovered above the Facility, ready to give support to the fortress against enemy invaders. Everyone in the fleet knew that the odds were greatly in favor of the Ribiyar being victorious, but they had to make a strike on the Facility if they had any hope of making real progress against their invaders. Before they could attack the Holding Facility, they had to draw the cruisers away from the base and destroy them, so they could focus their attention on the fortress and the fighters that would swarm toward the attackers.

Admiral Tinel, standing in front of the data display, pressed a button on it, activating the *Ironclad*'s communication array, and contacted the other ships of the fleet. "Attention all ships of the fleet, this is Admiral Tinel. All ships are ordered to hold position until *Thunderfox* and *Defender* have completed their task. Captain Syvon, you know what to do. I know this battle is not going to be an easy one, and if we are to secure our planet from these invaders it will certainly not be our last. But we are our planets' Defenders, and we will not give it up without a fight. So, let's give 'em one they will never forget. Admiral Tinel, out."

Location: Aboard the *U.S.S. Thunderfox*, near the Ribiyar Holding Facility positioned in the Atlantic Ocean.

"All right men, you heard the admiral. Let's get this done," Captain Syvon ordered. "Commander Ton, is the *Thunderfox*'s Laser Array ready?"

"Affirmative, Captain," Ton responded from his post near the front of the bridge. Like the other officers, he had strapped himself to his chair to prepare for the rapid flight maneuvers they were likely to engage during the upcoming battle.

"Then let's do this thing. Helm, take us out of the water, and set a course for the Holding Facility."

"Right away, sir," Ensign Maria Mooring, a tall woman with bright pink hair, who served as the *Thunderfox*'s helm officer, reported. Immediately, Captain Syvon felt the *Thunderfox* lurch forward as it rose to emerge from the surface of the ocean, where they had been hiding to remain undetected from Ribiyar sensors.

"Chief Payton, when we arrive at the island, focus the Laser Array at the cruisers above the Holding

Facility. If the fleet has any hope of attacking the fortress, we must divert those ships away from the island. To do that, we have to get their attention, and make them mad enough so we can lead them away from the island." Through the window at the front of the bridge, Captain Syvon saw the ship leave its refuge beneath the ocean's surface, and ascend higher into the air.

"Understood, Captain Syvon," Chief Tactical Officer Leonard Payton, a handsome man with a western accent and flowing brown hair, responded. Payton then began giving orders to the other tactical officers on the *Thunderfox* so they could act immediately when they were in position.

After a few minutes of flying (they had been a good distance away from the island while they waited for the fleet to get in position to avoid detection), they were over the shore of the island, rapidly approaching the Holding Facility that was positioned in the center of the land mass.

"Why don't they attack us?" Ensign Mooring asked, trying to comprehend why the Ribiyar would let them get so close to their stronghold.

"Because they don't think we're a threat," Commander Ton responded. "And they are essentially correct. If we didn't have the rest of our forces backing the assault, we wouldn't stand a chance against this many Ribiyar." Finally, the *Thunderfox* was in position to begin its assault on the cruisers stationed at the Holding Facility.

"Sir, standing by to commence firing on your orders," Chief Tactical Officer Payton reported.

Captain Syvon took a deep breath, knowing that once the battle began, it could not be stopped, and then gave the order everyone was waiting for: "Open fire on the Ribiyar cruisers. Fire the Laser Array at maximum power, and use our standard cannons to support the attack." On his command, the *Thunderfox* unleashed the full might of its arsenal, firing lava-red beams at the Ribiyar cruisers and slicing into their hull plating and weapon ports as the ship's cannons fired its ammunition into the cut's in the armor the Array created, maximizing the damage they caused as much as possible. The *Thunderfox* then jumped to full speed, targeting as many sections of the ships as they could reach. Though the lasers were doing damage to the vessels, the *Thunderfox* was no much for the might of the four Ribiyar cruisers, who began to move after the *Thunderfox* to intercept it.

"Sir, the cruisers are maneuvering to intercept us. Your orders?" Commander Ton reported.

"Unleash our entire armament of missiles on the cruisers, and continue firing the Laser Array. Do not alter course until directed to do so," Captain Syvon ordered. Captain Syvon kept his eyes on the window of the bridge, which had been covered by the protective metal plating on the outside of the ship, and a projector now shone brightly on top of the window, showing the events unfolding outside of the ship from camera's mounted on the exterior of the hull. Along with the laser beams continuing to drill into the cruisers' hull, a total of 38 missiles swarmed toward the Ribiyar, slamming into their hull. While the missiles were able to do a good deal of damage to the cruisers, even disabling one of their engines, overall, the damage was relatively minor. But the attack accomplished what Syvon had been hoping for. The cruisers were now firing at the *Thunderfox* and following it as it raced away from the island.

"Captain, the cruisers are continuing their pursuit of the *Thunderfox*," Commander Ton reported. "It appears that we were successful in getting their attention. However, even with the *Thunderfox* at full speed, the cruisers will overtake us within minutes; sooner if they manage to disable our engines." Captain Syvon gripped his chair as Ensign Mooring did her best to maneuver around the Ribiyar's energy blasts, but he could also feel the *Thunderfox* rocking beneath him as it sustained blasts that managed to strike his ship.

"Don't be concerned about it, commander," Captain Syvon replied. "Remember, we don't need to out run the Ribiyar for long. We just need to make it to our rendezvous point. Are we almost there, Commander Ton?"

Commander Ton checked the readouts on his computer interface, and replied, "Affirmative, Captain Syvon. We will reach the coordinates in roughly 30 seconds."

"Good. Let's just hope the *Defender* is ready for us." Captain Syvon desperately wanted to give the *Defender* a call and inform them they were almost there, but he didn't dare risk the Ribiyar intercepting the communication and discovering the location of the hidden vessel.

Commander Ton continued to give a countdown to the time of their arrival. "20 seconds... 15 seconds... 10 seconds... 5 seconds... 0 seconds. We have reached our rendezvous coordinates." A brief cheer of celebration went up in the bridge, but it quickly calmed while the officers returned their focus upon their duties.

When nothing happened after they passed their rendezvous coordinates, Captain Syvon began to fear that the *Defender* has been unable to detect their approach from beneath the ocean. But then it happened, the view screen showed a small, Ribiyar missile, rise out of the ocean, right as the Ribiyar ships approached that location, still chasing after the *Thunderfox*. But this missile was not a typical warhead, as the core of a nuclear warhead had been placed in its payload compartment. Unable to maneuver around the warhead in time or have time to target and shoot the missile down, the lead cruiser slammed into the warhead, causing it to erupt. The instant the warhead detonated upon the Ribiyar ship, a mighty explosion engulfed all four of the cruisers, creating a massive mushroom cloud into the sky, and sending a mighty shockwave that rocked the *Thunderfox*, even though it had travelled a good distance from the rendezvous point.

The bridge erupted in cheers as they watched the events unfold on the window screen. Captain Syvon sighed in relief of their fortune. The reports of the Ribiyar's weakness to nuclear warheads had been proven accurate. When the captains of the fleet learned of the *Atlanta*'s survival, they had theorized that they could wipe out the cruisers guarding the Holding Facility with one blow, if they used a nuclear warhead from the *Atlanta*'s arsenal, which were the only nuclear weapons they knew of that remained after the Ribiyar had disabled the supply of warheads that the nations of Earth had developed. Using the *Defender* to shield the warheads from detection, the fleet had been able to keep their small arsenal hidden from the Ribiyar as they made their way to the Holding Facility.

"Captain," Commander Ton reported as the applause died down, "The *Ironclad* reports that the infiltration team is now enroute to the Holding Facility, and that the fleet has engaged its bombardment of the Facility and the forces protecting it. The *Ironclad* is requesting assistance from the *Thunderfox* and the *Defender* with deterring the counterattack of the Ribiyar forces. Your orders?"

"Set course for the island immediately, and ready the Laser Array and all other weapons for deployment. This fight is far from over." The *Thunderfox* immediately performed a loop in the air, and sped toward the Holding Facility at full speed, eager to wreak havoc upon the Ribiyar forces.

Once the fleet engaged their attack on the Ribiyar forces, an oval-shaped fighter emerged from the ocean's surface, and quietly made its way toward the upper landing pad on the central tower of the Holding Facility. Within the fighter rode the infiltration team. Most of the team sat in chairs that had been installed before the launch, since the Ribiyar had no use for such devices, except Jack, who stood at the central console with his hands pressed upon it. Tiny strobes of electricity jumped off his hands and onto the console's surface, giving new instructions to the computer as he piloted the crafted to the fortress before him.

"Hey, Jack," Olo said as he finished adjusting the laser rifle he carried, "I've been thinking, we need to get you a cool name to call yourself. No offense, but 'Jack Vade' doesn't exactly strike fear into anyone."

"What kind of name are you thinking about?" Jack asked as he steered the fighter out of the way of several Ribiyar fighters that swarmed past them. Though the presence of the fighter might raise suspicion, since the craft should be engaging the forces attacking the Holding Facility, the fighter would most likely go unnoticed with the bombardment of the fleet underway. In theory, anyway.

"I don't know. I just think that you need a name that sounds heroic and patriotic and stuff, but at the same time, sounds intimidating and fearsome to these guys who are trying to take our planet from us."

Jack thought for a moment, and then replied, "I think I'll call myself... the Guardian."

"And what, pray tell, are you the guardian of?" Victor, clad in his Dark Serpent armor, asked.

Deciding to go as big with his name as possible, and to try to show up Victor at the same time, Jack responded, "I guard Earth, and all the people within in it, from any who try to harm it." Nearing the highest landing pad at the tower, Jack slowed the ship's engines, and after reaching the landing pad, slowly setting the fighter down onto the center of its surface, turning the ship so the docking ramp would face the opposite direction of the entrance, which gave the group time to exit the craft before the battle commenced. Though the fighter could be used to attack the Ribiyar on the landing pad, the fighter's weapons may inadvertently damage the pad, which would force them to jump from the fighter onto the walkway that led to the entrance. Furthermore, use of the fighter could lead to the Ribiyar deploying the Holding Facility's weapons against it, but if it was just the infiltration team attacking, it was the team's hope that the Ribiyar would just let the warriors stationed on the pad to deal with the intrusion.

The landing pad was a large, circular shaped structure, and a walkway, which led to the entrance into the Holding Facility, held the pad up in the air. Several fighters were dotted around the pad, with a large number of Ribiyar soldiers stationed around the ships, waiting to be deployed into combat. In addition to the troops, two of the ball-shaped Enforcer Pods guarded the way towards the entrance into the Facility.

"That's a big role to fill, tinman," Colonel Brown said as he unbuckled himself from his chair. "I'm going to hold you to that commitment. All right ladies," the major said as the rest of the group unbuckled from their seats, "here's the game plan. We're going to split up, take out fighters and the metal heads defending them. Oakland, while we're keeping the rest of the forces busy, have that little fur ball of yours take out those Pods. Rogers, Davidson, Aru will go with me to the left side of the pad. The rest of you, go right. We clear?" When all the officers replied yes, Brown punched a button on a panel near the end of the fighter, and the ramp quickly lowered onto the surface of the landing pad.

When the ramp lowered, several Ribiyar approached the entrance to investigate the fighter's unexpected arrival and looked in the vessel to see the team standing inside it. Before the surprised aliens could even reach for their weapons, the Dark Serpent lunged toward them, activating the Phantom Blade as he flew through the air, and sliced them all in half with one swing of the Blade.

"Finally, time for things to get entertaining!" Victor said as he deactivated the Phantom Blade, attached it to his belt, and disappeared from sight as his stealth device activated. Sighing from Victor's unwillingness to stay with his unit, Colonel Brown cocked a round into his rifle, and charged down the ramp of the fighter, and turned left as he engaged the Ribiyar on the landing pad.

Deploying his machine guns, which latched onto the side of his arms, Jack took the lead and charged down the ramp, turning right when he reached the surface of the landing pad, and fired relentlessly as the Ribiyar grabbed their weapons and began to fire back at him. The rest of his unit also began their attack as well.

Lieutenant Commander Stone used his specially-modified bow that allowed him to shoot three times the distance of a regular bow, and fired arrows that had been equipped with electromagnetic pulse emitters that were placed behind the tip of the arrow. The size of a small, rectangular box, the emitters activated the second the arrows pierced into the surface of the Ribiyar's metal surface, effectively frying all of their internal mechanisms. Beef Rogers, somehow chomping on a piece of jerky as he did so, launched waves of intense fire from his flame thrower, which Jack had recently upgraded with a small, Genetic Modulator in its fuel tank that created an endless supply of fuel for the weapon. Once a perimeter of fire had been erected around the aliens, Rogers let go of his flame thrower, which held onto him with the strap that went across him, and retrieved his laser rifle from his back, and expertly shot down the Ribiyar, with some assistance with Lieutenant Commander Stone.

Only a minute had eclipsed since the battle had started, and most of the Ribiyar had been destroyed, and it was then that Jack saw Batcat leap onto the top of the fighter they had traveled in, sitting in-between the top two engines and on the surface of a gun that laid between the engines. As his black cape flapped in the wind, Batcat stared intently at the foe he was about to engage, the two Enforcer Pods blocking the path to the entrance of the Holding Facility.

Knowing the arsenal of weaponry Batcat possessed, Jack almost pitied his alien adversaries, knowing the next minute would likely end in their destruction. During the period Batcat had been offline while Jack and Olo modified his software, Jack had also made several upgrades to Batcat's systems, including adding small fabricators within him that provided him with an endless supply of bullets for his machine guns, and he had also increased the potency of the bullets, allowing them to more readily pierce through metallic substances, and increased the firing rate of his machine guns, allowing them to fire even faster than before. Jack also installed another fabricator in Batcat's grenade compartment, providing Batcat with more grenades as he used them.

Just as Jack was about to return his attention to the Ribiyar soldiers, he saw the Enforcer Pods extend their spear-like legs as they stood up, and moments later, dozens of spherical devices shot out the backs of the Pods, twisting their shapes within moments to give them a sleeker design to allow for more precise, rapid flight, and flew toward the officers on the landing pad. Before anyone could react, Jack saw Batcat crouch down, and though he knew Batcat let loose his 'battle meow' when he moved his mouth, he could have sworn that he had said "move" to the missiles and the Enforcer Pods, as if warning them away if they wanted to survive. Batcat deployed his cannon-like guns on his back, devices that had enough firepower to blow open a tank, and leapt into the air with the grace of a ballerina. Batcat spun sideways as he flew through the air, and fired his cannons, somehow managing to shoot down every single missile as he flew towards the Enforcer Pods. Batcat disappeared from sight as he hit the ground and used his momentum to slide in-between the Enforcer Pods, and moments later, a blinding light flashed, and two Pods began sparking violently from the EMP grenades Batcat had deployed. The Pods collapsed, and, because of their proximity to the edge of the landing pad, they fell off, and plummeted to the ground below. And when the smoke from EMP grenades cleared, there sat Batcat, calmly surveying the landing pad with his crimson-red eyes, almost daring the Ribiyar on the pad to try and take the walkway from his rightful possession.

Jack seized the moment and attacked the Ribiyar, who were equally astounded by the display they had just witnessed Batcat perform. After a minute more of combat, the remaining Ribiyar were neutralized, and the group made their way to the small walkway that led to the entrance of the Holding Facility. Walking around Batcat, who had been calmly licking his paw as he waited, the group walked single file as they crossed the narrowing path, with Colonel Brown leading the group, and Batcat and Olo taking the rear. The group was halfway over the walkway when the path began to tremble below them as explosions destroyed the supports holding the landing pad. Apparently, the Ribiyar were still trying to keep them from entering the Holding Facility, and were willing to destroy the landing pad in order to do so.

"Let's get a move on people!" Colonel Brown yelled as he quickly led the group forward as fast as they could, desperate to get to the entrance before the walkway collapsed beneath them. They were nearly to the end of the walkway when it began to crumble. A huge explosion ignited near the middle of the walkway, severing whatever was left of the support structure beneath the walkway, and the structure began to slowly fall to the surface. The walkway began sagging downwards as the landing pad pulled it down, and still the team continued to run across the path to get to the entrance. Colonel Brown and Major Aru reached the entrance, which fortunately had its own structure to stand on and was in no risk of plummeting below, and turned to help the rest of the group up. As more of the group moved onto the surface leading to the entrance, the walkway snapped in half, and the landing pad, and the fighters on it, began falling to the ground. The collapse of the walkway jolted Olo and Batcat, the only officers still on the structure, and they lost their footing, and began quickly slide down the remainder of the walkway.

"Olo!" Jack yelled as he jumped off the area surrounding the entrance, deployed his wings, and quickly flew after him. Flying as fast as he could, Jack intercepted Olo as he reached his hand upwards for Jack to grab onto. Just before Jack grabbed Olo's hand, the structure dropped again a few feet lower, and Olo dropped out of his reach as he rocketed past him, and because of the high speeds he had been flying, he traveled a good distance away before he could begin to turn himself around. Turning as fast he could, Jack flew back towards Olo, who had almost reached the end of the remaining walkway. As Olo was about to go over the end of the structure, Batcat jumped onto Olo's chest and held onto him tightly, in a way that looked like the cat was hoping that he could save him from death. But as Jack neared Olo, desperately reaching for him, three sharp spikes emerged from the end of Batcat's tail. The end of the tail shot away from Batcat, revealing a rope that connected it to the cat, and the spikes pierced into the surface of the walkway. Batcat and Olo jolted to a stop at the end of the walkway's surface, and Olo was so close to falling that his legs dangled in the air. As Jack reached Olo and began grabbing ahold of him, the remaining supports holding the rest of the walkway to the Holding Facility gave way, and the structure began plummeting to the ground. As Jack grabbed Olo, Batcat's tail detached from the walkway, and the cat jumped into Olo's arms as Jack held Olo in his grip.

His engines straining from the extra weight of them, Jack managed to lift them back onto the area surrounding the entrance. When he was high enough, Batcat leapt onto the ground by the entrance as Lieutenant Fairchild and Beef Rogers grabbed onto Olo's arms and helped him onto the surface.

"Thanks for coming for me, Jack," Olo said as Jack landed on the ground, retracting his wings and deactivating his thruster as he did so.

"Anytime, Olo. I'm glad you're alright."

"As sweet as this reunion is," Victor interrupted, "I think it's time we get back to the task at hand. You know, trying to take control of this death trap of a fortress and save our fleet?"

"Always the sentimental one," Jack murmured as he moved past the officers, a difficult task because of the small area that had been untouched by the landing pads collapse, and reached the entrance, a triangular door, similar to the entrance that led to the bridge aboard the *Defender*. Jack pressed his right hand onto the computer interface that was positioned in the wall to the right of the entrance, and energy began pulsing off his hand and onto the interface, connecting him with the device. "Though it may take some time, I believe I can get through the firewall and open the door. Stand by." And with that, Jack went silent as he focused his attention on breaking through the encryption protecting the controls for the door. With nothing else to do, the rest of the group stood silently as they waited for the door to open so they could continue their attack on the Holding Facility.

Location: Aboard the *Defender*, near the Ribiyar Holding Facility positioned in the Atlantic Ocean.

"Captain! The Ribiyar fighters have taken out five more of our energy cannons on our left wing, and are coming around for another attack!" Commander Hayley reported. "Your orders?"

These guys just won't give up, Captain Rickman commented to himself. Even after the fleet had taken out dozens of fighters, and some of the outposts scattered around the island outside of the Holding Facility, the Ribiyar continued to fiercely defend their territory. And, because the *Defender* was a valuable asset of the fleet, it was the primary target for the Ribiyar to attack, forcing the ship to endure a large portion of the overall attack.

"Bring us hard to starboard, and lay down a heavy bombardment with the forward cannons. Modify the cannon's energy blast for maximum detonation radius." The eight, huge, tubular cannons that were positioned in the front of the ship fired an orb of destabilized energy. When deployed, the orb explodes in a small shockwave of energy, allowing for multiple targets to be neutralized with one shot. The *Defender* turned hard to the right, and fired several energy orbs into the squadrons of fighters that were attacking the ship, completely annihilating them, but the victory was short lived, as dozens of fighters remained, and continued their fearless attack on the *Defender*.

"Sir!" Commander Hayley reported, "Sensors are detecting five Ribiyar cruisers inbound from multiple locations, heading right for us. What are your orders?"

"Set a course to intercept the cruisers, and prepare another nuclear warhead for deployment."

"Sir, I strongly caution you against this action," Chief Tactical Officer Nickland protested. "While it may have been a good strategy to use the warheads when the cruisers had been a good distance away from us earlier, this is ship-to-ship combat we're in now. The risk of getting caught in the warhead's blast is very high, and the *Defender* isn't any more immune to the nuclear reaction than they are."

"I am aware of that, Chief Nickland. But we can't let that stop us from making a stand against the Ribiyar. Besides, these warheads can be modified to limit the extent of their nuclear blast. If we can work it right, we should be able to avoid the detonation. Position the ship between the fleet and the cruisers and prepare the warhead for deployment. It's time to see what the *Defender* is made of."

As the *Defender* raced forward in the direction of the incoming cruisers, Rick could only hope that he could fend off the approaching forces. But, ready or not, he had to take a stand against the cruisers, and hope that they would survive to continue the fight for the Holding Facility.

Chapter 24

Date: July 11, 2132.
Location: In the Ribiyar Holding Facility, positioned in the Atlantic Ocean.

The infiltration team had not been waiting long before the door began to split open, but it hadn't been Jack, who had still been attempting to break through the encryption protecting the controls of the door. When the sections of the door receded into the entrance, several Ribiyar warriors were revealed, standing on the other side of the entrance and aiming their weapons at the officers. But, before the aliens could attack, Lieutenant Fairchild fired his machine gun, managing to mow them all down before they could attack the group. With his gun barrels still smoking, Fairchild moved through the entrance, quickly surveying the area for anymore hostiles. When the coast was clear, the rest of the team moved past the entrance, and into the interior of the Holding Facility.

"All right ladies, let make these dome-heads regret ever stepping foot on our planet!" Colonel Brown yelled as he led the group deeper into the Facility, firing his AK-47 at the Ribiyar he encountered. The corridors in the Holding Facility were similar to the ones aboard the *Defender*. The hallways were colored a light silver, and the upper part of the corridors were angled in the shape of an upside-down V. The light through the corridors was produced by panels built into the support beams positioned periodically throughout the hallways. One of the few differences from the *Defender*'s corridors was that these were built taller and wider, most likely to facilitate the travel of the fearsome Enforcer Pods.

As the group charged forward, Colonel Brown and Major Aru led the group, while the Dark Serpent and the Guardian guarded the rear against anyone who attempted to assault them from behind. Moving in a tight formation, they quickly made their way deeper into the Facility, annihilating any Ribiyar they encountered. After advancing through the Facility for several minutes, they stumbled upon a large room containing dozens of Ribiyar. Before the group could retreat, the Ribiyar spotted them and fired a heavy barrage of energy blasts. The group quickly split up and dived behind several storage containers, while the Ribiyar continued blasting at the containers, and as others began making their way around the containers to reach the team.

Activating the Phantom Blade, the Dark Serpent cut down the Ribiyar that made their way around the storage containers, while Lieutenant Commander Stone threw several EMP grenades over the containers, briefing lighting the room in bright flashes as the devices activated and disabled several of the aliens. Once Stone stopped his EMP bombardment, Olo deployed Batcat into the battlefield, and the room shook as Batcat simultaneously launched both a grenade assault and a relentless stream of machine gun fire. Not two minutes passed before Batcat had eliminated the dozens of Ribiyar in the room. The group quickly moved through the room and into the labyrinth of corridors that lay beyond it. After traveling up a walkway that led to the next level above, the team reached a three-way intersection in the hallway, but the path that led to their objective, the lift that was stationed behind the door in front of them, was sealed shut. Jack pressed his hand on the interface and attempted to take control of the lift, but the firewall prohibited him from doing so, and it would take some time before he could break through the encryption.

"We have hostiles coming in multiple directions!" Lieutenant Commander Stone announced over the team's radio channel. From the three corridors that surrounded them, dozens of Ribiyar soldiers charged toward the team. Jumping into action, Jack activated his machine guns, and fired at the aliens. Though several of the Ribiyar managed to fire upon him before he mowed them down, their blasts only caused minor damage to his recently-repaired armor. Though he and the team were able to neutralize the Ribiyar, more and more aliens continued to charge toward them. Jack quickly moved back to the interface, pressed his hand on it and connected to it, and managed to access the door controls in the corridor. Farther down each of the three corridors, large, metal plating lowered from the ceiling and sealed off the intersection. After the group finished off the remaining Ribiyar, Jack activated his scanner, and surveyed the area around him to find a to continue forward.

"Colonel Brown, my scanners are detecting a secondary security processor in a room just beyond these two corridors. It is preventing me from taking control of the lift. We need to destroy it if we are to move forward. However, I'm detecting a large concentration of Ribiyar, likely about 150 or so, in the room as well."

"And how do you recommend we do that, tin head?" Victor remarked. "Not even Ollie's little fur ball could take out that many dome-heads."

"Maybe he can," Jack replied after thinking a moment. "Batcat can deploy a multitude of EMP grenades, enough to destroy all the soldiers and the security processor, while a few of us engage the Ribiyar in the room." Loud pounding sounds, accompanied by weapons fire, echoed dimly as the Ribiyar attempted to force their way into the corridor. The door protecting the way they had come through was already beginning to falter and would not last much longer. "While they engage the Ribiyar, the rest of us will protect the lift from these Ribiyar."

"This warp-brained idea of yours sounds risky, with a high change of us getting our brains fried by these aliens," Colonel Brown replied, "But then again, so did this mission, and that didn't stop us from coming. Oakland, take Batcat, Davidson, and Fairchild with you. You need to take out most, if not all, of the Ribiyar and those ball-tank things so we don't have so many aliens shooting at us. Now, get going!" Jack opened one of the two corridors that led to the room with the security processor, and after dealing with the Ribiyar on the other side of the door, Batcat lead the group away, leaving the rest of the team to fight a relentless swarm of robotic aliens.

5 minutes later…

"Now, go Batcat! Complete your mission!" Olo whispered to Batcat, who jumped to the top of a crate and disappeared into the shadows to do his task. The room was a lot bigger than the ones they had rushed through before. The ceiling was at least three stories tall, and the floor looked big enough to hold at least three Olympic swimming pools. There were several groups of crates scattered around the edges of the room, near the walls, but the rest of the room was stocked full of Ribiyar soldiers standing in formation, waiting to be sent out to combat the intruders. But worst of all, over a dozen of the feared Enforcer Pods hung from the ceiling, with several catwalks attached to the ceiling so the troops could move around, waiting to be unleashed upon their enemy. Olo and the others were currently hiding between a tall pile of crates that were out of the way of the two exits so they wouldn't be discovered before they could make their move.

"All right boys," Olo said as he inserted a fresh power cell into his EMP rifle, "Lets sing it loud, and sing it proud."

"I don't know what that means," Victor responded as he grabbed the Phantom Blade from his waist and attached it to his tail, "but if it means we go at them guns blazing, it's the best thing you've said since I first laid my eyes on you. It's finally time for the Serpent to be unleashed." Just as Victor finished speaking, he activated his stealth device and vanished into thin air.

Not wanting to draw attention to himself and Fairchild by calling after Victor, though he knew it would be useless as he would certainly ignore him anyway, Olo sighed at Davidson's recklessness, and silently climbed up the crates, getting into position to snipe down the Ribiyar.

"*Lek tar k fer! Don dek fektiz! Sep un tu qwar!*" One of the Ribiyar, presumably the general in charge, ordered. Olo couldn't understand what was being said, but he assumed that another group was being sent out, and from what he could see, nearly half of the troops were being deployed this time to destroy the rest of the team. Olo knew that those troops needed to be stopped before they could exit the room.

Before Olo could give the signal of attack to Lieutenant Fairchild, who was positioned behind a crate a few feet away from Olo, Victor suddenly appeared in the middle of the Ribiyar soldiers that stood attention in the center of the room.

"Hey Ollie," Victor yelled as all the Ribiyar in the room turned toward him, drawing their weapons as they did so. "I'd like to see Batcat do this!!!" Victor deployed his tail, which had the Phantom Blade attached to it, and the blade sparked to life, and quickly grew until it was over 30 feet long. Just as the Ribiyar began to fire at Victor, he spun around, swinging his tail-sword around with him. In that one move, over 50 Ribiyar were sliced in half. Enraged at the destruction of his troops, the Ribiyar general redirected the troops that had been leaving the room to engage the Dark Serpent, who was now laying waste to the other Ribiyar in the group that had been outside of the Phantom Blade's reach, simultaneously fighting with the energy blasters built onto his arms, and his tail-sword, which had shrunk down to its normal 12-inch size.

Taking advantage of the chaos that Victor had created, Olo and Fairchild shot at the Ribiyar that were coming back into the room, Fairchild inflicting considerably more damage with his Quick-Silver machine gun, which Jack had upgraded with a device that created an endless supply of ammunition. But no matter how fast they shot down the Ribiyar, more kept coming, and were gradually advancing closer to their location. Olo only hoped Batcat could finish planting the EMP grenades while there was anyone still alive to use them.

EXPLOSIVE SECURE. MOVING TO NEXT LOCATION TO INSTALL FINAL DEVICE.

Batcat quietly and swiftly moved along the catwalk (a fitting name for the structure, considering who was walking upon it) that was attached to the ceiling, high above the firefight between his team and the robotic aliens. Though Batcat's programming demanded that he leap down and destroy the Ribiyar, his current orders superseded those instincts. Besides, if his mission was successful, he would strike a great blow against his oppressors.

Batcat jumped off the catwalk and landed onto a tall pile of crates and began fixing an EMP grenade onto the security processor, a console in the center of the catwalk. Just as Batcat finished, all of the Enforcer Pods detached from the ceiling and fell to the ground. All of them fell near the middle of the room, except one, which landed on a tall stack of crates that had been moved under it. Ribiyar troops rushed to the Pods, except the one on the crates, which was out of reach for the aliens, and entered them, preparing to launch a counter-attack against the humans.

With his task complete, Batcat leaped back onto the catwalk and rushed back to his master to provide support against the oncoming threat.

Olo felt the crate shake below him as the Enforcer Pods fell from the ceiling, and he feared it was only a matter of time before the Ribiyar reached the Pods and obliterated Olo and the others.

"Meow," Olo heard, and he glanced behind him to see Batcat standing beside him, awaiting new orders.

"Good, your back. Now, we need to get out of here, and-"

Before Olo could finish the sentence, he felt his chest erupt in pain as the Ribiyar managed to shoot at him multiple times with their energy rifles. Olo was thrown backwards from the impact, and fell to the floor on his back. Above him, he could hear Batcat firing back at the Ribiyar who had hit him, and he was also dimly aware of Lieutenant Fairchild shouting at him from his position on top of the crates.

"Lieutenant!" Fairchild yelled as he lowered himself to the crate under the one he was on. "Hang on, I'm coming for you!"

Though Olo's concentration was slipping, he knew what had to be done. Olo did his best to focus, and spoke to Fairchild, his speech slow and slightly slurred as the life drained out of his body. "No… Lieutenant. I need… you and Victor… to get out while…you can."

"But, what about you? I can't just-"

"Forget about me. Our job… has been accomplished, and… you need to rendezvous get back to the others and get this mission… completed. The fate of the world… rests on our shoulders. Go... while you still can. I will activate… the EMPs." Fairchild hesitated, but reluctantly left as he informed Victor of their retreat on the comm.

Olo painfully used his arms to pull himself against the wall behind him, resting his back on it, and put his right hand over the wound on his chest while he used his left to fish the trigger out of his pocket. The trigger was a small, cylindrical object with a light under a cap that contained the detonation switch, and the light was rapidly pulsing green, indicating that the grenades were ready and awaiting activation. Olo was about to activate it when Batcat jumped down from above him, apparently finished enacting revenge on the Ribiyar who had wounded Olo.

"Batcat... listen to me. You... have a new mission. You are to protect... Jack Vade... at all costs, and he is to... be your new master. Do... you understand?" Batcat meowed, indicating that he understood. Batcat turned to leave, but then something Olo couldn't explain happened. Batcat's eyes suddenly stopped glowing red, indicating his attack mode had deactivated, and he moved toward Olo. Batcat moved his head under Olo's right hand and purred softly, giving him the sense that the cat was saying farewell. Touched by this unexplainable occurrence, as E.V.A.N. units had never been programmed to have the capacity for emotion, making them fearfully efficient killing machines, Olo weakly petted Batcat's head, leaving a stain of blood on his fur. Batcat moved away from Olo, and his eyes once again glowed crimson red. Moving quickly, Batcat quickly raced away from him as some of the Enforcer Pods began rolling out of the room toward the rest of his team. Olo waited about half a minute to allow Batcat time to escape, but he felt the ground tremble as another Enforcer Pod raced out of the room, and he knew he could wait no longer.

With Olo's dying breath, he lifted the trigger in his hand, and pressed the button, heralding a blinding flash and the dying mechanical screams of those who brought the end of his life.

Chapter 25

Date: July 11, 2132.
Location: Aboard the *Defender*, near the Ribiyar Holding Facility in the Atlantic Ocean.

"Direct hit, Captain Rickman!" Commander Hayley reported as a huge mushroom cloud erupted on the holographic display on the bridge. "The warhead has detonated successfully, and the final three cruisers have been destroyed!" The bridge crew gave out a few cheers, but they all knew that the battle was far from over. While the *Defender* had been engaged with the five cruisers, which had been destroyed after using two nuclear warheads, several more cruisers had engaged the ship, which led to the required use of more warheads. Now, almost a half hour later, 17 Ribiyar cruisers had been destroyed, at the cost of using the rest of the *Atlanta*'s nuclear warheads. Though the *Defender* hadn't been caught in the blasts of the nuclear explosions, by modifying the warheads remotely to increase or decrease the size of the detonations, the victories had not been without cost. The *Defender* had taken several critically hits during the engagements, and now three of its eight engines, along with several energy cannons along the wing and over the main hull of the ship, had been destroyed or otherwise rendered nonoperational.

"Captain!" Lieutenant Commander Nickland announced, "the Holding Facility's weapons are crippling several vessels from the fleet, and at the rate their firing, our forces are not going to last much longer! What are your orders?"

"Deploy all the drones that we have constructed, and program them to disable the weapons on the Holding Facility. With that many drones focusing their attacks on the weapons, they'll be able to do enough damage to take them out, and hopefully minimize overall damage to the Facility. The prisoners are still in there, and I'd like to keep civilian casualties to a minimum." Commander Hayley worked her console and instructed Chief Lexton, who was stationed in the Engineering Center and monitoring the conditions of the power core and other essential systems, to release the Recon Drones and program them to attack the Holding Facility's weapons. Next to the holographic display above the central console that showed what was happening around and in front of the ship, a new display materialized, showing video footage of the Drone's deployment. All over the *Defender*, dozens of hatches and docking ports opened, and a swarm of Recon Drones began pouring out of them.

"Chief Lexton, is the control system working?" Captain Rickman asked as he directed the *Defender* to intercept a swarm of Ribiyar fighters that were attacking the *Ironclad*. To ensure that the drones attacked in formation with each other and attacked in a well-coordinated and combined assault, Chief Lexton and Ambassador Shaan had created a computer program that would allow the *Defender*'s crew to direct the drones' attack.

"*Affirmative, Captain Rickman,*" Lexton responded over the comm. "*The Defender's computer has successfully taken control of the drones' systems, and they are now traveling to the Holding Facility to disable its weapon systems.*"

"Good work. Make sure the Drones are programmed to minimize the damage where they can. We're going to need those weapons to defend ourselves if and when the Ribiyar attempt to reclaim the Holding Facility." As the *Defender* blasted away the Ribiyar fighters, Rick hoped that Jack and the others were making progress toward the Control Center so they could end this fight. As good as the fleet was, Rick knew they couldn't last forever against this many Ribiyar.

Location: In the Ribiyar Holding Facility, positioned in the Atlantic Ocean.

Back at the lift, Jack and the rest of the team were busy holding off a seemingly endless horde of Ribiyar soldiers, who had broken through the two corridors that had been blocked off, the third one that Olo and the other officers had used still empty. Using his enhanced strength, Jack had pried several chunks of metal plating from the wall and placed them in a perimeter around the lift, providing an area for the officers to get behind to protect them from weapons fire. After several minutes of combat, he finally saw Lieutenant Fairchild and the Dark Serpent in the empty corridor, running as fast as they could. Before he could question why they ran so fast, the answer became apparent as seven Enforcer Pods appeared further down the corridor. The Pods bounced off the walls as they rolled after the two officers, quickly gaining the distance between them, and one of the Pods was so close that it was mere moments away from rolling over Fairchild and Victor.

Right before the Pod rolled over them, Victor shoved Fairchild out of the path of the Enforcer Pod, and slammed his tail into the ground and used it to thrust himself high into the air, activating the Phantom Blade as he did, and the Pod began to rush past under him. With a mighty roar, Victor brought down the Blade and sliced the Pod in half. As Victor landed on the ground, the halves of the Pod, and the Ribiyar that had been in it, crashed into the walls of the corridor, he stood his ground as the six other Enforcer Pods rolled to a stop, and stood as their spear-like legs deployed. As they worked to stand up, they also deployed their six, huge rectangular energy cannons, two positioned near the legs, two more placed near the top of the sphere, and the last two stationed in-between the two other clusters of weapons.

Beef Rogers let loose a huge stream of fire, forcing the Ribiyar near the team to fall back, while the rest of the group concentrated their firepower on the Enforcer Pods. Lieutenant Commander Stone released volley after volley of EMP arrows, managing to take out several of the Pods' weapons, and Lieutenant Fairchild managed to inflict even more damage with his machine gun as the Dark Serpent began slicing through the Pods, the team wasn't inflicting enough damage in the short time they had left, and the Pods quickly began powering up their weapons, preparing to eradicate the enemy.

Jack began to move toward the Pods and firing his weapons, knowing he wouldn't be able to take them down before they destroyed him and the rest of his team, when he noticed another Enforcer Pod emerge from the end of the corridor, rolling at twice the speed the others had used, and moments later, his sensors detected the EMP grenades activate, shorting out several light fixtures in the wall and sending down a shower of sparks as components and systems within the walls were fried, and the Pod just barely outran the blast of the pulse. As the weapons on the Enforcer Pods began to glow brightly, preparing to unload its firepower, the approaching Pod deployed its legs while it rolled, causing it to 'jump' into the air, its top sparking as it impacted against the ceiling. As it flew through the air, a dozen spheres shot out of the Pod, instantly reshaping into a more aerodynamic shape, and filled the corridor with the sound of jet noises as they streaked through the air, and Jack braced himself for the missile to strike him, unable to stop the projectiles before they hit their targets.

But instead of destroying the infiltration team, the missiles slammed into the Enforcer Pods, reducing them to scrap metal, and filling the corridor with smoke and debris. Dimly visible within the cloud of smoke, the remaining Enforcer Pod, the one that had fired the missiles, fell out of the air, bounced off the remains of one the Enforcer Pods, rolled into the intersection of the corridors, deployed its legs and cannons, and used its energy cannons to blast away the Ribiyar soldiers that had been attacking the group. Within moments, all the Ribiyar had been exterminated, and the corridors settled into an eerie silence, and the smoke finally settled.

The Enforcer Pod retracted its weapons, and then, a part of the back structure of the Pod began lowering to the ground, creating a ramp that led to the cockpit of the vehicle. The cockpit of the Pod, like the vehicle, was spherically shaped, with bright lights periodically placed around the floor of the interior. The cockpit was empty, except for an odd-looking chair. The chair was black, and had an armrest like object on the right side. The chair hovered in the air, and several black struts were placed underneath the seat, in front, behind, and on top of the chair. The struts had a hexagonal-surface attached to the end of it, and they produced small magnetic fields that kept the chair in the air, preventing the pilot from being tossed around due to the Pod's rolling motion. When the ramp lowered enough, the team saw the pilot controlling the Pod, and to everyone's surprise, it was someone they knew very well.

"You've got to be kidding me!" Victor said, understandably shocked, "Along with everything else he can do, that thing can drive a tank!?" The group continued to stare into the cockpit, where Batcat, the one everyone least expected, sat on the chair in the cockpit, the large chair making him seem small in comparison. The end of Batcat's tail was inserted into a circular, interface port on the armrest, which he was somehow using to connect him to the Pod, allowing him to pilot the vehicle. "How can that cat even manage the controls!?" Victor said, having trouble trying to understand how Batcat could possibly operate the machine.

"We don't have time to worry about that right now," Colonel Brown said, leading the group away back to the elevator door. "Guardian, you need to crack open this lift really quickly, and I mean right now. Those metal heads are going to be back soon, and I don't want to be here when that happens."

Jack quickly returned to the computer interface by the lift and continued working on taking control of the device.

"Hey, Fairchild, Davidson, have you two seen Oakland?" Colonel Brown said, looking down the corridors for him to see if he was coming. "Shouldn't he have been right behind you guys?"

Fairchild hesitated a moment, but then said, "Sir, I regret to report that he didn't survive the fight. He was shot by the Ribiyar, and we had to leave him there, while he activated the EMP's. He died a hero, sir."

"*What*!?" Jack yelled, shocked by the death of his friend. Just as he said that, Jack's programming was finally able to take control of the elevator controls, and the doors whooshed into the wall, finally allowing the team to enter. The lift was identical to the lifts aboard the *Defender*, differing only by the fact that its interior was three times the size as the other lifts, most likely so the Ribiyar could transport the Pods around the Facility.

"I... have taken control of the lift, Colonel Brown," Jack reported, shaking his head to clear his thoughts and try to focus on the mission, "and I recommend that we board it quickly, and proceed towards our objective." Though Jack was doing what he could to concentrate, he felt it difficult to maintain focus as a deep wave of emotions erupted within him over the loss of his friend. But he had to keep his feelings to himself to dwell on later. There was too much at stake to become distracted, no matter how much he hated simply putting aside his remorse for Olo.

"All right then," Colonel Brown said, "Lets complete this mission, and show the Ribiyar what we humans are made of." Deciding that it would be wise to bring the Pod with them, they allowed Batcat to maintain control of the vehicle, since he was the only one among them who had experience with it. The team entered the lift, with Batcat entering last, so the Pod would be the first thing to exit the lift, and they raced upwards to reach the level where the Control Center was located.

"Warriors, the organics have taken over the lift, and are now traveling towards our location," The Ribiyar general announced. Several dozen Ribiyar soldiers, along with three Enforcer Pods, had gathered themselves around the lift doors to confront their adversaries. "No matter the cost, they *must* be purged, before they reach the Control Center. From there, they could inflict untold destruction upon our forces. We cannot let that happen. *DO YOU UNDERSTAND?*"

"Yes, general," the Ribiyar troops replied.

"Good. The doors will open in 3 … 2 … 1!" The officers grabbed their weapons and aimed at the door. After they heard the noise of the lift locking in place, the doors whooshed open.

And they were immediately confronted with the fury of an E.V.A.N. unit in possession of an Enforcer Pod. The Pod rocketed out of the lift, rolling over several soldiers unlucky enough to have been in its path. Having built up the necessary momentum, the Pod deployed it legs and jumped into the air as the Ribiyar, and the Enforcer Pods, attempted to destroy it. Two dozen missiles were launched from the Pod and stormed toward the Ribiyar, as the vehicle simultaneously deployed its six energy cannons and launched a relentless bombardment upon the other

Enforcer Pods. The corridor erupted into flames as the missiles detonated, annihilating the Ribiyar troops, who were engulfed in the fiery explosion. Even the three Enforcer Pods were quickly obliterated from Batcat's unstoppable campaign of terror and destruction.

Batcat's Enforcer Pod fell to the ground, landing on its spear-like legs. The doors on the lift opened, which had been closed after Batcat had left to protect the team from being caught in the explosions during the fight, and the team began to cough as smoke poured into the lift. As the smoke from the explosions cleared, the remains of the Ribiyar soldiers began to emerge, littering the area around the lift, giving the area the appearance of a robotic graveyard.

"Guardian, how far are we from the Control Center?" Colonel Brown asked as he and the rest of the team walked out of the lift.

"Not too far. We simply need to follow this corridor," Jack said, pointing to a hallway to the right of the lift.

"Alright then. To save us some time, I think its best if we let Batcat pave through any Ribiyar." Brown activated his comm device so Batcat could hear him in the Pod, and said, "Batcat, lead the way to the Control Center, and plow through any Ribiyar that gets in the way."

When Batcat didn't respond to Brown's orders, Jack stepped forward, and said, "Allow me, Colonel Brown. Perhaps he will respond if I'm the one giving him instructions." Jack repeated the orders Brown had given, and the Pod immediately dropped to the ground as its legs reattached into its spherical shell and began racing down the corridor towards the Control Center, crushing the remains of several Ribiyar as it did.

"Why did that fur ball listen to you and not me?" Brown asked Jack as he and the rest of the team jogged after the Pod.

"I don't know, Colonel. It's possible he was instructed to follow orders from me if something happened to Olo. That would explain why he didn't respond when you gave him instructions."

"Well, I guess that means you're his new caretaker now. I know you have your hands full with everything else going on during this mission, but I need you to stay on top of things and make sure he doesn't get out of control. Alright?"

"Understood. But for now, I don't think we'll have a problem with Batcat going wild."

"And why is that?" Brown asked. A few moments later, the sounds of Batcat's Pod echoed through the corridors as it engaged a group of Ribiyar up ahead, crushing some while blasting away others.

"The way Batcat is right now, I have a feeling the Ribiyar, not us, will bear the brunt of any anger he needs to unleash."

Chapter 26

Date: July 11, 2132.
Location: Control Level of the Ribiyar Holding Facility, positioned in the Atlantic Ocean.

"All right, Guardian," Colonel Brown said, "do your techy gizmo magic and get this door open." The group stood in front of a 9-foot doorway that guarded the Control Center. Behind the group, Batcat, still controlling the Enforcer Pod, stood guard over the group, ready for action should any Ribiyar be foolish enough to provoke the fury of the E.V.A.N. unit. "On the other hand, if you can't get in, we could always let Batcat bust the door open," Brown added, provoking a few chuckles from the group, though Jack could tell a few of them wanted to let Batcat do it so they could watch the fireworks that would erupt from his attack.

Jack walked to the doors control panel and pressed his hand on the computer interface, but before he had a chance to connect to the door's controls, the door whooshed open as the Ribiyar opened it themselves, and Jack's world was lit up from a barrage of energy blasts. Activating his machine guns and V-guns, Jack charged into the room, taking care not to destroy any of the equipment. The Control Center was shaped like an oval, with several computer interfaces placed around the room, and there was also another entrance on the opposite side of the room. Several displays clung to the sides of the upper walls, showing readouts of the Holding Facility's status and security footage of prisoners in different locations around the Facility. Along with those displays, a holographic display was being shone on the walls of the ends of the oval, showing a view of the outside of the Holding Facility, which was still covered in darkness from the night. In the center of the room, a small platform, or a workstation, was poised over the ground, and it was about a third of the size of the room. The platform was held in the air by four arches that emerged from the walls, and it could be reached by two ramps that started at the back of the room on the bottom floor, and then made its way up the wall, and used a walkway to reach the workstation. It was from the platform that several Ribiyar were attempting to gun Jack down, along with the other aliens stationed at the consoles on the bottom floor.

As Jack charged forward, shooting down the Ribiyar on the first level, the aliens on the second level fired a barrage of energy blasts at his team. Though most of the team was able to jump out of the way, several of the energy blasts stuck Lieutenant Fairchild all over his body, burning into his uniform and skin, causing him to collapse in pain.

"Batcat," Jack said, contacting him over the comm, "exit the Enforcer Pod and engage the Ribiyar in the Control Center. Focus your attack on the Ribiyar on the upper level." The moment Jack finished talking, the ramp to the Pod lowered, and Batcat leapt out of the Pod and sped past the group, who were beginning to charge deeper into the room behind Batcat while Major Aru, who was the field medic of the team, attempted to stabilize Fairchild's condition and treat his wounds. While Beef Rogers burned several of the Ribiyar near the doorway, being careful to not let his flames go wild and damage any of the equipment, the rest of the group moved forward, exterminating any Ribiyar they encountered. Batcat jumped up onto the workstation above, and it lit up as he fired his machine guns. Parts of the Ribiyar stationed up there began to fly out of the workstations as Batcat's machine guns blasted them off the aliens.

With the efforts of the team, the remaining Ribiyar were soon neutralized. Jack quickly surveyed the Control Center and confirmed that all the aliens had been destroyed, which gave them access to much of the Holding Facility's equipment, including its weapons and its computer core.

"All right, Guardian," Colonel Brown said, "it's your time to shine. Link up to this computer core gizmo, and get us a win for the fight against the dome heads."

"Colonel Brown," Major Aru called, as he stood up, "I'm afraid Lieutenant Fairchild's injuries were too severe for me to stabilize. He's dead." Major Brown walked over to the officers, his appearance weighed down by his inability to heal Fairchild.

"I'm sure you did all you could to save him, Major," Brown responded. "I know you wish you could've saved him, but you can't dwell on that right now. We need to focus on our mission, and keep the Ribiyar from taking any more lives. Guardian, I recommend you do what you need to do and get this thing started as soon as you can. I don't know how long we can keep the Ribiyar away from the Control Center."

"Understood, Colonel Brown." Jack jumped up to the workstation above, pressed his hands on the computer interfaces, and connected to the Holding Facility's communication system, since his personal communication gear wouldn't reach the *Defender* effectively from this distance, and modified the system so the Ribiyar couldn't block or listen in on the conversation.

"Vade to *Defender*, we have taken command of the Control Center, and I am standing by to create the link between the *Defender*'s computer system and the Holding Facility's computer core." Because of the complexity the Omega Virus, Jack would need to channel all his mental focus on the procedure, leaving him completely vulnerable to attack, which is why the remaining members of the team would be leaving the room and standing guard over the Ribiyar, who would be reaching the Control Center within moments. Because of the intensity of the computer link, it was possible that Jack's neural circuits could be damaged from the strain of the interface, or his brain could even be completely destroyed, but Jack knew that this was the only way they could take over the Holding Facility's computer core. The program was too complex for Jack to do himself, and it wouldn't be potent enough to take control of the system. Also, the only way the interface could be established was a direct link with the computer from the Control Center, which Jack would be providing. There were no other options if they wanted to take control of the Holding Facility.

"*We read you, Jack*," Captain Rickman responded over the comm system, "*and we are now bringing the* Defender *closer to the Facility to provide optimal performance of our computer, and we will be in range within 2 minutes. But we must move fast. We have already lost the Tsunami to the armada of Ribiyar fighters, and the Ironclad has also taken heavy damage. Good luck, Jack. Captain Rickman out.*" Jack placed his hands on the computer interface, an oval shaped screen placed in the middle of a balcony on the front of the workstation, and prepared to begin the interface.

"Colonel Brown, I recommend that you take everyone but Batcat to protect the entrance to my right. Batcat can secure the other door."

Brown eyed Batcat skeptically. "You really think this little fur ball can hold those Ribiyar off by himself?"

"Batcat could probably hold them off under normal circumstances, and with that Enforcer Pod, combined with his anger over losing Olo, I doubt they'll stand much of a chance of overpowering him. I have programmed the computer to let you and the rest of the team enter the Control Center, so you will still be able to access the room in the event that I am incapacitated, and unable to open the door for you."

Colonel Brown nodded grimly, understanding the risk that Jack was about to take. He led the group to the door, which Jack had opened for them, and as he left, Brown turned to Jack and saluted him. "It has been an honor serving with you, Jake Vade. We couldn't have done this without you. Good luck." Jack returned the salute, and the group left the room, and the door immediately closed behind them.

With little time before he had to initiate the connection with the computer, Jack turned to Batcat, who was sitting on a ledge on the back end of the balcony. "Batcat, I need you to use the Enforcer Pod and protect this room from any approaching Ribiyar. Do not exit the Pod unless ordered by one of the members of our group. If I should perish during the procedure, Colonel Brown, and whoever is left of our team, excluding Victor, is to be your new masters. Do you understand your orders?"

Batcat meowed in response, and Jack assumed that was his way of saying he understood what was needed.

"Good. Hurry to the Pod. I will close the door once you leave the room. Good luck, Batcat." Jack rubbed Batcat's fur, which had been stained with blood (Jack sickened at the realization that it was likely from Olo), and Batcat jumped from the balcony and boarded the Enforcer Pod, and as the ramp lifted up behind Batcat, the door to the room slid closed, leaving Jack alone in the Control Center.

"*Jack, we are now in range for the computer link,*" Chief Lexton reported over the comm, "*and we are standing by to initiate the link. Are you ready?*"

Taking a moment to gather his courage, he placed his hands on the computer interface. "Affirmative, Chief Lexton. Begin the procedure."

Energy bolts began to be produced from the nodes on his hands, and the energy arched off his hands and landed on the computer interface, linking him to the computer, just as he had first done on the *Defender* when he first took control of its systems. Unlike the first time, when he had to wait a minute before the process began, Jack immediately began to feel his consciousness begin to transfer into the Holding Facility's computer core. Before Jack completely lost his hold on reality, he launched Recon to do what it could to stabilize his mental satiability, and add whatever processing power it could spare. The drone latched onto his back with its crane-like arms, and it began to hum as it rerouted power from its other systems to its computer processors.

Jack braced himself as his vision began to blur and grow darker, and darker, until there was nothing but darkness.

Location: Unknown.

Two days had passed since the two commanders had met with each other, and they now once again conferred with each other in the dark meeting room.

"Tell me, were you successful in gaining the support of our forces?"

"I was. Fortunately, while many did not agree whether we can trust the aliens under attack of the Ribiyar, it was unanimously agreed that our forces should strike while the Ribiyar are preoccupied with the invasion of this planet. We have been given command of the fleets Qadron, Tronar, and Kepton to use in the fight against the Ribiyar. I have received word that they will be prepared to leave orbit tomorrow, and I recommend that we do everything possible to leave even earlier than that. We have a lot of space to travel across to reach the planet, and the Ribiyar are well into their invasion of the planet. If we are to save the aliens, we must move swiftly."

"Agreed. Alert the engineers in our fleets to prepare the engines for maximum thrust, and ask them to make any improvements they can to increase the speed without risking the integrity of the engines or the starships."

"I will get to it right away. If you need me, you know how to find me. Now, get some rest. We have a long journey ahead of us."

Location: Unknown.

Jack opened his eyes to find that he was in a room exactly like the one he had found himself in when he had linked to the *Defender*'s computer core. Jack couldn't see the walls or the ceiling in the room, and the room was also void of any light. Then suddenly, the room was covered in light, and as before, Jack turned to see a red energy form of a Ribiyar.

"*Kon kar cho?*" Jack didn't respond to the computer's question, not that he understood it any way, but he readied himself for the imminent battle.

"*Par tu cho. Ko zepar.*" The Ribiyar lifted his left hand, and a red beam moved over Jack's body, attempting to determine what he was. Trying to defeat the computer before it realized he was a threat, Jack deployed his Laser Cannon and fired at the Ribiyar before the alien could finish its scans. The Ribiyar lifted its right arm in defense as the Laser Cannon burned into its armor, but before Jack could do more damage, the Ribiyar formed a sword 40 inches long, twice the size of the one the *Defender*'s computer had wielded, and threw the sword at Jack, slicing through his Laser Cannon and rendering it useless.

Just another sword materialized in the Ribiyar's hand and it moved to attack, Jack saw another Ribiyar appear in the room, except this one glowed blue and had the Omega symbol on its chest. It appeared that this was the computer from the *Defender*, but instead of fighting against Jack like before, they now fought together against the Holding Facility's Ribiyar.

"*Sep un tu qwar!*" The blue Ribiyar yelled as it lunged toward the red Ribiyar while swinging its sword at its foe. The two swords clanged together as they struggled against each other, though the red Ribiyar quickly managed to overpower the blue one, shoving him down to the ground. Roaring loudly, the red Ribiyar began moving his sword downwards as the blue Ribiyar grabbed onto it and tried to hold it away from him.

Jack activated his flight systems and sped toward the red Ribiyar, punching it with his right fist and knocked it a few feet away from the blue Ribiyar.

"Listen to me!" Jack yelled to the *Defender*'s computer, "You have to use the Omega Virus now!" Jack barely finished talking when the red Ribiyar charged towards Jack and swung his left fist widely and threw him several feet away. Before he was able to get back to his feet, the two Ribiyar were already locked in brutal combat with their swords. Swinging his sword rapidly, the red Ribiyar knocked the blue Ribiyar's sword out of his hand, and it then thrusted its sword into the blue's chest. Jack feared the battle was already over, as he knew that strike would kill the computer, when the blue Ribiyar lifted his left hand and caught the sword. The red Ribiyar struggled against the blue Ribiyar's grip, attempting to lower the sword into his foe, but the blue Ribiyar did not let him, moving his right hand on the red Ribiyar's arm that was holding then sword. The blue Ribiyar then began to glow even brighter, and blue veins began to streak across the sword, and then up the red Ribiyar's right arm. The red Ribiyar attempted to let go of the sword and shake free of its grip, so the computer would lose its connection to him, but the blue Ribiyar tightened his grip as more and more blue veins spread across his arm, and onto the rest of his body.

Just as Jack got to his feet and rushed to help his ally, the red Ribiyar was able to free his arm and his sword, and the alien swiftly jabbed his sword into the blue Ribiyar's chest. The blue Ribiyar began to convulse violently, losing his grip on the red Ribiyar and falling to the ground, while the red Ribiyar kept its sword deep within the blue Ribiyar. The blue Ribiyar began to dissolve, growing dimmer and dimmer, but before he died completely, he reached out to Jack, who was now within reach, and grabbed him. Jack felt the Omega Virus within his system as he began to glow blue and the Omega symbol materialized on his chest. Just as the transfer was finished, the blue Ribiyar dissolved completely, leaving Jack alone to face the red Ribiyar, who raced toward him, swinging his sword wildly.

Location: Outside the Control Center in the Ribiyar Holding Facility, positioned in the Atlantic Ocean.

Batcat didn't have to wait long before Ribiyar began to approach the doors of the Control Center. Dozens of soldiers marched in an orderly manner as they traveled towards the Center. They didn't think it odd to see the Enforcer Pod standing by the door, since they likely expected a scout had already arrived and disposed of the intruders posted at the door, and awaited reinforcements before storming the Control Center.

What they didn't expect was that one of their enemy's greatest warriors sat in the Pod, lying in wait to unleash its wrath upon any who approached. And now, the first unfortunate souls had arrived. It was time to strike. Before Batcat deployed his cannons and began his attack on the Ribiyar, he activated the audio emitters on the outer shell of the Pod to deliver the last sound the aliens would hear before the carnage, and their ultimate demise.

"Meow." With that one word, Batcat then began his assault on the surprised Ribiyar forces. Batcat's Pod lunged at the aliens as it deployed its energy cannons, crushing several Ribiyar beneath it as it landed on its legs. Batcat then proceeded to unleash a furious attack on the aliens, firing the Pod's cannons as fast as possible. And though the Ribiyar pelted the armor of the Pod with their weapons, it was insufficient to make Batcat falter in the protection of his master.

No matter how many warriors came, no matter how powerful their weapons, Batcat would not allow them to inflict harm upon his new master.

Batcat would either protect his master from harm, or he would die trying.

Location: Unknown

"*Sep un tu qwar!!!*" The red Ribiyar roared as he threw his sword at Jack. Jack dived to the side just as the sword sliced through the air he had been moments earlier. Dodging the red Ribiyar as it attempted to grab him, Jack reactivated his thruster and flew away from the alien. As he turned to face the alien, he noticed that he was slowly beginning to grow weaker and found that it was becoming harder to focus on what he was doing. He realized that he was suffering from the strain of the computer link, with the *Defender*'s computer no longer able to support him, and it wouldn't be long before he was too weak to fight against the computer, and he also didn't have much time before his neural circuits suffered irreparable damage from the strain as well. He had to act fast and transfer the Omega Virus to the Ribiyar, before it was too late.

The red Ribiyar jumped several feet into the air and began to dive toward Jack, its sword ready to slice him in half. Jack readied for the alien, but in a flash of insight, he realized the move was similar to the one he had observed in his training program, and he knew exactly what to do. Jack sidestepped to the side right as the alien thrusted his sword into the ground, and before he could remove it, Jack quickly jabbed him with his right leg, throwing a few feet from his weapon. Before the computer had the chance to recover, Jack lunged onto the alien, placing his right foot on its chest, and held down both of his hands to keep him constrained. Veins of blue light began spreading over the Ribiyar from where his hands and foot where in contact with its body, but, it progressed considerably slower that it did than when he had taken control of the computer on the *Defender*. Jack guessed that the Ribiyar wasn't affected the same way as the computer on the *Defender* because the Holding Facility's computer was much bigger, resulting in more systems to take over, prolonging the infection process, and the computer also had stronger firewalls to protect itself against his reprogramming. The Ribiyar strained to free itself from Jack's grasp, and he did all he could to keep the computer restrained, knowing his strength would soon give out.

Finally, his onboard systems reported: **OMEGA VIRUS DELIVERY COMPLETE: COMPUTER SLAVING IN FULL OPERATION.**

More and more blue veins continued to spread across the Ribiyar's body as the Omega Virus gained control of an increasing amount of the computer systems, but even near its defeat, the computer did all it could to resist Jack's attack.

"*Sep... un to... qwar!*" Summoning its faltering strength, the Ribiyar finally managed to rest his right arm out of Jack's grip, a sword quickly materializing in its hand, and the computer stabbed the sword through Jack's chest. The circuits within his chest sparked as they began to short out, and he now felt his concentration and control rapidly fading. As his world faded into nothingness, he closed he eyes as he slumped and fell to the ground, comforted with the knowledge that the loss of his life would serve as payment in the fight to save his people from their invaders.

Chapter 27

Date: July 11, 2132.
Location: Aboard the *Defender,* holding position near the Holding Facility located in the Atlantic Ocean.

"Chief Lexton, what is happening at the Holding Facility?!" Captain Rickman asked impatiently, anxious to know what was happening. Rick had almost lost control of his emotions when Chief Lexton had reported that the *Defender*'s computer had been overwhelmed during the download process, and had then lost its connection with Jack, and the Ribiyar computer. While he didn't completely understand what that meant, he knew it wasn't good news for Jack. Could he have suffered damage from the computers defeat? Was he attempting to complete the transfer all by himself?

"*I don't know, Captain Rickman!*" Chief Lexton responded over the comm, more than a little agitated over her inability to fix their problem. *"The readouts from the computer show that the Omega Virus was transferred to another computer source before it was overwhelmed, and it appears that-"*

"Sir," Tactical Chief Nickland interrupted, "the Holding Facility has ceased its attack on the fleet, and it is now firing its weapons on the Ribiyar fighters and the outposts on the island! They're being overwhelmed!" The bridge erupted in a roar of celebration for their first major victory against the Ribiyar.

"Commander Hayley, instruct the infiltration team to open all the entrances into the Holding Facility that they can, and program the Recon Drones to hunt down the Ribiyar in the place. Also, inform the fleet to send officers from their ships to the Facility once the battle is over to help with-"

"Captain!" Nickland yelled, immediately silencing the rest of the crew in their celebration. "Sensors are detecting a Ribiyar Warship descending from the atmosphere, and it is headed right for our position!" The central holographic display switched from a shot of the Holding Facility, and now showed the sky above them. Moments later, the clouds parted to show a Ribiyar Warship quickly approaching them, it's massive dual-domed structure overshadowing the horizon around it, with its large, revolving trench cannons glowing with energy, ready to rain their wrath upon *Defender* and its allies. The dual-ringed engines orbiting the vessel were ablaze as they lowered the ship down into the atmosphere, and towards the Holding Facility and the Defender's fleet.

Unsure of how they could defeat their foe, all the crew turned toward Captain Rickman, hoping he would have a way to save them and the fleet.

"Lieutenant Commander Nickland, are there any nuclear warheads left?"

"I'm afraid not, sir," Nickland grimly replied. "We used all of the warheads in our fight against the cruisers. And, captain, if you're thinking of taking that thing on, I don't think that the *Defender* possesses enough firepower to destroy it."

"Captain," Commander Hayley spoke cautiously, "This might be more than what we can fight against. We just don't have the means to engage this ship."

Captain Rickman sighed, knowing that, even with the advances the *Defender* possessed, it was no match against the approaching foe. Rick was just about to order the crew to ram the *Defender* into the battleship, the best chance they had at doing any real damage to it, when Chief Lexton, who had been listening in on the discussion, asked "*Captain, what if we used the* Atlanta *to take that thing down?*"

"Chief, what in the world are you talking about?" Captain Rickman responded, confused by her question. "We've already used the nuclear warheads from the *Atlanta*, and its remaining missiles won't do anything against that ship."

"*I know, Captain Rickman. But the ship still possesses its nuclear power core. If we made the appropriate adjustments to the core, and dropped the* Atlanta *onto the ship's hull, the collision with the Ribiyar's hull, combined with the detonation of the* remaining missiles in the sub, should cause the core to breach, creating a nuclear reaction. While the blast won't be as powerful as a nuclear warhead, the blast should contain enough nuclear radiation to create a chain reaction in the Ribiyar's power systems, which will result in the ship destruction."

"Are you sure we should just sacrifice the *Atlanta*, Captain Rickman?" Commander Hayley asked. "We'll have to get awfully close to the warship to get into position, and we're sure to take get a beating with us at point-blank range of their cannons. What if the blast isn't strong enough to destroy the battleship?"

"We don't have any other options, and we are running out of time. Commander, use the *Defender*'s computer to download all the information you can from the *Atlanta*'s computer core. Personal logs, mission reports, everything." Hayley nodded, and quickly began working the computer interface to initiate the download.

"Chief Lexton, will there be any physical adjustments that need to be made to the core to cause the breach?"

"*No, captain. All the adjustments we need to make can be done from here.*"

"Alright. Do what you need to do. Stand by to release the docking clamps holding the *Atlanta* on my signal. Helm, set a course for the battleship. Take us to maximum thrust if you need to, just get the *Defender* above that thing before it reaches the fleet." Rick grabbed the edge of his chair (which he had been able to install in the bridge before the mission had begun) as the ship bolted forward. Though the magnetic boots provided from the *Thunderfox* where aiding the crew as the ship was thrown around, Rick was certain that Doctor McGriffen would still have a lot of bumps and bruises to deal with if they survived this stunt.

"Captain, the battleship will be in position to fire on the fleet in just over two minutes. This is going to be close!" Lieutenant Commander Nickland reported.

"Sir! The download from the *Atlanta*'s computer has been completed," Commander Hayley announced. Now in range of the battleship's weapons, the vessel's massive spherical weapons began rotating at an extraordinary rate, and then began letting loose their armament on the *Defender*, with a firing rate comparable to a machine gun. Though the *Defender* shook beneath the crew as the vessel was attacked, the ship remained steady as she continued to race higher in the sky. But the *Defender* didn't endure the attack silently, as she used her forward cannons to blow apart many of the spherical weapons, and she also used her energy cannons along her wings and across the hull to attack the engine rings of the battleship. The *Defender* soared past the weapon trench of the Ribiyar ship, and now flew just above the surface of the top dome on the battleship.

"Chief Lexton, is the *Atlanta* ready for deployment?" Captain Rickman asked over the comm link, eager to do everything possible to expedite the process before the *Defender* suffered critical damage.

"*Affirmative, captain. All we need to do is drop the old girl and watch the fireworks. I do recommend that we drop the* Atlanta *at a distance so that we can escape the blast radius. The* Defender *is just as vulnerable to the nuclear reaction as we are.*"

"Understood. Helm, take the *Defender* 100 feet above the battleship. Commander Hayley, once we reach that height, drop the *Atlanta* on them." On the holographic display above the central console, currently showing the battle ship beneath them, Captain Rickman was shocked as he saw the battleship beginning to rotate sideways, still in flight with the engine rings supporting the vessel, and with the battleship's rotation the weapon trench was slowly being brought upright so the attack could be resumed. And while the battleship was being moved, many weapons on the engine rings were blasting away at the *Defender*, bashing her already badly damaged hull.

"Aye, captain," Commander Hayley replied feverishly, aware of how close the drop was going to be to the time when the battleships spherical cannons were in position. The *Defender* continued to gain altitude as it flew higher into the atmosphere, and they quickly reached their desired height as the battleship continued its descent toward the ocean's surface. The moment the *Defender* was 100ft above the battleship, the docking clamps holding the *Atlanta* retracted, and the sub plummeted down to the sub below. Though the Ribiyar fired upon the descending sub, its amour kept the ship more or less intact as it grew closer and closer to the battleship. Jumping to high speeds, the *Defender* rocketed away to avoid the imminent explosion.

Just as the weapon trench rotated to blast the sub away, the *Atlanta* plunged into the weapons, erupting in a mighty explosion. But as impressive as the *Atlanta's* fire show was, it was nothing compared to the size of the explosion the battleship created. The entire sky seemed to ignite as a thunderous shockwave stretched over the sky. The force of the shockwave, fortunately free of residual nuclear radiation, rocked the *Defender*, momentarily causing the ship to lose control of its flight before it stabilized, and set course back to the Holding Facility, which was only a few miles away from where the battleship had been. If the *Defender* had been only a half-minute later, the battleship would have been able to destroy all the ships in the fleet, and the Holding Facility as well.

"Commander Hayley," Captain Rickman said as the crew celebrated on the bridge, though several frequently glanced at the displays to make sure another battleship wasn't descending toward them, "I want you to lead a team that will take command of the Control Center while me and the other commanders in the fleet try to determine our next move against the Ribiyar. We still have much work to do if we want to get the Ribiyar off our planet."

10 minutes later…
Location: Control Level of the Ribiyar Holding Facility, positioned in the Atlantic Ocean.

UNIT IS ONLINE.

RUNNING DIAGNOSTIC CYCLE:

MEMORY: PARTIAL DATA CORRUPTION DETECTED.

DECODING PROTOCOLS HAVE BEEN ACTIVATED AND ARE ATTEMPTING TO RESOLVE ERROR.

WEAPON SYSTEMS:

MINOR DAMAGE AND WEAR ON EQUIPMENT DETECTED.

MAINTENANCE ON SYSTEM RECOMMEND, BUT NOT NECESSARY FOR SYSTEM FUNCTIONALITY.

OVERALL WEAPON STATUS: 96% FUNCTIONAL.

MOTOR FUNCTIONS: OPERATING AT 98%.

OPTIC, AUDIO, SENSORY RECEPTORS: FULLY FUNCTIONAL.

SCANNING... UNIT FUNCTIONALITY IS AT 94%.

WARNING: DIAGNOSTIC SCANS SHOW NEURAL CIRCUITS ARE UNSTABLE AND IS LIKELY TO DETERIORATE FURTHER IF REPAIRS ARE NOT PERFORMED IMMEDIATELY.

UNIT CONSCIOUSNESS WILL BE RESTORED FOR 17MIN, 43SEC TO FACILITATE REPAIRS BEFORE DEACTIVATION WILL OCCUR TO CONTINUE MENTAL SYSTEM RECALIBRATION AND REPAIRS.

BRINGING UNIT CONSCIOUSNESS ONLINE AND REACTIVATING ALL OTHER SYSTEMS.
ENGAGING...

"Jack? Can you hear me?" Chief Lexton asked Jack, who stood dormant by the console on the balcony in the Control Room, with his hands still holding onto the console he had used to connect himself to the Holding Facility's computer, though no energy pulsed from his hands, signifying he wasn't still connected with the computer. A Recon Drone, attached to Jack's back, hummed softly as Lexton attached an interface chip, a small circular device that would link the drone's computer to her scanner, to its computer module, and used the scanner in her hand to try and figure out what was wrong with Jack. Once the device was activated, it began to send information to her scanner, and Lexton focused as she searched through the information to see what she could do for Jack.

But before she got far in her search, a high-pitched whine was produced from Jack's equipment as he began to reactivate. Jack opened his eyes, and nearly fell to the ground as he tried to stabilize himself.

"Jack, are you okay?" Chief Lexton asked as she tried to help him to his feet, a difficult task because of his bigger mass, and the Chief's lack of overt muscular strength. "What happened to you during the Omega Virus download? We thought we lost you."

"I... don't remember what happened during the download process. Some of my memory has been corrupted. Possibly from the stress of the Omega download. I do remember needing to administer the Omega Virus on my own, after something happened to the computer. That would explain the deterioration and fragile state my neural circuits... my mind I mean, is in." Just as Lexton lifted Jack to his feet, he fell to the ground again, this time taking the chief down with him.

"I apologize, Chief Lexton," Jack said as he tried to grab onto the balcony and lift himself while the Chief got to her feet. "My diagnostics show my mental infrastructure is extremely weak, and it may take some time before I regain full control of my systems. I would appreciate any help that you and the other engineers can provide."

"I'll do what I can Jack, but you will have to show me what you need fixed. No one knows much about how your systems work, even me, after spending hours poring over your schematics, and we don't want to do anything that might make your situation worse. Unfortunately, it may take some time before anyone can help you. Our fleet took a lot of damage during the fight, and we're diverting most of the engineers in our fleet focusing on repairing the ships that weren't destroyed."

Jack finally managed to pull himself up and stand, though he heavily leaned on the balcony to hold himself upright. "How badly was the fleet damaged?"

Chief Lexton sighed. "We got hit real hard. We lost the *Tsunami, Pocahontas,* and the *Un-Holstered* during the assault. All the other ships took a lot of damage as well, including the *Defender*, which is the vessel that took the most damage and is still operational. The GMs on the *Defender*, or the fabricators, as you call them, are going to be working for days to create all the parts we will need to make our repairs."

"Do you think that we will have enough time to administer the repairs on the ships?" Jack asked, concerned that another attack force could attack at any moment. "Wouldn't the Ribiyar attempt to attack us while we are regrouping?"

"For the moment, the Ribiyar have yet to attack us," Commander Hayley answered from the lower level of the Control Room. "It is possible that they are trying to determine how to deal with us, now that we have command of one of their Holding Facility's, in addition to the *Defender*, and the other fighters and equipment in this place. In the meantime, we are going to do all that we can to strengthen the Holding Facility's defenses, and the weapons and equipment on the ships in our forces. It is time that we are properly equipped to fight against the Ribiyar."

"I couldn't agree more," Captain Rickman said as he walked through the entrance in Control Center, with Batcat and Colonel Brown following close behind. Seeing Jack in the balcony, Batcat ran up the stairs that led to the workstation, and purred as he walked between Jack's feet. "Which is the other captain and I have decided to make the Holding Facility the new base of the Defenders in our fight against the Ribiyar."

"Colonel Brown," Jack asked as Brown walked up the path to the workstation, "it's good to see you're still alive. Did we lose any more of our team members while you defended the Control Center?"

"Fortunately, no. And as much as I hate to admit it, we can thank Davidson for that. As much as I can't stand that guy, I have to admit that he knows his way around that laser sword of his." Brown hesitated before continuing. "Guardian... Jack, I mean, I wanted to let you know that we found Oakland's body, back in the room with all those Ribiyar and the ball-tanks in it. I heard that you two had been friends a while back, and I thought you should know that we're planning a memorial service for him, along with Fairchild, and the rest of the brave soldiers that gave their lives in the battle today. We will be giving him special recognition for the part he played to help us get to the Control Center."

Jack closed his eyes as the grief of his friend came fresh to his mind. Opening his eyes, he nodded his thanks to Brown, grateful that his friend's sacrifice would be honored, and remembered by the people that he helped save. "Thank you, Colonel. He deserves nothing less for what he did for us."

Jack and the other officers in the room continued to talk for several minutes, discussing how the parts for the repairs will be distributed, which ships should be repaired first, and other matters, when Commander Hayley urgently spoke up, and asked the group to listen to what she discovered.

"Captain Rickman, I have been going through the Holding Facility's database, looking for other bases we could attack, when I came across several reports that indicated that the Ribiyar have detected a military base hidden in Hawaii."

"What?!" Captain Rickman exclaimed. "When do they plan to attack? Can we send in the *Defender* and the rest of our ships in time to stop them?"

"I am afraid it is too late for that, sir," Commander Hayley replied soberly as she typed commands into the computer console, which the computer had translated from the Ribiyar langue into English so the operators could work the interface. The holographic display in the front of the room displayed an orbital view of earth. The image zoomed in closer and closer, until it showed a clear image of Hawaii. Or rather, what was left of it. Several of the officers in the room gasped in horror as they saw the smoldering remains of the islands that had comprised Hawaii. The few parts of the islands that hadn't been blown apart by the Ribiyar were either in flames, or flooding as water rushed gushed over the fragments of dirt that had once comprised the islands.

"This footage is from two hours ago. The Ribiyar have cut the computer link that connected the Holding Facility to the rest of their fleet, and judging from the video, there wouldn't have been anyone left to rescue if we had heard about it sooner. Still, we should have been there to do something." Commander Hayley said, tormented and angered over the destruction caused by the Ribiyar's crusade of conquest.

"What do we do now?" Jack asked, hoping that the officers had some idea of what action they could take.

"Now," Captain Rickman said as he looked again to the display. Drawing strength from his will to fight against humanity's biggest threat yet, he turned to face the other officers in the room. "Now, we find a way to hurt the Ribiyar like never before, and put a stop to them. For good."

The trilogy continues with book two: Genocide
Coming sometime in the future
Whenever that will be

ACKNOWLEDGMENTS

While I was writing this book, I knew that I would need a lot of characters to introduce, since the military was going to be involved, and I would need to put officers in the appropriate places on the ships and installations I used. So, I asked some people if they wanted to be in the book, and I used some of the ideas they gave me to create the some of the characters throughout the story. To recognize their contribution, I have decided to introduce the people who played as various members of the 'cast' in the book. Thanks for your help guys. Without you, the characters you played, such as Batcat and Victor Davidson, would likely never have been born, and my characters wouldn't feel as real as they do without you guys. Thanks a bunch!

Carli Way as Carley Lace of the *U.S.S. Pocahontas*.

Evan Mitchel as E.V.A.N., Evan Adler, and, of course, Batcat.

Jim Fox as Captain Jim Syvon of the *U.S.S. Thunderfox*.

Zach Bedwell as Captain John Whitefield of the *U.S.S. Ocean-Walker*.

Daven Dyal as Colonel Vern Brown.

Drew Dyal as Larry "Beef" Rogers.

Delton Dyal as Lieutenant Johnny Fairchild.

Chris Nicholas as Major Buck Aru.

Seth Tiebout as Lieutenant Commander Simon Owen Stone.

Seth Krouse as Victor Davidson, AKA the Dark Serpent. Thanks for letting me use your ideas for him.

Addie Freeman as Doctor Sadie McGriffen.

Berakah Cook as Chief Gabrielle Lexton.

Maddux Wilson as Captain Max River of the *Tsunami*.

Grace Wilson as Captain Grace Gold of the *U.S.S. Un-Holstered*.

Lastly, Michael Mishoe as (I'll let you try to figure that out yourself. Good luck with that.)

Thanks again guys, and I apologize if I left anyone out in the role call.

Thank you, dad, for suggesting that I should write down the daydreams I have about this series and taking time to teach me the things in life, such as cars and lawnmowers, that I have no idea about that will help in the future. It may take a few years, or decade's, but hopefully I will finally complete my task.

Thank you, mom, for reading some of the earlier chapters of the book, even though you aren't much into sci-fi, and thank you for putting up with us while we watch through the seasons of *Star Trek* while we eat the meals you often make for us. Thanks for all the mom stuff you do behind the scenes that I don't know about.

Thank you, my sister Emily, for being there to talk to about my wild ideas, and be there to make me laugh, even if you don't always get the ideas that I have. I've really liked what I've read of what you've got written of your book, and I hope that it, and the other future works, take off with success, and that your acting career takes off brilliantly.

Thank you, Seth Tiebout, for being an awesome friend and being there for me. It's really awesome to have your interest in my series, when so few take the time to let me talk about it, and even fewer that let me go into deep detail like I do with you. Your support is very much valued, especially since I know you aren't as much into the sci-fi world as I am. Thanks a million bro.

Thank you, Dale Kirkpatrick, for the time you spent to go through my book, and helping me find my many, many mistakes I made in the writing process. It was definitely very helpful for me. And also, I wanted to thank his son Casey Kirkpatrick for the work he did for the cover picture. It really was awesome work, great job on it man. Thank you for the time you guys spent volunteering to help me out for free. It was a huge blessing for sure you guys!

And thank you Jesus, for giving me the imagination I need for this book, and all that come after it, and for sending Your Son to die for us. Yours is the ultimate story that mine can never compare to.

And real quick, I'd like to take a moment to speak to the dreamers out there reading this book. You guys provide so much for this world, whether it's through art, writing, construction, fashion design, work and jobs, and tons more. Know that you don't have to be famous people like Gene Roddenberry and Picasso to make a difference.

I'm not a famous person. I'm just the guy walking past you on the street, serving your food, living my life. But here I am, writing novels.

Never let anyone tell you that you can't be who God made you to be. Use the gifts you've been given, change the world, and continue dreaming the impossible.

And then, make it possible.

ABOUT THE AUTHOR

Michael Mishoe is a true sci-fi fan at heart, enjoying many Tv series such as Star Trek, Star Wars, Doctor Who, and others, but also enjoys heavy reading as well, and is well acquainted with series such as Michael Vey from Richard Paul Evans and The Mindwar Trilogy from Andrew Kalavan. Endurance is his debut novel, and the start of the sci-fi series Galactic Defenders, which will likely span around 20+ books. He lives in Cookeville, Tn, with his parents, sister, dog, and a collection of bouncy balls and fidget spinners.

Made in the USA
Middletown, DE
06 August 2018